MISSING, PRESUMED DEAD

EMMA BERQUIST

GREENWILLOW BOOKS
An Imprint of HarperCollins Publishers

Missing, Presumed Dead
Text copyright © 2019 by Emma Berquist

The text of this book is set in 13-point Adobe Jenson.
Book design by Paul Zakris
Library of Congress Cataloging-in-Publication Data

Names: Berquist, Emma, author.
Title: Missing, presumed dead / Emma Berquist.
Description: First edition. | New York, NY :
Greenwillow Books, an imprint of
HarperCollins Publishers, [2019] |
Summary: "Jane's ghost is haunting Lexi, who has the ability
to foretell by touch when and how a person will die,
in order to seek revenge on her killer"— Provided by publisher.
Identifiers: LCCN 2018052589 | ISBN 9780062642813 (hardback)
Subjects: | CYAC: Ghosts—Fiction. | Psychic ability—Fiction. |
Revenge—Fiction. | Murder—Fiction. | Magic—Fiction.
Classification: LCC PZ7.1.B4634 Mis 2019 | DDC [Fic]—dc23
LC record available at https://lccn.loc.gov/2018052589

19 20 21 22 23 PC/LSCH 10 9 8 7 6 5 4 3 2 1
First Edition

GREENWILLOW BOOKS

TO THE ONES WHO WENT AHEAD,
AND THE ONES WHO STAYED BEHIND

1

I TAKE THE PILLS WHEN THEY TELL ME TO. NOT THE
Haldol, only the Ativan. I don't need the antipsychotics;
I just need to rest. I'm not sick. Or at least, not the kind
of sick that drugs can fix. I know, I've tried them all;
they don't make it stop. Nothing does.

I have about twelve hours left of my seventy-two-
hour stay. It's a voluntary psychiatric hold, so they can't
keep me any longer unless they're willing to go to a lot
of trouble. I only come here when it gets to be too much,
when I can't take one more death brushing against my
skin. LA County Mental Health isn't particularly nice,
or even particularly clean, but it is quiet. Quiet and white
and no one tries to touch me. For seventy-two hours
I can sleep the sleep of the drugged in a locked ward,
my own personal sensory deprivation tank. Our sense
of touch is controlled by a complex system of neurons
and pathways called the somatosensory system. Sensory
receptors in our skin respond to stimuli and send signals

to the spinal cord and brain. When you feel everything, sometimes it's better to feel nothing at all.

I stretch out between the scratchy hospital sheets, the edge of the benzos starting to creep up. I tongued the other pills, then tucked them into the crease of my jeans. I don't need them, but someone else at the club might.

"Good evening, Lexi," a voice says, and I roll over and blink heavy-lidded eyes. It's dark, but I can just make out the figure standing over the bed.

"Oh," I say to the older man in a white coat. "Hey, Dr. Ted."

"I didn't expect to see you again so soon."

I struggle to sit up. "Had a rough week. The last job . . . it was a kid."

I hate it when they're kids; they don't understand that they're dead. And I can't explain that their tantrums are drawing too much attention, that people are starting to notice the flickering lights. All I can do is tell them it's going to be okay, right before I push them over to the other side. It feels like they're dying all over again.

"I'm sorry to hear that." Dr. Ted sounds like he means it; hell, he probably does. He's too soft for his own good, the sort of person who thinks if you're kind enough you can trust people. You'd think this place would convince him otherwise, but he's still here, still trying.

"It's not your fault," I say. "I needed a break. I'm leaving tomorrow."

"How is your grandfather?" he asks.

I shrug. "Deda is Deda."

Dr. Ted nods. "And you? How are you doing, Lexi?"

I rub my face. The drugs are pumping through my bloodstream, slowing down my heart, and it's hard to think clearly.

"I'm . . . surviving," I say.

Dr. Ted is quiet for a moment. "I suppose that's a start."

There's a click and the door to my room opens, letting a shaft of light spill in. A nurse stands backlit, glowing like a saint in stained glass.

"Who are you talking to?" she asks suspiciously, her eyes darting around the room.

"No one," I say, shaking my head. "I'm . . . praying."

One corner of her mouth purses, but she's only paid enough to check that we're still breathing. The door closes and I'm cushioned in darkness again.

"I won't keep you up any longer," Dr. Ted says. "Sleep well, Lexi."

"You, too, doc," I say, but only to be polite. Ghosts don't sleep.

The hours go too quickly, most of them slept away. The doctors don't bother me much; free clinics are a refuge for the poor and the drug-addicted and the runaways. There are too many of us for them to get attached, and they dole their care out in small doses so they don't get swallowed whole.

I sign myself out around noon, squinting against the sun. There aren't enough trees in LA, not enough shade. The palms don't do anything except bend over during the Santa Ana winds and leave huge fronds in the street that people swerve to avoid.

I walk to the bus stop, zipping up my hoodie even though it's already warm out. I hate riding the bus—too many people, too many chances for contact—but I didn't want to leave my grandfather's Buick parked over here for three days.

A man leans against the bus stop shelter and I make sure my hood is up as I turn away and shove my hands in my pockets. He barely glances in my direction, no doubt writing me off as a surly teenage boy. I keep my dark hair shaved close, a few centimeters of fuzz covering my head. That, combined with a number of tattoos and curves that are more like slight waves, give a certain impression. People don't bother boys the way they do girls, don't try to crowd them, don't try to touch them. Up close the illusion fades, but I don't let people get too close.

When the bus arrives, I head for the back, as far away from the others as I can get. I tuck my arms in tight, just trying to make it through, but I forget about the people behind me. The bus lurches and a hand clamps around my shoulder as a woman stumbles forward.

My breath stops as her death sings to me; sixty-two, breast cancer. She mumbles an apology, but her hand is still on me, and it only gets worse the longer she touches me. The smell of iron clogs my nose as the image of her pale and withered body shoves its way into my mind. I twist away, ignoring the insulted look she gives me, and lurch into the nearest empty seat. Shivers roll over my skin and I cross my arms tight against my chest until they pass. I let my head fall back against the seat and close my eyes, wishing like anything I could have stayed in that white room forever.

The bus goes to Van Nuys, which is technically Los Angeles but also definitely not. It's not near the beach, it's not pretty, and the only actors who live here are the ones who play bodies on TV.

LA is where dreams go to die. We pretend it's perfect, hot yoga and green juice and beaches, but underneath it's all despair. Our sunsets are beautiful because of pollution from the cars choking the 405. Hollywood is filthy, nothing but strip malls and garbage and tourists taking disappointed selfies. Homeless people pee in the middle of the sidewalk in Santa Monica because they have nowhere else to go. Venice Beach is littered with needles and rich kids pretending to be hippies.

Everyone comes here with the same stupid dream, and everyone gets crushed under the weight of it. This place is for people trying to claw their way out, or people who have already given up. All you have to do is drive by Skid Row to realize no one gives a shit about anyone else in this city. Including me.

I get off not far from my apartment but I'm not headed there just yet. My grandfather's nursing home is a few blocks away, close enough for me to visit every day when I'm not locked up in the psych ward.

"Good morning, Lexi," Nancy says when I walk in the door.

"Hey," I say, breathing in the scent of antiseptic and piss. "How's he been?"

"He won Mr. Hardin's pudding cup playing poker."

I shake my head. "He cheated. He always cheats."

Nancy smiles. "He was worried about you," she says softly. "Maybe you can tell him next time you're not going to make it?"

I wince. "Yeah. Sorry, I will."

"He's watching TV, go on in."

"Thanks."

Sherman Assisted Living isn't terrible, but it isn't great, either. The staff are decent enough, but it's old, the rec room stuffed with Salvation Army couches, the food tasteless.

The rec room still smells like pee, but at least there's a layer of burnt popcorn to cover it. I find Deda in front of the TV, his long body draped over a ragged armchair, his oxygen tank propped at his side.

"Deda," I say, pulling up a folding chair to sit next to him. "I'm back."

"Alexandra." Deda's shaggy brows draw together. "Do you not watch the news? Where have you been?" He gestures at the TV, where the anchor is reporting the latest missing person. People go missing in this city like socks, bunched up and discarded, but not like this. Not four in a row, young men and women who seemingly disappeared off the face of the earth. One of them should have at least turned up on Urie's doorstep by now, but there's been no sign.

"I'm sorry," I say quietly. "I went to the clinic; I should have told you."

He sighs, leaning back in his chair. "I wish you would not go to that place."

My grandfather looks like a golden age movie star on a slight decline, a Russian Errol Flynn if he lived past fifty and wasn't a total creep. He always dresses impeccably, crisp pants and shiny dress shoes. I don't think I've ever seen him wear jeans, or a shirt that wasn't tucked in. And I would never tell him, because he worked so hard to lose it, but I love the slight trace of an accent he still has and his habit of avoiding contractions.

"Some days . . ." I swallow hard. "I can't handle it, Deda. I can't see one more death without screaming."

"Our gift makes us different, Alexandra," Deda says. "But you do not have to cut yourself off. If you would go back to school—"

"No," I say, interrupting him. I'm not having this

fight again, not now. "Deda, please, can we . . . can we just watch TV for a while?"

Deda's mouth gets tight, but after a moment he nods. I scoot his tank to the side and lean against his armchair, and for an hour we pretend we're just two ordinary people, as long as we ignore the elderly ghost slumped on the couch behind us.

I don't know why we can do what we do, why I can feel every person's death like a brand on my skin, see things no one should have to see. Deda calls it a gift. But every time I ask "From who?", I get a different answer. Once he told me we're descended from Rasputin and his magic runs in our blood. Once he said we were hexed by Baba Yaga after tricking her out of her best cow. Once it was my great-great-grandfather who tried to beat death in a game of chess.

I don't think it's a gift. At least not the kind anyone asks for. It scared my mother. She tried her best, but she couldn't handle a kid who talked to nothing, who saw her death before she could walk. It was bad enough her father couldn't hold her. When her kid started flinching from her hugs, I think it broke something inside her. She stayed, though, and I'll always be grateful for that. She stayed until it was too late to leave. Until she learned she was right to be scared.

I doubt Deda even knows what the truth is. It skipped his grandfather and his older brother, but not his father. It popped up in a few cousins still in Russia. It skipped Mom but not me. Maybe it's a gift, maybe it's a curse, maybe it's just a gene mutation. Whatever it is, it's ours to keep.

My apartment is a piece of shit. It's a studio, barely big enough to fit my bed and a dresser, but eighteen-year-olds with no money don't have a lot of options. I could move to the larger complex in Echo Park where most of the people who work for Urie live, but I've always kept to myself. I don't care that it's small and there's no water pressure and the window sticks; it's enough that I have someplace that's just mine.

I take a shower, wash three days of hospital stink off of me. I'm too tall for the ancient showerhead, but it doesn't take much to get shampoo out of short hair. I put on my cleanest black pants and pull a gray hoodie over my head so only the tattoos on my hands are visible. Finger bones connect to wrist bones, the outline continuing halfway up my arms. They were some of the first marks Theo put on me, spells for strength and health. They're more than that to me, though; the bones are a reminder of what's inside, lurking just beneath the surface. Peel back a layer of skin and we're all the same; ashes to fucking ashes, everything gets ground back into the dirt.

I'm going to be late for work again, especially if there's traffic. And there's always traffic. I'm pulling on my boots when there's a flicker at my left eye, and I bite off a yelp.

"Fucking hell, Trevor, can you not do that next to my *face*," I yell.

"Where have you been?" he demands, scowling at me. "You know the news is saying people are getting abducted by aliens, right?"

"That is not what they're saying."

"You didn't tell me you were leaving *again*."

"Yeah, that's because I didn't want you to follow me."

Trevor steps back, looking hurt, and I sigh. He's just a kid; barely sixteen, or at least he was when he died. I don't know when that was exactly, but judging by his faded jeans and swoopy hair, I think it was sometime in the nineties.

"I'm sorry," I tell him, sitting back on my bed. "I needed a break from everything."

Trevor sits down next to me and bumps his shoulder

against mine. I think he looks like he did when he was alive, but I didn't know him then; maybe his bronze skin is a little paler, his dark lashes a little hazier. He feels solid, and warm.

That's what people always get wrong about ghosts; they aren't cold. They don't make your breath cloud, or give you goose bumps. They're heat and weight and the taste of metal coating your tongue. They're energy, pure energy that makes your skin crackle and your hair stand on end. When people die, their life force doesn't disappear; it just changes. It's the first law of thermodynamics: energy cannot be created or destroyed, only transferred from one form to another.

"Hey," Trevor says. "I'm sorry, too."

"Not your fault," I say, leaning my head against him. It's nice to be able to touch someone without feeling sick. Even if I still taste copper in my mouth. Even if that someone isn't quite a someone anymore.

"Did you tell *anyone* you were going?" Trevor asks, raising his eyebrows.

I shake my head, and he looks somewhat mollified.

"Not even Phillip?"

I push Trevor away and stand up. "Okay, enough prying. I'm late as it is."

He spreads out on my bed and I try to ignore the red streak that blooms across his chest. He was in a bad car crash.

"Trevor," I say, jutting my chin to his shirt.

"Oh," he says, looking down. He closes his eyes for a second, and the light flickers overhead.

"Easy," I mutter. If they concentrate hard enough, ghosts can sometimes affect electromagnetic radiation: lights, radios, once even my microwave. I have a theory, untested, that violent deaths create the strongest ghosts because they fight so hard to stay alive that the kinetic energy builds up and carries over to the other side.

"Sorry," Trevor mumbles. He opens his eyes, and the blood blinks away. He's an old ghost, with the control that comes from practice. He still won't change his clothes, though.

"You better not be in my bed when I get home," I tell him.

"Mm-hmm," he answers, waving me away. "Say hi to Phillip for me."

I give him the finger as I shut the door behind me.

I like LA better in darkness. The night hides the ugliness, smudges sharp corners into soft edges. The low-slung houses melt into one another until all you see is palm trees glowing in the traffic lights.

None of us ever sees darkness, not true darkness. Even without the headlights, even without the high-mast lighting, it would never be truly dark. Not the way it used to be, not the way it should be. We can't see the Milky Way anymore because of light pollution across the continent. People don't sleep like they should, can't see the stars like they should. We build these cities and fill them with light and garbage and people, and then we wonder why we're so unhappy.

I take the exit slowly, running into the usual traffic as I get closer to Hollywood. Everyone comes out to play at night, and the bars are already spilling music and drunks into the street. My destination is farther down, but trying to find closer parking is a waste of time. I pass two full lots before I find a garage, and I have to drive up three flights to get a spot.

It's too hot to be wearing a hoodie, but I don't take it off. I need something to separate me from the women in slinky dresses, from the men in tight jeans. I am not one of you; I am not here for you. The trick is to look straight ahead, to look mean and angry at the world. It's not exactly a reach for me. I stomp down the street, but the crowd is dense and drunk and I can't avoid all of them. Shoulders bump mine, and I grit my teeth as deaths wash over me in a sticky gray wave. I only get flashes, but it's enough; all these plump, dimpled cheeks, thick hair, and painted nails, I glimpse the way it ends. Throat cancer, aneurysm, pneumonia. They beam even white teeth, and all I can see are the skulls smiling beneath.

Elysium is on a corner, a tall, gray stone building with an elaborate carved façade. I hate it with a passion, but a job is a job. The club has four levels, all equally loud and awful, but a line still stretches down the street. Of course, that's what happens when you spell people's drinks. Not a spell strong enough for them to notice, just enough to tweak their body chemistry, make them happier than normal, lighter, more willing to dance and ignore the pain in their feet. No other place can satisfy you quite like Elysium can, so yeah, there's always a line.

The bouncer nods at me as I duck past the front door and head down the darkened alleyway. The side exit is locked, but I pound on the door with my fist. Then kick it with my boot, for good measure.

A second later the door shoves open and a bald, angry face leers out.

"Give it a rest, I'm—oh, hey, Lex." Georgie's face clears as he recognizes me. "You working tonight?"

"Yeah," I say, and he opens the door wide enough for me to sneak past without getting too close. I've been here long enough that security knows I don't like to be touched.

"Haven't seen you in a few days," Georgie says as he lets the door slam shut behind us.

"Been busy." I walk quickly, knowing my way around; the service elevators are to the left, much plainer and emptier than the glitzy ones in the main lobby.

"Phillip is around," Georgie says, far too casually. "He's been asking about you. Want me to send him up?"

I stomp into the elevator and punch the number four.

"No," I say firmly, and the door closes on Georgie's face.

I lean back against the wall and shut my eyes while the elevator starts to move. I certainly didn't *intend* to get involved with Urie's son. Well, at least not the first time.

Maybe I should have told Phillip I was working tonight. And maybe I should have answered one of the dozens of messages he sent me. I owed him a proper breakup, but I didn't know what to say. How do you tell someone it's hard to kiss him when you keep picturing him dead?

Phillip wouldn't understand; he's not like me. He has a healing gift he inherited from his mother, something small and helpful. He still has to hide what he can do from outsiders—we all have to—but it's not the same. He can be around people, go to school, live in the light. He gets to have a life.

The elevator dings and I pad down the hallway, my boots quiet on the carpeted floor. On the other side of the wall music blares, the bass reverberating in my chest. I brace myself, then pull open the door that leads to the club, and the noise is inside my head.

It's early enough that the crowd is sparse. It'll fill up in a manner of hours, but nowhere near as packed as the first two levels. It's why I stick to the top; people are usually distracted by strobe lights or DJs before they make it all the way up here.

I weave across the slick wooden floor, avoiding the people occupying the leather couches along the walls. The bar is long and backlit, and I wave at the girl with golden skin and fire-engine red hair behind it.

"Lexi!" she says, giving me a relieved smile. "There you are."

I slip behind the bar and take off my hoodie, shoving it beneath the counter.

"Thanks for covering for me, Nic," I tell her. "I really appreciate it."

Nicole is kind to me; she's the closest thing I have to a friend, if I allowed myself to have living friends. She has a touch of psychic ability herself, enough to know which people to kick out when the mood in the club turns sour. Everyone who works here has at least one foot in the unknown. That's why we're here, because Urie found us and gave a place. He protects most of us magic types, the charmers and the forgers, the psychics and the witches, and whatever it is that I am. You need a healer, you see Urie. You need a loan, you see Urie. Without him, half of us would be living on the street, more missing kids on the news. He keeps us working, keeps us hidden, keeps us out of jail or someplace worse.

"No problem," she tells me. "I needed the money. Urie was looking for you, though."

I run a hand over my peach-fuzz hair. "Aw, shit. What did he say?"

So far I've avoided Urie needing me when I'm gone, but it was bound to happen eventually; ghosts have been popping up all over the place, the undercurrent of unrest in the city stretching to the undead. The money's nice, and I owe him, but the more jobs he sends me on, the more I want to run to the hospital.

"He was worried," Nicole says. "Didn't you hear about Marcus?"

I shake my head. "No. Who's Marcus?"

Nicole's mouth goes flat. "Fifteen-year-old with a talent for locks. He's a good kid, really outgoing, never stops talking. He went missing from around the warehouse."

Shit. Urie keeps good track of his people; we don't just go missing.

"How long?" I ask.

"A few days. Everyone's a little rattled."

"Maybe he'll turn up," I say, but even I don't believe that.

"Yeah," Nicole says. "Maybe."

Someone shouts at us from across the bar, and our conversation ends as we start pouring drinks. I try to remember what Marcus looks like and come up with an impression of a scrawny kid with messy hair. I don't socialize with the others if I can help it. Now I feel doubly guilty about not answering any of Phillip's messages.

I focus on the shouted drink orders, try to put it all out of my mind. I'm a crap bartender. I can't make Manhattans properly, I always mess up martinis, and half the time I don't know what I'm putting in an old-fashioned. It doesn't matter; people don't come here for the taste of the drinks; they come for the feeling inside them. It's a simple spell, really, that bonds to any type of alcohol.

I pour three shots of whiskey for a group of button-downed bros, not entirely sure it's the kind they ordered.

"Aren't you a little young to be behind the bar?" one of them yells over the music.

"No," I lie, pushing the drinks across. Urie doesn't care regardless, but I do have a flawless fake license a forger made me. Even the feds wouldn't be able to spot it, though each of them would see something different.

The man shrugs and takes the drinks with a wink at Nicole. She smiles brightly at him, which is why she gets tips and I don't, but also why she gets hit on and I don't.

"He's gonna ask for your number," I tell her, leaning against the bar. "Don't you dare give out mine again."

Nicole laughs, an open, delighted sound that almost tempts me into a smile. Then the laugh cuts off as she spots something over my shoulder.

"Uh-oh," she says, "playtime's over."

The stink of thick cologne wafts over me before I turn and scowl.

"Hey, sexy Lexi," Ilia drawls.

"What do you want, Ilia?"

He just grins and reaches across the bar to grab a cherry from the container. Urie's nephew is twenty-two, his second-in-command, sometimes my partner and sort of friend. At least when he's not being a pain in my ass.

"Nice of you to finally show up," he says, tossing the cherry into his mouth. "Where the hell have you been?"

"I was off," I tell him, crossing my arms. "I don't have to answer my phone if I'm off."

"Yeah, well, Urie's been climbing up the walls trying to account for everybody, so next time a heads-up would be nice."

"Yeah," I say grudgingly. "I got it."

"Good. He wants to see you."

"Now? I just got here."

"So tell it to him." Ilia shrugs.

I sigh and look over my shoulder at Nicole.

"Sorry," I say, tugging my hoodie back on.

"It's fine," she says, giving me a sympathetic smile. "I'll see you later."

"Is he pissed at me?" I ask, following Ilia out from the bar.

Ilia glances at me. He's annoying as hell, but he's always straight with me.

"More worried than pissed," he says. "I wouldn't disappear again anytime soon, though."

"Noted," I say. "Any news on Marcus?"

Ilia shakes his head curtly. "Nothing. Where were you, anyway?"

I chew on my lip. People like us don't go to doctors; if we're sick, we see healers. If we're lost, we see palm readers. We don't confide in outsiders, and we definitely don't check ourselves into clinics.

"Nowhere," I say. "Just turned my phone off. The last job—"

"Yeah," Ilia says, running a hand over his face. "I remember."

It wasn't easy for him, either. I had to deal with the ghost, but he had to deal with the mom who lost her kid.

We walk in silence down the hallway, both of us plagued by bad memories. We turn the corner and find a lanky young man slouched in front of a closed door.

"Hey, Jordan," Ilia says. "He's expecting us."

I nod and Jordan nods back; when he's not playing guard dog, he's a skilled witch, specializing in repelling spells.

"One sec," Jordan says, pushing off the wall, and turns and taps lightly on the door. A muffled voice says something, and Jordan twists the handle and pops his head inside.

". . . here to see Mr. Porch . . ."

I only catch snippets of his low voice before he straightens back out.

"Go on in," he says, opening the door wider with a teasing flourish.

I take my hands out of my pockets and run a nervous hand over my hair before I step into the office.

2

URIE PORCHOWSKY HAS ALWAYS MADE ME anxious. I guess in some ways he's like Deda, one of those serious, hardworking immigrant types. But while Deda can be sharp and demanding, Urie is polite and distant, the kind of man who keeps you reaching for reassurance. I've known him since I was a kid, and I still live in fear of disappointing him. Not that it matters; once Urie takes you in, you're under his care for life. The only way to break faith is to endanger the community, and god help you if you do that. Never piss off people with magical powers.

The office is dark and chilly, with CCTV footage of the club playing across screens on one wall. Urie's other businesses are under surveillance, too; the supply warehouse, the apartment office, even the grocery store we all shop at. Two men with earpieces sit and watch the screens carefully, Urie standing behind them with his arms crossed over his chest. He's not as tall as me, but stocky, his blond hair just starting to go white at the edges.

"Alexandra," he says, his blue eyes bright. "I was beginning to become concerned."

I swallow some moisture back into my mouth. "I'm sorry I was gone," I say.

"People are going missing," Urie says. "And you decide it's a good time to run off?"

"I had some personal business I had to take care of."

He frowns. "Your grandfather?"

I don't know if Deda would call Urie a friend, exactly, but when you work for someone your whole life, I suppose there's some sort of relationship. Urie hasn't visited him, but he pays for the home and asks about him.

"He's fine," I tell him, but my hand curls into a fist, the fig sign to ward off evil.

"I'm glad to hear it," he says. "I trust your personal business is now taken care of?"

I nod curtly. "Yes."

"Good. Then I have a job for you."

I knew it was coming, but my shoulders still slump. Bartending isn't my real job, just something to keep me occupied while I wait for this work. Urie picks up a sheet of paper from his desk, but instead of giving it to me, he hands it to Ilia. In the two years I've worked for him, Urie has never once made the mistake of touching me. At first I thought it was because of his own gift, but Urie's control over his pyrokinesis is legendary. It's for my benefit, not his; he doesn't want me to have to carry the knowledge of his death. I don't know if he gave Deda the same courtesy, and I'm afraid to ask.

"I'll get the car," Ilia tells me, folding the paper away. "Meet me out back."

He leaves, and then I'm left facing Urie alone.

"Is this about Marcus?" I ask.

"Someone betrayed our confidence," Urie says, eyes flashing. "And now Marcus is missing."

"His marker?" I absentmindedly rub the tattoo at the back of my neck. Theo tattoos everyone who works at the club with Urie's symbol, a Slavic thunder mark at the base of the neck. It proves we're under Urie's protection, tells us who we can trust, and, in worst-case scenarios, we can use it to track someone.

Urie shakes his head. "Unresponsive."

He meets my gaze, and we both know what that means. It's possible the spell is being blocked; more likely it means the boy is dead.

"Find out what you can," he says.

"Right," I say softly, and I turn to leave.

"Oh, and Alexandra?" Urie calls after me.

I stop and turn back. He watches me with pale blue eyes, like shallow pool water.

"Next time you will clear your schedule with me, understood?"

I nod.

"Understood?" he asks again, louder.

"Yes," I say, clearing my throat. "Understood. It won't happen again."

"*Spasibo*," he says, nodding. "Send Jordan down to the first floor on your way out; tell him to find Ivan."

I duck out of the room without another word and shut the door behind me.

"Headed out?"

I jump. Jordan is standing next to me. He has a bruise on his jaw, right where someone would swing a fist. I stare at it, and his mouth quirks to one side.

"You should see the other guy," he says.

"I bet. Boss wants you on the ground," I say. "Find Ivan."

"Should've guessed," he says. "He's been extra cautious since Marcus."

"Think it'll help?" I ask.

"Can't hurt." Jordan shrugs. "Stay out of trouble, Lex."

"Too late," I mutter back.

I tug up my hood and slouch down the hallway back to the elevator. I punch the button inside as I yawn. My peaceful nights of drugged sleep are already wearing off.

The elevator dings at the ground floor and the doors slide open.

"So," Phillip asks. "Were you just going to leave without saying hello?"

Fucking Georgie.

I shove my hands in my pockets and step out of the elevator. "That was the plan, yeah."

He looks exactly the same, long blond hair falling around delicate features. He has Urie's coloring, but he's slender and long-limbed. "Where have you been? You didn't answer any of my messages; I thought something might have happened to you."

"I'm sorry," I say, and I'm getting tired of apologizing. "I didn't mean to scare you, but I'm fine."

I slip past him and walk down the hallway, and he falls into step beside me. We're the exact same height, our strides matching perfectly. I used to like that.

"So, what, you're never going to talk to me again, is that it?"

"There's nothing to say, Phillip."

"Oh, I think there's plenty to say."

He stops and grabs the pocket of my hoodie to swing me around to face him.

"What did I do wrong? Was it something I said? If you just tell me—"

"It's nothing you did; it's me," I say. "I can't do this anymore."

It's cruel. I know it's cruel, but it's better this way. I try to pull away and he grips my hand instead, and I cringe at the rush of contact. Skin to skin is the worst, nothing dulled by clothing, the images shoving themselves into my brain.

"Don't give me that bullshit, Lex. I want to know why."

Because being with you makes me lonelier than being alone. Because I can't stop picturing your body on a cold metal table.

"Please," Phillip says softly. "Just talk to me."

He looks at me like I'm a painting he's never seen up close before. Like I'm priceless, like I'm something to be admired and pored over.

"Lex," he says. He threads his fingers through mine and I wince. "I was really worried. All I could think about was that something bad had happened, and how awful it would be that I never got to tell you—"

And I don't want to hear it; I don't want him to finish that thought. So I grab his face and kiss him roughly, even though it hurts, even though I shouldn't. He opens his mouth eagerly, and then his tongue is on my teeth and I'm backed against the wall while he presses into me. The rush of longing pushes back the rush of death, and it's so close to being normal. My hands circle his neck and run over his shoulders while Phillip slips his fingers up beneath my shirt.

"You want to get out of here?" he whispers into my mouth, and I almost nod because it's so familiar and easy.

But after this part, after tongues and teeth and sheets, there's the other part. The part when he tries to hold me, when his death creeps around me, until the feel of his skin against mine makes me sick.

"No," I say, pulling back.

Phillip blinks heavy-lidded eyes at me. "Don't you want to?"

"I have to go," I tell him, stepping away from his arms. I shiver, cold without his heat pressed against me. "Ilia's waiting."

"Lexi—" He stares at me, confused and hurt, and I shake my head.

"I can't give you what you want, Phillip. I'm sorry."

And because I'm a coward, I run away. His voice calls after me, but I'm already in the alley, weaving through the dumpsters until I see the headlights of Ilia's sleek car. I slide into the front seat, trying to slow my breathing.

"What happened to you?" he asks, frowning at me.

"Just drive," I tell him, and shut my eyes.

"Ooooh," he says as the car starts to roll forward. "Phillip, huh?"

I don't answer, and he chuckles to himself.

"My cousin has it bad for you. I don't know what you did to him, but—"

"Shut. Up," I grind out.

"I told him to let it go. Does he ever listen to me, though? No."

"I swear to god—" I say, my eyes flashing open.

"Damn, Lex, I'm just messing with you," Ilia says, holding up his hands in surrender. "Don't you ever laugh?"

"Maybe I would if something was funny."

"Ouch. I'll have to work on my tight five."

I lean back in the cool leather seat, hug my arms to my body, and watch the club grow smaller and smaller behind us. *Objects in Mirror Are Closer Than They Appear.* The mirror's convexity means we gain a larger field of view but we sacrifice perspective. Isn't that the way of things? There's always something lost, always something traded. Always a cost to seeing more.

"Heart attack?" Ilia asks me, breaking into my thoughts.

I look away from the mirror to glare at him.

"You're right, too blasé," he says, shaking his head. "And I'm in excellent shape."

"I'm not doing this, Ilia," I tell him dully.

"It's not cancer, is it? It better not be cancer; I can't lose this hair."

I clench my jaw, try to ignore him.

"I got it!" Ilia says, snapping his fingers. "Peacefully, in my sleep, surrounded by naked models."

"Actually, I kill you, Ilia; that's how you die. I stab you with a fork because you won't shut the hell up."

"You wouldn't stab me," Ilia says confidently. "Poison me, maybe, but not stab me."

"Where are we going?" I ask, done with his games.

The playfulness falls from his face, and for a moment I feel guilty. He doesn't like doing this any more than I do. I deal with the dead, Ilia deals with the living, and either way it burns when people look at you with fear in their eyes.

"Here," he says, shifting so he can pull out the paper from his pocket.

I take the sheet from him, unfold it slowly. A name is scrawled at the top in slanting letters, followed by an address off Olympic.

"What happened to him?" I ask.

Ilia glances over at me, then looks back at the road. "You really wanna know?"

I shrug. "Guess not." I'll find out soon enough.

Ilia's car hums along the road with enough speed to press me back into the leather. The lights start to blur together, the gas stations and BBQ joints and hotels, until the night becomes one long streak of neon. He only slows down when we hit the neighborhoods, taking the turns with slick precision. Finally we pull up in front of a yellow apartment complex, the paint faded and the grass outside patchy. It's nicer than my place, but only just.

"Ready?" Ilia asks.

I take a deep breath. Already my skin is crawling with the awareness of what's waiting inside.

"Yeah," I say, and step out of the car.

3

ILIA HAS KEYS TO THE BUILDING, AND I DON'T
bother asking how he got them. We go up the staircase,
my boots echoing hollowly in my ears. At the second floor
Ilia opens the door for me, standing well out of my way.

I hesitate on the landing as Ilia halts in front of the
first door on the left. He unlocks the door and then
looks back at me.

"Lexi," he says. "Come on."

I bite the inside of my cheek, and his mouth goes thin.

"We need to do this," he says tightly. "Please."

It's not the *please* that moves me forward; it's the look
in his eyes. If I didn't know any better I'd say it was
worry, and I remember why we're here.

Ilia opens the door to the apartment and I step
inside, bracing myself. The air in here smells stale, old
cigarette smoke mixed with oil, and beneath it something sweet and rotting. It's bare except for a coil of cable
wire sticking out of the wall and a roll of paper towels on

the kitchen counter. The carpet is matted and stained, and I move deeper into the apartment, my focus on the bedroom at the back.

"You getting anything?" Ilia asks over my shoulder.

I could lie. It would be easy to say no, to get back in the car and drive away.

"Yeah," I say flatly. "He's here."

The thing is, not everyone stays. Sometimes they don't need to; some people love so well, live so hard, that when they die there's nothing left to tie them to this world. They go quickly, with no backward glances. And some spirits are too weak to materialize, so they linger in the in-between spaces, never fully forming and never moving on.

Even those that stay aren't always quite human. Sometimes they've been dead so long, their spirits slowly unravel until they don't remember what it was to be a person, until they don't understand words. They become something else, a presence in a house, a spot of warmth between your shoulder blades.

And then there are the ones that always stay, the vengeful, the murdered and the murderers. Those ghosts are unpredictable and burn the death sense like acid. They never leave this side, fueled by an anger that will last far longer than the last breath of this world.

"Good," Ilia says, relieved. "Let's just get the information and we can get out of here."

We, he says, like he's going to do anything but stand there and watch me. There is no *we*; there's never been a *we* where I'm concerned.

"Be quiet," I tell Ilia, settling my back against the wall. My fingers curl into my palms and I close my eyes, let my death sense swell and curl out.

"James." I whisper the name from the paper, my lips barely moving. "James Eliot Sanderson."

I turn in lazy spirals, waiting, watching. Slowly, so slowly, the reddish black behind my eyes turns darker, deeper. My magic brushes against something, something warm and soft and near.

"James. There you are."

I open my eyes and walk straight into the bedroom; heat blasts into my face and a small, slight man stares back at me. There are bruises all over his face and arms, and a deep ring of them circles his throat.

"I'm sorry," I say, because it's the truth. I'm sorry for what happened to him, and I'm sorry for what I'm about to do.

"What do you want?" he asks, his voice hoarse.

"You know what I want. You know who sent me. Give me the name."

He shakes his head rapidly. "No. His boys already tried, and I didn't tell them anything. And I made sure no one can ask me again."

"Tell us who you told, Sanderson," Ilia says, his eyes trying to pinpoint what I'm looking at. "We know you were selling on the side. That puts us all in danger."

"I'm dead, you little shit," Sanderson huffs at him, even though Ilia can't hear him. "There's nothing you can do to me now."

"Yes, there is," I say, and my hands tighten into fists. I grit my teeth and I start to push, pressing my magic against the ghost until my muscles strain.

Sanderson's eyes go wide, his mouth gaping like a fish, and his form goes even paler, the edges flickering in and out.

"What are you doing?" he chokes out.

"Give us the name or I'm sending you to the other side," I tell him.

"You can't—please," he says, shrinking in on himself. "I have a daughter. They'll come after her."

My stomach twists and I ignore it, bearing down harder. If you want Urie's protection, you keep your mouth shut. History is full of stories of people who covet magic and people who fear it, but the constant is that when others find out about people like me, we end up dead. We protect one another because no one else will, and putting our community at risk is the worst betrayal anyone could commit. Urie will always sacrifice the few to save the many.

"You knew the risk when you took it," I say, shoving aside any sympathy. "And you know the price. Give me a name if you want to watch her grow up."

"No," Sanderson pleads. He fights me, shoving back at my magic with everything he has. It's not enough. Sweat drips down my neck, and something in my back spasms.

"I won't let you," he yells, and he runs at me, his fingers scrabbling at my face, his eyes desperate and wild. I grab him by the wrists and *shove* my magic at him, force it down his throat and into his pores.

"A boy is *missing*, you asshole," I pant. "Probably because of you. Now give me the name or we go visit your daughter next. Your choice."

He screams, loud and full of pain and despair. And it's not a choice, not really. He's not ready to go. Even though he killed himself, even though he'll never speak to his daughter again, he wants to stay. Because at least this is a semblance of life, a last bit of consciousness, a chance to see the girl grow up, to protect her. I don't know what's on the other side, if it's heaven or hell or nothing at all. All I know is that most ghosts fear it the way we fear death. When push comes to shove, they always choose to stay. And I'm always the push.

Sanderson gives me the name and I repeat it to Ilia, who writes it down carefully. I don't envy the fate of whoever's on that paper.

"Keep yourself hidden and don't cause any scenes," I say when it's over. I don't think he has enough energy to mess with much, but sometimes they can surprise you. "Don't make me come back here."

"Go to hell," Sanderson says dully. He looks at me with eyes so empty I almost wish I saw hate instead. His ghost flickers out, maybe to see his daughter, maybe to get away from me, leaving behind only the burnt taste of his pain.

"You all right?" Ilia asks, moving toward me.

"Fine," I say, holding out a hand to stop him. "Can we go?"

"Yeah," he says, not meeting my eyes. "Yeah, we can go."

"Great." We walk out of the apartment, and I touch one finger to my cheek. One of his nails caught my face, but the spells on my arms kept him from breaking my skin. It's a small scratch, just enough to sting, just enough to hurt.

We drive back to the club in silence, each of us guilty in our own separate ways. We have to keep a hard line; that's what I tell myself, what Urie says. We do this so no one is exposed, so the others can live without fear, without looking over their backs. But it's hard to shake the hate in Sanderson's eyes when he looked at me, hard not to feel like a monster when I shove unwilling ghosts to the other side. They're only ghosts, that's what everyone thinks, but they're real to me. They're skin and heat and solid weight, the line so thin between living and dead that it blurs into nothing. What difference is there between pain and the illusion of pain? Between the idea of a thing and the thing itself?

After the amputation of a limb, over 90 percent of patients report phantom sensations. Some sensations are mild, and some are markedly painful. Doctors don't know the exact cause of phantom pain, only that the lack of a limb doesn't make the pain any less real.

The car slides into a reserved spot at the front of the club, and Ilia cuts the engine. My ears feel hollow, the silence stretching between us. His reasons are different than mine, but no less complicated. Family is family, and blood is thicker than guilt.

"You need anything?" he asks me finally.

I shake my head and get out of the car, the night warm and suddenly loud. I don't want to be here anymore. I don't want to serve drinks and watch Nic smile and listen to ordinary people talk about their uncomplicated lives. I want to go home, I want to go back to the hospital and the scratchy sheets and the silence.

"Lexi, wait up, I—"

The front door bangs open as I pass it and a group of shining girls and laughing boys spills out. I freeze in place but it's too late; metal and death scream from every direction. Cancer, pneumonia, heart attack, everything is teeth and sweat and death. The sting of it makes my eyes water, perfume mixing with iron.

My stomach lurches and my shoulders curve in and then—someone's forehead collides with my chin and I stumble back.

"Shit!" a voice says, laughing. "I'm sorry."

I try to back away but small hands grip my arms and a stone hits my chest, knocking the breath out of me. *Let go of me*, I want to say, *you have to let go*, but I don't have the air to speak. The girl is beautiful; her mouth is painted red and shaped like a heart, and something shimmers along her cheekbones. But that's not why I can't breathe.

"You okay?" Her hands tighten on my arms, dark eyes concerned, but all I see is her face, open and staring and bloodied.

She's going to die. Tonight. Painfully, brutally, and that long neck won't look the same after.

Bile rises up in my throat, and I tear myself out of her grip.

"Hey, hey, easy," she says, holding a hand out like I'm a wild animal. "Are you all right? Can I call someone?"

She takes a step toward me and I stagger back, trying to shake the truth out of my head. She should go home, run, save herself. But I don't tell her to. It wouldn't matter if I did. Death always finds you.

"What's wrong?" she asks.

"She's fine." Ilia is at my shoulder, leaving barely an inch between us. "I got her."

The girl looks from me to Ilia and back again. "Are you sure?" she asks me.

"I—I'm okay," I manage to force out.

She narrows her eyes, hesitating, but I can't take it anymore.

"Thanks," I say, and I duck past her, pitching through the open door as bloody images slice into my mind.

I run down the hall and tuck my back against a wall, my throat burning with unshed screams. My arms won't stop trembling, so I press them against the knot in my stomach and try to breath.

"Jesus, Lexi," Ilia says, catching up with me. "Are you okay?"

I shake my head, too sick to answer. *No, I'm not okay. I'll never be okay.*

"Can I . . ." His hand flutters up and I recoil.

"Don't touch me," I gasp. I can't take any more, not now.

"I wasn't going to," Ilia says. "Fuck." He sighs and scrubs his face with his hands. "What did you see?"

I close my eyes, as if it could help. "That girl—her death is bad. Really bad."

When he looks at me, there's no pity in his eyes, only a kind of sadness.

"Come on," he says. "I'll take you home."

"My shift's not over. And my car—"

"You can't drive like this," he says. "Don't worry about it. I'll take care of it."

A tremor of relief runs through me.

"Are you sure?"

"Yeah. Come on. I just have to stop by the warehouse real quick."

I push off from the wall and my legs barely hold me. Ilia doesn't try to help.

Urie's boundaries stretch from the club up to Echo Park and west to Koreatown, making a triangle that most of us operate within. The warehouse is off Wilshire, a solid block of a building without windows or an obvious entrance. Inside are industrial shelves stocked with every magical component you could hope to find. It keeps our witches and the club in operation, but Urie also ships rare ingredients to the other pockets of magic throughout the country—Salem, New Orleans, Cleveland.

"Stay here," Ilia says, parking illegally at the curb. "I'll be right back."

I nod, my head thrown back as I try to massage away a pounding headache. Ilia closes his door gently, and the small kindness sits strangely on my heart.

But I can't get the image out of my mind: the girl, a gleaming red smile slashed across her throat. Suddenly the car feels too small. I open the door and stagger out, taking in deep breaths. The air smells like fried food and cigarette smoke, but it calms me, settling into my lungs with a familiar bite. I look up, stare at the telephone wires strung across the night sky, fill my eyes with the silhouette of palm in place of death.

Something prickles at the base of my neck, and I turn around. There's nothing there, just a quiet street with parked cars. I frown and push my magic out, my hands tingling at my sides.

"Marcus?" I ask softly. "Are you there?"

I push out farther, pressing against the night, and I swear I can *almost* feel something. It's like my fingertips are reaching out to brush someone just as they move away, leaving nothing but a slight disturbance of air.

"Marcus?"

Nothing answers, nothing moves, and the tickle at my back fades so quickly I think maybe I only imagined it.

"Lex?"

Ilia's walking toward me, carrying a small box in his arms.

"What are you doing?" he asks, nearing me.

"Nothing," I say, getting back in the car. "Just needed some air."

I stare out the window while Ilia starts up the

engine, but everything is still. The only movement is the flickering of a streetlight casting a pool of white light over the lot.

The sky is turning bubblegum pink when Ilia drops me off. I drag myself up the stairs and collapse across my bed without taking off my shoes. My head is still pounding, and the muscles in my back are twitching with shivers that won't stop racking my body. I should eat something, but my eyes are closed before the thought is fully formed.

I don't know how long I'm out before I feel a pocket of warmth and a soft tug on my ear.

"You look like shit," Trevor says, his voice close to my head. "Did you eat anything today?"

I make a sound that might be a yes and might be an insult and burrow deeper onto my blanket.

There's a sigh and then a weight presses against my side, the heat much stronger than a human body. My breathing eases, something tight in my chest uncoils. Only the ghosts know how lonely it can be, how much I crave being touched. I let myself drift back into sleep, sink into the warmth and pressure at my side. I'll take whatever comfort I can find.

4

I DREAM ABOUT THE GIRL. I SEE HER NECK SLICING open, flesh parting to reveal white bone, and when I look down I find a bloody knife fisted in my hand.

I wake up covered in sweat, the back of my shirt soaked through. Trevor is gone and I'm alone again, still dressed and starving.

The sun is streaming in through my small window, and I push back the curtain all the way to let a breeze into the stale air. My phone says it's almost one and I have missed texts from Phillip that I ignore. I pull off my wet shirt and take a quick shower, staring at the stained tile and peeling grout while I wait for the water to warm up.

I run the soap through my fingers, and the slipperiness feels uncomfortably like blood. I look down, half expecting to see my hands smeared with red. They might as well be. It doesn't matter that I'm not the one who killed her; I feel just as guilty. I stood by and let it happen, left her to die alone and afraid. I didn't have a choice; if you try to cheat death it will punish you, it will take what it's owed and then more. But what would that excuse mean to the dead?

My phone is ringing when I step out of the shower. I grab a towel that's stiff with age and hastily wrap it around me.

"What?"

"Well, hello to you, too," Ilia says.

"Give me a break," I say, "I just woke up."

"Good morning, then."

"*Ilia*," I growl.

"Your car is out front," he says, unruffled. "I had Theo drive it over."

"Oh," I say, feeling guilty for snapping. "Right. Thanks."

"No problem. You off today?"

"Yeah," I tell him. "Why, you need me to come in?"

"No, just making sure. You doing okay?"

"I'm fine." I pause, suddenly suspicious. "Did you call to *check up* on me?"

"Wouldn't dream of it," Ilia says dryly. "But maybe get some rest today."

"I'm hanging up now."

I throw the phone on the bed and glare at it for a moment. Is he trying to be *nice?* If he is, it's a mistake; nice doesn't get you anything, and I'm not about to reciprocate.

My stomach growls and reminds me I'm starving and dripping water on the floor. I wrap the towel more firmly around me and rummage around a pile of dirty laundry until I find a decent-smelling shirt. I'm late to see Deda, and I can get lunch at the home. It's not exactly flavorful, but right now the only things I have in my small fridge are mustard and milk that's definitely spoiled. I need to get groceries, I need to do laundry, both of which cost money I don't have—I sigh and sink down onto the edge of my bed, a headache building behind my eyes. I don't know if it's from the bad dreams or from the impossible weight of living. I guess it doesn't really matter; the solution is the same. I find a dusty bottle of painkillers, take two pills, and I keep going.

They don't put enough salt in the mac and cheese here. I shovel it in my mouth anyway, Deda watching like a hawk to make sure I'm eating.

"You want some?" I ask.

"I already ate," he says. "Only young people eat lunch this late."

"It's not even two."

"Exactly," he says. "Where were you?"

"Sleeping," I say. "I was up late."

"Did you go back to that . . . place?" Deda asks, frowning. He doesn't like to say *hospital*, like if he doesn't say it, maybe I'll forget about it.

"No," I tell him, giving up on the mac and cheese and switching to the pork chops. "I had to work."

Deda makes a sound in his throat. "Tell me."

I poke at the meat with my fork, avoiding the answer.

"Alexandra."

"Someone leaked information. Urie sent me to make sure it was contained."

The deep lines around his mouth deepen. "Any trouble?"

I shake my head. "He wasn't strong. And he has a daughter."

"Foolish man," Deda says. "You did well."

"I did my job."

I try not to let the bitterness color my voice. It's not like I was going to be a teacher or a doctor or a lawyer. I was never going to college; I dropped out of high school my junior year. Deda fought me on it, but there was no point in going anymore. It was awful, trying to sit in class and pretend everything was normal when the teenage suicide that haunted homeroom would start to cry. Awful to walk down the halls and have so many people shove against me, the darkness pressing so roughly my nose would start to bleed. I had no friends, couldn't have friends, and the counselors didn't know what to do with me and eventually stopped trying. Then Deda got sick, the brakes on the car went out, and rent was due. It was time. I got my GED, picked up where Deda left off with Urie, and there was no going back.

A gnarled hand covers my arm and I look up at Deda, his eyes seeing too much. It's different, between the two of us. Whatever the magic is, it shields us from each other, like two magnets being repelled. I can't see Deda's death and he can't see mine. Maybe the magic knows it would be too hard, to have no one.

"I am sorry," he says, and his voice is thick with regrets.

Deda never wanted this for me. It's not the kind of gift you're grateful for. He was so happy when Mom didn't have it, even though it cut her off from him. And then I came along. And I was like him, and it broke his heart. It still breaks his heart, every damn day.

"It's not your fault, Deda," I tell him. "I'm fine. Let's just eat."

I put a piece of rubbery pork in my mouth and chew.

We play gin in the rec room, the TV blaring in the background. I sort my cards, putting a group of fours together, my mind only half on the game. I never win anyway; no one can beat an old man when it comes to card games.

I'm still tired, and the weak coffee from the machine here isn't helping much. I add more sugar so it will taste like something besides water.

"Are you working tonight?" Deda asks, his eyes staying on his cards.

"No," I tell him. "I'm off till . . ." I pause. I don't remember what day it is. Saturday, maybe? It all starts to bleed together, the sleepless nights, the too-bright days. I have no markers, no anchors, no way to track the hours. "For the next couple days," I finish lamely. "I'll come by, take you out. We can see a movie."

Deda huffs and rearranges his cards. "You spend enough time with me. I can play cards with my friends here; you go out with yours."

"You don't have any friends, Deda," I tell him bluntly. "And neither do I."

"You could make some. You could go back to school. You are so smart and you are wasting—"

"I'm not having this conversation again."

Deda once asked me what I wanted to be when I grew up. A molecular biologist, I said. I wanted to study cells, see them magnified until they looked like stained-glass mosaics, until I could see what makes people *people* on the most fundamental level. Why, Deda asked, and I was young then, and I didn't understand yet that sometimes lying is kinder than the truth. Because I want to fix us, I said.

"You need to be around people, Alexandra," Deda insists. "The living, not the dead. And not the almost dead."

"If it's so easy, then you go make new friends," I tell him. I nod at the shuffling ghost of an elderly man watching our game with interest.

"He won't talk to me." The ghost pouts, his mouth disappearing into wrinkles.

"I do not talk to you because you have nothing of interest to say, Edgar," Deda says, not looking at him.

"Sorry, Ed," I tell him.

"It is too late for me," Deda says, "but it is not too late for you."

I shake my head, knock on the table, and lay out my cards.

Deda looks at them and sniffs.

"Oh, come on," I say as he starts to ruin my sets. "How is that even—"

And my breath catches in my throat.

"What is it?" Deda asks, frowning, but my attention is locked behind him, on the TV. On *her*.

The picture they're showing is wearing less makeup, more clothes than the girl I ran into, but it's still unmistakably her.

". . . disappearance of eighteen-year-old Culver City High School senior Jane Morris. If anyone has any information on her whereabouts, please contact . . ."

The newscaster drones on. *Jane*, I think, *her name is Jane*. It doesn't sound right; it doesn't fit. It's a name for the nameless, for the lost girls and the unclaimed dead. She's too vivid for a name like that. *Was. Was* too vivid.

There are five liters of blood in the human body. The heart pumps out about seventy milliliters of blood with each beat, and it beats around seventy times a minute. If the carotid artery is severed, death from massive blood loss can result in less than three minutes.

I wonder how long those three minutes felt. Did she

pray, did she call out for help? I wonder if anyone heard her. I bet the three minutes felt much longer.

"Alexandra?"

I tear my gaze away from the TV, dizzy and sick and guilty.

"Are you all right?" Deda asks, leaning toward me.

"No," I tell him. "I think it's too late for both of us, Deda."

One day at a time. That's what the therapists at the clinic always say, even if they don't remember who they're saying it to. Take it one day at time, one hour at a time, one minute at a time. The respiratory rate for an adult at rest is twelve to twenty breaths per minute. Sometimes all it takes is knowing you made it from one breath to another. I'm not sick, not like the other patients in there. But I am damaged.

I take two sleeping pills, spread out on my bed, and wait for the drugs to work their way through my system. They're not strong, not like the ones the doctors give me, but I just need enough to keep the bloody dreams away.

"You don't have Harry Potter or anything?" Trevor asks, squatting in front of my small stack of books. "Not even one of them?"

"You can't turn the pages anyway," I remind him.

"I could pretend. *A Thousand Interesting Science Facts? Modern Biology?*" He reads the names of the secondhand textbooks and thrift store encyclopedias. "Who actually reads this shit?"

"I do," I say, closing my eyes.

I always liked science. I'm not looking for an answer anymore, a buried defect in a cell that would explain why I am the way that I am, but I still like learning. Not just biology, but astronomy, geology, ecology. Maybe I can't make sense of myself, but there's reason in the world around me. My head is full of random bits of information picked from old textbooks I find at thrift shops. Hydrogen is the most abundant element in the universe, acceleration is the change in velocity divided by time, black materials appear black because they absorb all wavelengths of visible light instead of reflecting them— my knowledge is incomplete, a shape without the details filled in, a skeleton without flesh. I still have so many whys to answer.

"You're boring," Trevor says, bouncing onto the bed.

"Then find someone else to haunt."

"Very funny," he scoffs. "You ever seen any famous ghosts? Like James Dean? Or the Black Dahlia?"

"No such luck," I tell him.

"What about Walt Disney? Or wait, can you even become a ghost if you're cryogenically frozen?"

"Urban legend," I mutter.

"What?"

"It's an urban legend," I repeat. "Disney's buried in Glendale."

I roll over onto my side, away from the heat and the hot-tar smell of him.

"Hey," Trevor says, poking me in the back. "I'm trying to have a conversation here. Why are you in such a bad mood?"

I'm too tired to be anything but honest. "Because I'm unhappy. And I don't know how not to be."

"Oh." He goes quiet for a moment, and then I feel a thin, warm hand on my shoulder. "I'm sorry you're unhappy, Lexi."

My limbs feel heavy, immobile and thick, but I turn back toward him and we lie face-to-face. His eyes are light brown, fixed in a glassy stare, and I ask, even though I have no right to ask.

"Did it hurt?"

His mouth tightens, and bruises roll across his face like storm clouds.

"The dying part?" His voice is so soft I don't breathe in case I miss it. "No. But the before part. I would have done anything to make it stop hurting. Dying . . . it was a relief."

I want to say *I'm sorry*. I want to say *I wish I could have saved you*. Instead I close my eyes, try to shut out the truth written on his face.

"Lexi?"

"Mmm?"

"Tell me an interesting fact."

I sigh, but I answer. "Babies are born with around three hundred bones, but an adult skeleton has two hundred and six."

"Really? What happens to them?"

"A lot of them start out as cartilage that ossifies and fuses as we grow."

"Weird."

The drugs rush through my veins and waves rock my body, tugging at my bones. Fully grown, we're so brittle with our fused skull plates and spinal columns. We start losing as soon as we're born. We are always less than what we were.

5

I READ THE NEWS THE NEXT DAY WITH MY COFFEE. It's Sunday, my phone says. Jane is the fourth person to go missing downtown in the last six months. It should say the fifth, but they don't know about Marcus. The police are still looking for leads and have a tip line set up. I skim the sites, searching for more information, but nothing comes up; they haven't found a body.

My phone buzzes and I jump, my heart skittering in my chest. Too much coffee, too many nightmares.

"I'm still fine," I tell Ilia crossly.

"Good," he says. "'Cause I'm coming to get you."

"For what? I'm off today."

"Change of plans. Urie wants to see us."

"Ilia—"

"Cops are at the club," he interrupts. "Not the ones on our payroll, real cops."

My stomach drops. "What do they want? Is it

Marcus?" There's no way Urie would have let that leak beyond his people.

"No," Ilia says, his voice strained. "There's a missing girl. I'm on my way."

Shit.

Ilia screeches up to the curb and I slip into the car, my hands white-knuckled around my coffee.

"Tell me what's going on," I say as he peels away.

"The girl was seen at the club last night. Cops looked at the security tapes with Urie. He's still with them. Apparently they saw us near her at some point."

I swear under my breath, and Ilia's head snaps toward me.

"You remember her?" he asks.

"It's that girl I ran into outside the front door."

"How do you know which—" Ilia stops as it dawns on him. "Oh, *fuck*."

"Yeah." I try to swallow moisture back into my mouth.

"The girl's dead? You're sure?"

"I don't make mistakes, Ilia."

"You should have told me," he says, slamming a fist against the steering wheel. "We could've prepared for this, made sure our people were the ones looking into it."

"I'm sorry, all right?" I say. "I wasn't thinking clearly."

"No, you weren't."

"I *said* I'm sorry."

Ilia hisses out a long breath and pinches the bridge of his nose.

"Marcus?" he asks me.

"I don't know."

He's quiet for a moment, his face pained. "We need to get our stories straight," he finally says.

"We tell the truth," I say dully. "I ran into her; she asked if I was okay."

"Don't embellish," Ilia orders. "Don't add details. A bartender would barely remember running into someone, you got it?"

"Yeah, I got it."

"Then look alive," he says, slamming on the brakes. "We're here."

The door to Urie's office is wide open. There's two of them, one man and one woman, both in bulky LAPD uniforms, their cumbersome belts taking up too much space. Urie's face is the same calm mask it always is, but I can feel the waves of tension rolling off Jordan as he stands outside.

"How's it going?" Ilia asks him quietly before we go in.

Jordan shakes his head. "I don't like this," he says. "They're asking a lot of questions."

"Like what?" I ask.

"They want a list of employees," he says, his face pale.

"We can't give them that," I say. "That's a list of practically everyone in this city with magical abilities. If that list gets out—"

"Urie won't let that happen," Ilia says.

"Ilia," Urie calls from the office, and Ilia straightens.

"Come on," he says, nodding to me. "Remember, no details."

"Officers," Urie says, gesturing toward us. "These are two of my senior employees."

My heart is in my throat as the cops turn to look at us. The man is young, clean-shaven, the stench of his cologne rivaling Ilia's. It's the woman who worries me more; she's in her late thirties with a down-turned mouth and eyes that look too sharp for a beat cop.

"Hello," the woman says, nodding at us. "I'm Officer Tisdale; this is Officer Green. Can we ask you a few questions?"

I glance at Ilia, who nods politely. "Of course," he says

in his best newscaster voice. "Whatever we can do to help."

They split us up, Green taking Ilia into the hallway and leaving me with Tisdale. Urie's eyes linger on me before he closes the door, the warning in them clear: *Say nothing that will endanger us.*

"What's your name?" Tisdale asks, her pen poised over her notebook. She gives me a perfunctory smile that I think is supposed to put me at ease.

"Alexandra Ivanovich," I say grudgingly. I don't like giving my name to people I don't know, don't like the way she writes it down, like she's taking something from me.

"We're looking for a missing girl," Tisdale says. "Jane Morris. She was last seen two nights ago, leaving this club." She pulls up a picture on her phone and holds it out for me. "Do you recognize her?"

I look at the picture, the same one they used on the news, and my pulse jumps.

"I don't know," I say slowly. *Keep it simple, no details.* "Maybe? She looks a little familiar, but we see so many people."

"We reviewed the security footage from that night, and it looks like you saw her. Do you remember running into someone? Outside the front of the club?"

"Oh, yeah," I say. "That was her?"

"Yes. Did she say anything to you?"

"Um," I say, screwing up my face like I'm trying to remember. "I said I'm sorry, and she asked if I was okay. It's not—I wasn't really paying attention."

"It looked like you were in a hurry?"

"I'm always in a hurry." I shrug.

"Had you ever seen her before that night?"

I shake my head. "I don't think so. Not that I remember."

I wait, my shoulders tense, the silence broken only by the soft scratching of her pen.

"Is that it?" I finally ask.

"For now," Tisdale says. She puts her pen in her pocket and pulls out a card. "If you think of anything else—anything, no matter how small—please get in touch."

I nod, taking the card without letting our fingers brush. "Sure."

"Thanks for your time," she says, opening the office door. She steps into the hallway and I let out a long breath, scrubbing my hands over my face.

Urie strides back into the office and Ilia follows,

shutting the door behind him.

"How'd it go?" Ilia asks.

"Fine," I say, crumpling the card into a pocket.

Urie comes around the desk and stands in front of me. "Is what Ilia tells me correct?" he asks quietly. "You know the girl is dead? You saw that night?"

"Yes," I say. "I'm sorry I didn't say anything."

"Alexandra," Urie says. "I will not allow anyone to compromise the safety of our people. Not even you."

"She didn't mean for it to hurt us," Ilia says, but he lowers his eyes when Urie turns to him. "Sir."

"Is Marcus dead?" Urie asks, his eyes snapping back to me.

I grip one hand with another. "I never touched him; I don't know how he dies. I haven't seen his ghost. I tried at the warehouse, but nothing came. There might have been . . . *something* there, but I can't be sure."

"If the girl is dead, and Marcus's mark isn't responding . . ." Ilia trails off.

"We assume he's dead," Urie says flatly. He takes a deep breath, and I would say he's trying to steady himself, except Urie doesn't get rattled. "We have a problem. Someone is using our properties as a hunting ground."

"We don't know that for sure," I say, and Ilia shifts

uncomfortably. My eyes dart to him, and he won't look at me. "What? What are you not saying?"

"The other missing people disappeared around the same areas," Urie says evenly. "All within our boundaries."

I suck in a breath. "Did you see what happened?"

"Whoever is doing this is hiding it well, taking people from the streets we don't have under surveillance."

Anger bubbles up in my throat. "And you didn't think to tell us?"

"They weren't our people or our responsibility," Urie says. "Marcus changes that. This ends now. No one goes anywhere without backup, and we double security."

"Do the police even know about Marcus?" I ask, my voice tight.

"No, and it stays that way," Urie says. "We can't have the police looking too hard at us. We solve this internally. Ilia, tell Ivan I want everyone's movements accounted for over the last week. Get Jordan to set up a meeting with the witches to strengthen our protection spells and put a trace on *anyone* who attempts harm within our boundaries."

"Got it," Ilia says. "You think whoever it is will try for one of us again?"

"If they do, it will be the last time," Urie says.

"What about the girl?" I ask.

Urie strokes his chin, thinking. "I'll have someone call the tip line with a sighting of her. Put her south, San Diego. That should keep eyes off us."

"But—" The protest is out of my mouth before I can stop it.

"Yes?" Urie asks me, blue eyes cold.

"They'll never find her body if they're looking in the wrong place," I finish.

"That is not our concern," Urie says, frowning.

I look at Ilia, but he shakes his head. "She's already dead, Lexi. It's not like we can help her. Our people matter more."

"Do I need to remind you of your loyalties again?" Urie asks, a dangerous edge to his voice.

"No," I say quickly, gritting my teeth. "You don't. And I'll make this up to you, I promise."

"You can start now," Urie says, settling into his chair. "I have another job for you."

"Where are we going?" I ask once we're back in the car.

Ilia glances down at his phone quickly. "Los Feliz."

My coffee from this morning is still in the cup holder.

It's gone cold and thick, but I take a long drink anyway.

"Tired?"

"Didn't sleep well." I shift in my seat and brace my head between the window and the headrest.

"I had to tell him," Ilia says abruptly.

"I know."

"Yeah, but—" He sighs, runs a hand through his slicked-back hair. "Look, I'm sorry, kid."

"Not your fault," I tell him, my face turned away. "And don't ever call me *kid*."

I close my eyes against the sun and stop speaking, so Ilia starts to sing along to the radio, and eventually I drift into a sort of half stupor, my cheek smashed against the hot glass of the window. I don't even realize the car has stopped moving until Ilia clears his throat, more gently than I would expect.

"We're here," he says.

I blink a few times and wipe my mouth on my sleeve. We're parked outside a square, compact house, terra-cotta tile on the roof and thin white bars over the doors and windows.

"And who lives *here* exactly?" I ask.

"She supplies the spells for the drinks at the club. Urie owes her a favor."

"What kind of favor?"

"Not sure, exactly," Ilia says. "He said to give her whatever she needs. Ready?"

I swallow, my mouth dry from sleep, and nod. "Yeah."

I let Ilia take the lead; it's best if they see his face first, because I don't look like the kind of stranger you invite into your house. He walks up to the porch and rings the doorbell, smoothing his hair back out of his face, adjusting the collar on a terrible salmon-colored shirt. The door opens and I catch a glimpse of an older woman with thick glasses, her pale skin making the circles under her eyes even starker.

"Hello," Ilia says, his voice polite. "Are you Mrs. Hallas? Urie Porchowsky sent us. He told you we were coming?"

"Yes," the woman says in a low voice. She smells strange, like sage and sulfur, and it takes me a moment to place it—asafetida. They're always using that disgusting herb in their spells.

I don't care for witches, much. They're not like the rest of us—their magic isn't inborn; it comes from spells and books. It's crude at best and destructive at worst, and they always leave blood and chicken bones everywhere.

"Please come in," the woman says.

"Thank you," Ilia says. The witch nods, not really hearing him, and holds open the door for us. I cross the threshold and a shiver runs down my spine. There are screams trapped in these walls.

"This way," the woman says, leading us into a living room and gesturing toward an old-fashioned couch, cream colored and patterned with roses. Inside the house is dark, thick lace over the windows and candles burning on stacked shelves, an ancient television in the corner.

"It's nice to meet you," Ilia says, so convincingly I almost believe him. "I'm Ilia, and this is Lexi."

"Anna Hallas," the woman says, twisting a button on her shirt. "Urie said . . . you could help me."

"Of course, Mrs. Hallas. What can we do for you?" Ilia asks.

There's that *we* again. He's good at this part, though, the talking part. I keep silent, sitting with my hands threaded in my lap while death whispers at me. Whoever is haunting this place is strong—strong, and close, and angry. Mrs. Hallas goes to turn on a lamp and the light flickers on and off, then starts to burn brighter and brighter before finally blowing out with a pop and a sizzle.

"It's my daughter-in-law," the witch says with a sigh. "I know it is. Emily. She died two years ago. She won't— she won't leave me be."

Ilia and I sit as she settles into a matching armchair across from us.

"She's haunting here?" I ask, frowning. "Not her own house?"

"She was. But it's empty now," she says. "My son— he's not there anymore. But she follows him, too."

Ilia glances at me, raising his eyebrows in a silent question. I nod and settle back into the couch.

"Give us a moment, Mrs. Hallas," Ilia tells her. "We'll see what we can do."

I close my eyes, let my senses creep out in tendrils, digging under doors and slipping through cracks. She's close, hovering on the edge of my perception.

"Emily," I whisper, my lips barely moving. "Come out, come out, wherever you are."

I brush up against something warm, and I open my eyes to find her face staring back at me an instant before I slam headfirst into pain and rage.

"Oh, fuck," I say, and a wave of acid hits me so hard my nose starts to bleed.

"Lexi?" Ilia says, his eyes going wide.

Wrong, wrong, the feeling screams at me, pulsing sickness into my veins. I start to shake, sweat running over my arms and down my back, and I have to clamp my lips together to keep my stomach down.

"Lexi, what is it?"

I try to speak, try not to let the death crush me. "Murdered," I choke out.

His face goes pale, pale as the skin of the ghost who watches me with rage-filled eyes. Her chest is a mess of blood and skin, wet and raw with bone shining through.

"Get out of this house," she hisses at me, her voice dragging nails down my throat.

"Emily," the witch moans. She can't see her, but the candle flames roar higher, leaving black streaks on the walls.

The ghost turns around with awful slowness, her lips peeling back over her teeth. "You think you can save yourself?"

"Please," Mrs. Hallas says, wringing her hands together, pleading with something she can't see or hear. "He can't forgive himself."

"He's rotting from the inside out," Emily says, laughing a hollow, mirthless laugh. "The guilt will eat him alive."

"Lexi?" Ilia asks, his face hovering in front of my own. His eyes are dark with concern, but he doesn't touch me, knowing it will only make it worse.

"Emily, please," I gasp. "I can help you."

"It's far too late for that," she says, and then there's a screech and the television erupts, spitting out a shower of sparks. Mrs. Hallas cowers away from it, and Ilia rushes to help her.

I'm the only one who can stop this. I wrap my arms around my chest to keep from shaking and lurch forward off the couch. Emily pauses as I stagger toward her, her head tilting to watch me.

"Go," I say through gritted teeth, sweat beading over my lips as I push my magic at her.

She flickers out, then back in, and her mouth splits in a terrible grin. "I'm not finished," she says.

I try again, my knuckles white as I hammer against the blaze of her rage. It's like pushing at a wall, my muscles straining as she slowly advances on me.

"You can't stay here," I say, even as my magic buckles under the force of her. Maybe if I had Deda to help, but she's too strong, too angry. She shrieks, lunging at me, and my tattoos protect me from the pain of her grip, but not from the wall behind me. Emily slams me up against the plaster, and my head bounces off the hard surface.

"You can't make me leave," she whispers into my face.

She raises her hand and I lift mine just in time to catch her fist in my left hand.

"Get off me," I grit out, and then I slam my right hand into her chest. I can't push her out permanently. But I can force her outside, if only temporarily.

Emily screams as I *shove* at her with everything I have, dredging up every last bit of power. My magic forces its way into her chest, heat burning my hand and racing up my arm. Her eyes go wide and furious, and then with a sound like a lightning crack, her ghost snaps out of sight.

My knees go wobbly and I start to slide down the wall. The next instant Ilia is by my side, propping me up and moving me back to the couch. I shrink away from his touch, and he lets me go as soon I sit.

"Are you all right?" he asks stiffly.

I nod, even though my limbs are shaking and my face stings. I reach up trembling fingers to touch the back of my head and they come away smeared with blood. The color looks so bright in the gloom of this house, almost cheerful.

"What the hell happened?" Ilia asks.

"Too strong," I mutter, leaning back against the couch. I lock eyes with Mrs. Hallas, her face drawn. "You should have told me."

She glances from me to Ilia, her mouth tightening. "It was an accident," she says.

"An accident?" My voice is ragged. "He shot her in the chest by *accident*?"

She flinches like I struck her. "He's in prison," she says. "He's paying for what he did. But he won't eat, can't sleep; every time I visit more of him has gone. He's dying—"

"He deserves to," I say harshly.

"I know he does." Her eyes behind her glasses are huge and desperate. "I loved her like a daughter. But he's all I have left."

"You don't get it," I tell her. "That's not Emily. That woman died, and her ghost is nothing but vengeance and rage. I'm not strong enough to get rid of her for good—ward your house if you want her to stay away. It won't keep her out forever, but it will make it harder."

Mrs. Hallas crumples and I look up at Ilia. "Get me out of here," I say.

He reaches for me, then pauses. "Are you sure?" he asks quietly.

I nod and he hauls me to my feet, one arm around my waist. I grit my teeth, tamp down the images that flood my mind.

"Wait," the witch says, "please."

"I'm sorry," Ilia tells her. "I'll tell my uncle he still owes you."

"But my son," she begs. "What do I tell him?"

I turn back to look at her as Ilia leads me to the door.

"Tell him she'll leave when he's dead."

She gives a strangled cry, and we lurch out of the house without a backward glance. The sunlight is too bright after the darkness and the pain, and I only make it a few steps down the walkway before I vomit into the grass.

I feel sick the whole ride home. I try to ignore the acid in my stomach, the smell of burning copper and frayed wires in my nose.

"Well, that was intense," Ilia says after a while. "You okay?"

"I don't want to talk about it," I say, turning to look out the window. It's hazy, the tips of the skyscrapers downtown disappearing into a smeared sky.

"I'll make sure Urie knows you did everything you could."

I don't answer, closing my eyes against the clouds.

"I didn't know," Ilia says quietly, "that it was gonna be like that. If I'd known . . ."

He trails off, and I don't know if he's trying to convince me or himself. We both know it wouldn't have made a difference. Not for him, and not for me.

My face feels hot and prickly and I angle the AC to blast directly at me.

"Next time I'll check the details before—"

"What part of I *don't want to talk about it* do you not understand?" I snap.

"Okay, okay, jeez." Ilia holds up one hand in surrender. He glances at me and puts on a tight, fake smile. "So, what is it? Skydiving accident? Drown in a hot tub?"

"Don't," I say. "People are dead, Ilia. You can ignore it, but I don't get that luxury. People are *dead*, and I don't want to play this game with you."

"Well maybe if you started paying attention to the *living* around you, we wouldn't be in this situation."

"You really want to know how you die?" I ask him viciously, because he's right, because I'm angry, because death is like copper on my tongue. "Fine. You have an aneurysm at twenty-seven. No warning. Just—gone."

Ilia's face goes white and slack. "That's—that's not true."

I look back out the window, the sky as sour as my stomach. "No, it's not true. Or maybe it is. But either way, I don't think you really want to know."

Ilia's voice comes out low and deep, reverberating in my chest.

"You can be a real bitch, Lexi. You know that?"

"Yeah," I say, still staring at the freeway. "I know."

He drops me off outside my apartment without another word. I brush my teeth twice, rinse the taste of death and vomit off my tongue.

Later, when Phillip texts me, I answer.

6

"DID THESE HURT?" PHILLIP ASKS, RUNNING A FINGER along the black lines on my arm.

His bed is bigger than mine, softer, and the sheets are always clean. Of course, if I was rich and had a maid, my sheets would be clean, too. His room isn't even in the huge main house; it's part of the guesthouse. The privacy is nice, but who has a *guesthouse*?

"You got one; you should know," I say. I touch the thunder mark on his neck, try not to think about Marcus lying dead somewhere, his marker dull and useless.

"Ilia got me drunk beforehand," Phillip says. "It bled a lot, but I didn't feel anything."

"Theo's good," I say, moving my hand away and flexing my knuckles. "It only hurts when it gets close to nerves. Otherwise, it just feels like . . . a pinch." I squeeze the skin in the crook of his elbow for emphasis. This close, I can't avoid the caustic smell beneath his skin, but I try to focus on the flowery scent of the sheets.

"You want to get another one?" I ask.

He grimaces. "My mom would kill me."

"Mama's boy," I tell him. Not that I can blame him; Katya is the kind of mom who still makes Phillip his birthday cake from scratch every year. Only on his actual birthday, never before, one of those nonsensical Russian superstitions.

"Guilty," Phillip says, grinning. He flops onto his pillow, his hair falling into his face.

I shift onto my elbow so I can move the strands out of his eyes. I like seeing his face. Phillip is always smiling, even when I tease him, even when I leave.

"So why'd you change your mind?" he asks, like he can read what I'm thinking.

I nestle down next to him, pretend it doesn't hurt. "I needed to get away. Needed to get out, just for a while."

"What happened?"

"Had a run-in with an unfriendly ghost," I say, trying to keep my voice light. The dead are not bedroom talk.

"Is that why there's blood in your hair?" He runs his fingers over the knot on my head, and his healing magic starts to fizz against my skin.

"It's just a bump," I tell him, but I let him fix it. "You

know head wounds bleed a lot."

"I'm sorry," he says, pulling his hand away. "I mean, I'm sorry you got hurt, but I'm not sorry you're here."

I almost smile. "Thanks."

"You hungry? We can go out and get something to eat."

I raise an eyebrow. "Go out? Like on a date?"

Phillip laughs. "Yeah."

"I don't think so," I say. I sit up and reach for the bundle of clothes on the floor. "I should get going."

"Of course." Phillip sighs. "I knew that would scare you off."

"I'm not scared," I tell him, tugging my shirt on. "I just—it's hard for me to be around people, Phillip."

"Even me?" he asks, frowning.

I pause and look over at him. He only knows half of what I can do; no one knows all of it, except Ilia and Urie and Deda. Even within our world, I have to keep secrets. Talking to ghosts isn't exactly common, but it's not unheard of: psychics can sense ghosts; mediums can communicate with them. But knowing when people die? That's the kind of thing that scares people. And once they know what you know, they'll never look at you the same. But right now I hurt Phillip's feelings, and his bottom lip is sticking out in a distracting way. I lean over and kiss him.

"Yes, even you," I say. I swallow, block out the knowledge that screams in my head. "But I do it anyway. That's got to mean something, right?"

"You just can't stay away, can you?"

I shove him back and shake my head. "Idiot."

I put my boots on and stand up, running a hand over my fuzzy hair.

"Are you going to call me?" Phillip asks, watching me. "Or am I not going to see you for another month?"

I look down at him and chew on the inside of my cheek. "I don't know. But thanks for tonight."

"Anytime," he says.

He takes my hand and I let him pull me down for one more kiss.

"You could stay," he says. "I'll order something."

I push his hair out of his eyes, read the words that are written there.

"Not tonight," I tell him. "I'll see you around, Phillip."

"Yeah," he says, his voice trailing after me. "I'll see you around."

◆ ◆ ◆

I go out the back gate, passing Katya's minivan and setting off the motion lights, hoping Urie isn't looking out one of the dozens of immaculate windows. Fucking Brentwood. I hate this neighborhood. Everything is manicured and exact, tall hedges hiding faux-Venetian columns, xeriscaped gardens and wrought-iron fences. It screams money and perfection, and it makes me itch for chaos.

I sit in my car, in a neighborhood I hate, in a city I hate, in a life I hate, all of it inescapable. I let myself wish, just for a moment, that things were different. That I was different. That I didn't have this *thing* inside of me, this gift that isn't a gift at all, that I could cut it out of me like a tumor.

I lean my head against the seat and stare at the soft glow of light that filters through the houses along the street. I'm not ready to go home yet, back to my unwashed sheets and a scrawny ghost for comfort. I could go to the clinic, but it won't change anything. My life is always waiting when the hours are up. I wonder, Are the people inside these houses as lonely as me, or do beautiful things keep the longing away?

My phone rings and I jump, startled. I go to put it on Silent so I can ignore Ilia when I see the number.

"Nicole?" I say, answering.

"Lexi, thank god," she says, her voice an octave higher than normal.

"What's wrong?"

"I—I don't know exactly," she says. "Can you meet me at work?"

"Now?"

"Please," she says. "I don't know who else to call."

My heart thumps in my chest at the panic I hear her trying to suppress. If Nicole is afraid, then something is wrong. The dead girl's face flashes through my mind, and I turn the key in the ignition.

"I'm on my way."

"Thank you," she says, and my phone goes dark.

I drive as fast as my car can handle, the pedal almost flat against the floor. I roll the windows down and let the wind tear into my face. The lights sear my retinas as they streak by; bass blasts from someone's car stereo. The air is hot and smells like smoke, and I don't know if it's my tires or if the hills are on fire again. Everything around me is burning. I breathe the acrid smell deep into my lungs, not caring that it fizzles and sparks as it kills my cells. My ink-covered fingers squeeze the steering wheel. Something builds inside me and for one brief, blinding moment I want to scream at the sky. Then my exit flashes ahead, and the scream dies on my lips. I swallow it down, where it lodges in my chest, burrowing deep beneath my ribs to wait for me to call it back up.

I park as close as I can and break into a half run, half walk down the neon strip, dodging bodies and creeping cars. My legs are tired but I keep going; I should've eaten something with Phillip instead of running away the first chance I got. But that's all I ever do.

I finally reach Elysium and duck into the alleyway, kicking at the side door until Georgie sticks his bald head through.

"Jesus, Lexi, give it a rest, will you?"

"Where's Nicole?" I ask, barging past him, wincing as his arm brushes my side.

"I don't know," he says, slamming the door shut. "She got off a while ago. Not my job to keep track of you when you're off the clock."

I'm already dialing her number, and she answers on the second ring.

"Lexi?"

"I'm here."

She lets out a shuddering breath that hisses in my ear.

"I'm in the coatroom," she says.

I rush down the hallway toward the front of the club. The coatroom is the go-to place to hide during breaks or to sneak off to smoke weed. It's dark and cool and no one wears a coat in LA so no one ever needs to use it. Over the years we've filled it with spare chairs, a mini fridge, and a soda can tower that's steadily reaching the ceiling.

A murmur of soft voices greets me as I head through the door.

Nicole is huddled in a shabby green armchair with Theo perched next to her, his arm slung loosely around her shoulders.

"What the hell happened?" I grab a rickety wooden chair and settle directly in front of her.

Nicole shakes her head, her bright red curls tumbling around her face. "I don't know, I don't know," she says, pressing her palms into her eyes.

I look up at Theo and his lips press together.

"I found her in the hallway," he says, his dark eyebrows pinched. "She was shaking so bad I thought she was gonna pass out."

I frown; Theo doesn't exaggerate. He's the steadiest person I know, one of the two reasons he's the only person I trust to ink my skin. The other is that his death is one of the less painful types, pneumonia at eighty-eight. It still hurts, but not unbearably, and Theo doesn't pry if I flinch under his gloves or need to take breaks away from his touch.

"Nicole," I say softly. "You called me to come help you, so you need to tell me what happened."

She takes a deep breath, her hands falling from her face.

"I got off about an hour ago," Nicole says, her voice shaky. "Everything was fine; it was slow tonight. I was walking to my car, same way I always go, behind the club and then down through the alley behind Xanadu," she says, naming the place down the block. She stops and takes a deep breath. "I was walking, looking at my phone, and then—I'm not sure what it was, but I felt something. Something really bad."

"Bad how?" I ask her.

"Bad like . . . like a monster under the bed, only you know it's real. Like something you never want to see because you'll never get over the nightmares. Bad like *wrong*."

"Did you see anything?" Theo asks.

She shakes her head again. "No. But I knew something horrible would happen if I stayed there, the same way I knew I had to call you. So I ran back and that's what I did."

I brace my elbows on my knees and clasp my hands together.

"When you say you knew you had to call me, is it the same way you know about other stuff? Who's going to start a fight, who's going to call in sick?"

Nicole nods. "It's sort of like déjà vu, like I'm remembering something I dreamed."

Shit. There's only one reason Nicole would have to call me and not someone else.

"Well?" Theo asks, glancing from Nic to me.

I let out a sigh, lean back in the chair. "You did the right thing."

"It's a ghost, isn't it?" Nicole asks, swallowing. "I've never felt anything like that before. Is that what it always feels like to you?"

"Not always," I say.

"Do you think it's Marcus?" Theo asks. "What are you going to do?"

"Don't worry," I say, not answering the questions. "I'll take care of it."

Nicole sits up straighter, pulling away from Theo. "God, it all sounds so crazy now."

"Everything we can do sounds crazy," Theo says, his eyes meeting mine for a second. "Doesn't make it less true."

"Alvarez, you gonna be a gentleman and take Nic home?" I ask him.

"I'll be fine," Nicole says. "You don't have to babysit me."

"I'm going that way anyway," Theo says, which is clearly a lie, since Nicole lives with her aunt and Theo lives in the big complex with Ilia and the others.

I stand up and run my hands over my hair. "Stick to the streets this time. I'll let you know when the alley's safe."

Nicole stands up and raises her hand toward me. I go still, refusing to flinch and upset her further, but she doesn't touch me. Her hand hovers by my shoulder, close enough that I can feel the heat of her palm as she caresses the air. It's almost real, almost enough, and then her hand drops to her side.

"Thank you," she says softly. "For coming."

"I owed you," I tell her, uncomfortable. "I'll see you later, okay?"

Nicole nods and I turn to go, my skin feeling tight and the scream in my lungs itching to get out.

"Lexi?" Theo calls after me, and I look back over my shoulder. "You need backup?"

I shake my head, tapping on my arm where he inked a knife for protection. "I have backup."

Theo takes me at my word and doesn't argue. "Be careful" is all he says.

I nod once, and then I leave them behind as I go to meet what I know is waiting for me.

The streets are dark, the buildings so tall they block out the glow from the streetlights. I cut through the lot behind Elysium, turn left at the corner by the converted bank, avoid the dumpsters and the pools of water and oil. It smells like piss and gasoline, old beer and rotting food. The only sounds are the drip of leaking air conditioners and the constant soft roar of traffic.

"Where are you?" I whisper, and I don't know if I'm talking to myself or the darkness.

My boots click on the rough concrete as I turn down the long alleyway behind Xanadu, and suddenly I'm too warm, heat pressing against my face and gathering at my back. I smell rusted iron and exhaust fumes and something weighty, something desperate, pushes against me.

"I know you're here," I say to the death pulsing in the air. "Marcus? It's Lexi. You can come out."

It unfolds from the darkness in the alleyway, a patch of shadow peeling away. It makes no sound as it comes forward, steady and relentless.

My stomach drops. She stands in front of me, the blood and the heat and the fury.

"Oh," I say, my lips numb. "It's you."

7

MY BREATH CATCHES IN MY THROAT AS MY BRAIN tries to reconcile the *after* with the *before*. She's wearing the same outfit she had on that night, but her shirt is soaked with blood. The pink cheeks are still there, but her neck is marred by a brutal gash from ear to ear. She's still beautiful, even as a ghost, even with eyes the pearly color of death. She's still the kind of beautiful that makes you ache.

"You can see me," she says, her voice lower and rougher than I remember. Jane. Her name is Jane.

I swallow, my mouth tasting of iron. "Yes," I whisper.

She moves forward, her feet sliding silently along the cement, and I fight the urge to back up.

"You can really see me," she says again, almost to herself.

And then she's reaching out and grabbing my arms. When her fingers close around solid flesh, her eyes go wide and she looks up at me with something close to awe, like I'm her savior, like I'm holy.

"You have to help me," she says, her grip so tight it's almost painful. "I tried to go home, but no one can hear me, no one can see me. Please, they don't know I'm dead, you have to tell them, you have to—"

"Jane," I cut her off, and her eyes snap to mine. For two days she's been screaming at people who can't hear her.

"That's . . . do I know you?"

I shake my head. "No. Not—no."

She blinks at me slowly. "Yes, I do. I remember your hair. It was that night," she whispers. "You were there."

"Jane—"

"*Who did this to me?*" she screams in my face, the lights in the alley burning brighter and brighter.

"Jane, stop," I order. "I don't know what happened, I swear."

She doesn't listen; the murdered ones never want to listen. She pulls me even closer, and it's too much, the heat and the anger and the acid; my legs go weak, and wetness trickles down from my nose.

"Please," I say. She's not intentionally trying to hurt me, so my spells aren't kicking in. I don't want to have to force her away, but I'm close to passing out. "I don't want to hurt you."

She starts to laugh, the sound hollow. It fills up the small space between us, ugly and bitter, and then cuts out.

"I died," she says. "What else can hurt me now?"

"I can," I say, and I shove my magic at her with just enough strength to make her feel it.

Jane's mouth opens and she abruptly drops me; I fall to the ground as she backs up, her eyes darkening from white to brown.

"What was that?" she asks, pressing her hands to her chest like she's looking for a wound. "How did you . . ." She sees me on the ground, blood dripping onto the asphalt.

"Oh, god," she says, hurrying toward me. "I didn't mean. . . ."

"It's okay," I say, holding out a hand to stop her. "It's okay."

Her face crumples up and she screams then, slamming her palms against the rough stone of the building. "I'm so *angry*," she yells, her voice cracking. "What's wrong with me? I can't stop it. I don't want to stop it."

I press my sleeve to my nose and swallow, tasting blood on my tongue. "I'm sorry," I say, and I wonder if she has any idea how much I mean it.

She lowers her hands from the wall and looks over

her shoulder at me. "Who are you?"

"My name is Lexi," I say, my voice thick.

"You were there that night," she says.

"Yes. I work at Elysium. But I wasn't the one who hurt you."

"No," she says. "No, that part wasn't you." She frowns, blinks. "I keep trying to remember that part."

"Jane—"

"How can you see me when no one else can? How can I touch you?"

I try to stand up, and the ground tilts dangerously beneath me. "It's what I do," I say simply. "And now I'm getting something to eat before I pass out."

The mini-mart across the street is empty except for the bored-looking cashier. I buy a carton of milk and a bag of powdered donuts, my hands trembling as I dig out my wallet.

I sit on the curb in the dark, licking powder off my fingers and waiting for the sugar to hit my bloodstream. Jane sits next to me, her back straight, body rigid. If someone drives by us, I wonder what they would think of what they see; a girl, or maybe a boy, sitting alone on a curb in the middle of the night.

"How much do you remember?" I ask Jane quietly.

"Not enough."

Her eyes go unfocused, staring at something I can't see. This is what I must look like when I see the dead.

"The last thing I remember clearly is the alley. After that it gets foggy. I think I was somewhere else when I was dying," she says, her lips barely moving. "The blood felt like warm water spilling out of me. I remember the pain. It was . . . sharp. And then it was deep."

Blood starts to bubble up from the slash in her throat, cherry red and shining. Jane blinks, her face calm and detached, and presses a hand against the cut.

"Jane."

She lifts her hand up, examines her wet fingers, and I feel my neck start to crawl.

"I'm sorry," I say, curling my own fingers into fists.

"Not your fault," Jane says, and I flinch. I didn't hold the blade, but I'm still guilty. I let it happen.

"What else?" I ask, my skin hot from being this close.

She frowns. "I remember you. Looking afraid. Like you needed help."

"I was having a bad day," I say, which is almost the truth. "Anything after that? The person who . . . ?"

"No," she says. "Nothing, until I woke up like this.

With this . . . this *rage* inside me. Not that I was dead, but that someone killed me." She glances over at me, but I won't meet her eyes. "I tried to go home. They haven't found my body yet, have they? That's why my mom thinks I'm still alive."

I tear a donut into pieces. "No, they haven't."

And they won't, because Urie's going to make sure they'll be looking for her alive, and somewhere outside the city. Because of me.

"If they can't even find my body, how are they going to find who did this?" Jane looks down at her shirt, at the bloody fingerprints on it.

"They'll keep looking," I say. They'll just be looking in the wrong place.

"Not good enough," Jane says, her hands curling into fists. "I want a name. I want a face. I want justice."

I wipe powdered sugar on my pants and stand up. "I need to make a phone call," I tell her, taking a step away.

Ilia answers on the second ring.

"What is it?" he asks, sounding harried.

"About that dead girl?" I say. "I have a lead."

"What sort of lead?"

"I'm looking right at her," I say, my eyes flicking to Jane.

Ilia swears. "Does she know who killed her?"

"She doesn't remember much," I tell him. "Just bits and pieces."

"Keep her calm," Ilia orders. "I'll talk to Urie. See if you can figure out where her body is; maybe she can feel it. We can't have people stumbling across it and calling the police. And get her to remember what happened."

"How do I do that?"

"Retrace her steps, see if it jogs anything," Ilia says. "Talk to her friends. Hell, hypnotize her if it helps— just *get me a name*."

"I'll try," I tell him. "Tell Urie I'll try."

I hang up the phone and turn back to Jane.

"You're going to help me, aren't you?" Jane asks.

I failed her that night, when I turned my back and let her die. I won't fail her again. Her, or Urie.

"Yes," I say. "I am."

Silence stretches between us, taut and brittle. The neon lights from the mini-mart sign flicker and buzz, bathing us in a red glow like the inside of a heart.

"So what now?" Jane asks, standing up, and exhaustion hits me like a gut punch.

"Now I go home," I tell her. "I've been up for . . . I don't even know how long."

"Where am I supposed to go?" she asks.

"Look, we can't do anything tonight," I tell her. "Just go home."

"No," she says quickly. "I don't want to go back there."

I start walking back toward the club and my car and Jane stays beside me, her blood black under the streetlamps.

"Why?" I ask.

"It's—" She stops, presses her lips together. "I can't touch anything. My clothes, my books, everything is just *there*, waiting for me to come home. And my mother . . . " Jane pauses, swallows down her words. "No. I'm not going back there."

I shove my hands in my pockets. "Then stay here. Go to a friend's house. Go to Disneyland for all I care."

Jane shakes her head. "Being around people who can't see me, can't touch me, it's worse than being alone. It's like being nothing, less than nothing. You don't know how lonely it is."

I pause, glancing over at her, something uncurling beneath my ribs.

"I do," I say. "I do know."

Jane meets my eyes, weighs what she sees looking back, and finally nods.

"Good," she says. "Then I'm going with you."

I open my mouth, shut it, open it again. I try to come up a reason to say no, but I'm far too tired to argue anymore.

"Fine," I tell her. "You better not keep me up."

We only pass two clearly drunk people, but I don't talk to her until we get to the car. Then, like an idiot, I open the door for her; it's not like doors can stop ghosts. She waits until I move aside anyway, and I shut her in and walk to my side.

"Guess I don't need to bother with a seat belt," Jane says, but the joke comes out flat.

Her heat presses against my right side and I turn up the AC.

"My place isn't nice," I tell her, pulling out into the street. "Whatever you're expecting, it's worse."

"I don't care," she says. "You can see me, talk to me. It makes me feel like a person."

I turn onto the highway, grip the steering wheel hard.

"Is it normal?" Jane asks. "That I can't remember?"

I frown; most of the ghosts I come into contact with remember their deaths, even the violent ones. "I'm not sure."

"Will it get better?"

I swallow, avoid looking at her. "I don't know. Maybe."

"I wish I could remember the face."

I keep my eyes on the road, watch the exits disappear behind me.

"It's somewhere in there," I say. "Whoever it is, they can't hide forever." Our sins always find us out.

"Who the fuck are you?"

"Trevor," I snap. "Stop it."

I shut my door behind me and lock it before I turn to deal with the two ghosts facing off in the middle of my apartment. Trevor looks outraged, his arms crossed over his chest, while Jane's face is cold and impassive.

"Trevor, Jane, Jane, Trevor."

"Get out," Trevor says.

"Trevor, Jane needs a place to stay, okay? It's not for forever."

"She's covered in blood, Lex," Trevor says, sounding disgusted.

"That would be the slit throat, asshole," Jane growls at him.

"Oh, boo-fucking-hoo," Trevor snaps back. "I was almost decapitated and you don't see me sulking around like a stuck pig."

Jane's lips pull back over her teeth, her eyes starting to film over, and then she goes still.

"How?" she asks slowly.

"What?"

"How are you not bleeding? If you were hurt like that?"

Trevor looks at me in disbelief. "You didn't tell her?"

"I haven't gotten to that part yet," I tell him. "I just found her."

"What is it?" Jane asks.

I gesture at Trevor to go ahead while I sit on the bed and start to unlace my boots.

"You can control how you look," Trevor explains. "None of this," he says, motioning at his body, "is real. It only looks like this because it's how I see myself. You see yourself the way you were at the end. I don't like . . . being like that. That's not who I was, not how I want to be."

"Show me how to do it," Jane orders.

"Just picture yourself the way you looked before," Trevor says. "You have to focus, and sometimes you'll slip. I still slip. But since you were murdered, you should have energy to spare."

Jane closes her eyes, a line deepening between her brows, and I glance at Trevor.

"Are we good?" I ask him.

His chin juts out, but he shrugs. "Fine. As long as she understands her residency is not permanent."

I shake my head, then duck into the bathroom to take off my jeans and pull on a pair of soft shorts.

When I come out, Jane is opening her eyes, looking down at her body. "It didn't work."

"You just need to practice," Trevor tells her. "You're still new."

I sprawl onto my bed, punch my pillow into place.

"As long as you practice quietly," I say. "I'm going to sleep."

They don't answer, and I lift my head up to see the two of them sitting across from each other on my floor, Trevor watching as Jane scrunches up her face. I fall asleep to the sound of whispers, the dead outnumbering the living.

8

I WAKE UP GASPING, BLANKET TANGLED AROUND my legs, my shirt damp with sweat. I wipe my face, try to catch my breath, and I feel the strange weight of eyes on me.

"Bad dreams?" Jane asks, watching me calmly from the chair next to my dresser.

I grunt something and struggle out of the sheets, throwing open my small window and sticking my head into the early morning air. It's chilly, the sun barely up, and my sweat turns cold on my skin. I take two deep breaths, clear out my lungs, and then turn back to face the source of the heat.

The bloodstains on her shirt are gone, the white cotton crisp and clean, and her eyes are a clear, focused brown.

"You've been practicing," I say, sitting back down on my bed. "Where's Trevor?"

"He said he had a yoga class," Jane says, smiling

a little. "Why can't I pick up a book but I can sit in a chair?"

I sigh and drag my hands across my face. God, it's too early for this. I want to go back to sleep, not explain the intricacies of being dead to a ghost.

"Because you're not really sitting in it," I tell her.

"If I'm not sitting, then what am I doing?"

"You don't have a body so you're not actually sitting," I say. "You're thinking yourself into that position. It's the same reason you don't sink through the floor but you can walk through doors."

"Oh." Jane looks down at her feet, like she can see through the wooden boards to the room below. "Why don't you have a TV?"

I lie back down, punch my pillow into shape. "Because I don't need one."

"Trevor says you should get one," Jane says. "So he can watch it when you're gone."

"This isn't Trevor's apartment," I say, annoyed.

"Then why do you let him stay here?"

"He's my friend, I guess."

Maybe it's true. I don't know if Trevor even likes me much, or if I like him. We wouldn't be friends if he were still alive; he'd be in his thirties by now, probably living somewhere in West Hollywood with a husband and a dog and a couple kids. But death intervened the way it does and now we're stuck with each other and maybe that's enough. I never make him leave; the nights are less lonely when he's around.

"I had friends," Jane says, her eyes looking somewhere far away. "Macy and Delilah. And they don't even know I'm dead." Her gaze snaps back to me. "You could tell them," she says. "You could tell them; you could tell the police—"

"No," I say quickly. "I can't do that. You don't understand the way this works. We don't talk to outsiders."

"I'm an outsider," Jane says.

"Not anymore," I say, frowning. Jane's in my world now; whoever killed her pulled her into this, and there's nothing to stop it from happening again.

"But—"

"There are some things I can't do, so don't ask me to," I tell her. "They wouldn't believe me anyway. They'll think I'm lying or I'm crazy, and either way it won't help you."

"Morning!" Trevor says, appearing right in front of my face.

"Christ," I yell, scooting back on the bed.

"Sorry," he says, sounding not at all sorry. "You're wound too tight, Lex, you should try yoga."

I shove his shoulder and climb out of bed. "What happened to jazz dance?"

"It's not as fun without a partner. Although," he says, turning his attention to Jane, "that could be arranged. What do you say, newbie? They can't charge us, and you get a spot right next to the instructor."

Jane looks at me, her mouth a straight line.

"Maybe later," she says. "I have a killer to find."

"I get it," Trevor says. "Vengeance first."

"If you won't tell anyone I'm dead," Jane says to me, "then how do we do this?"

I pick up my toothbrush and stare at the dark circles under my eyes in the mirror. "Do you know a kid named Marcus? Fifteen, shaggy hair?"

"I don't really hang out with a lot of fifteen-year-olds," Jane says.

"What about any of the latest missing people?"

"The ones on the news? I didn't know any of them," Jane says. "You think whoever killed me killed them, too?"

"It's possible." I spit into the sink and rinse out my mouth. "Maybe there's someone you have in common with them, someone who connects you to the others."

"No one I know could have done this," Jane says angrily.

"You're more likely to be killed by a relative or a friend," I tell her. "Do you remember anyone else who was there that night?"

"Just you," Jane says, eyes narrowing.

"Fine, point taken," I say. "But maybe whoever was with you saw something. We need to make you remember. Can you tell me anything about where you died? Where your body might be?"

Jane shakes her head. "I told you, the alley is the last clear place. That's why I went back there. My body could be in Ohio for all I know."

"They still haven't found it?" Trevor asks. "Bummer."

"No one's found *Jane's* body," I say slowly. "But you're not the only one who's gone missing. I think I know someone who can help us."

The sun is almost up by the time I'm dressed and out the door, a breeze breathing down the fine hair on my neck. The Santa Anas are coming; I can feel it in the air, an electricity that turns the sky yellow and people savage. The winds come from the high-pressure air masses of the desert and channel through the mountain passes as they sweep out to the low-pressure area of the coast. But it's more than that, more than just air; women kill their husbands during the Santa Anas, people throw themselves off bridges, and the fires spread and jump across freeways, always looking for something more to burn. The winds bring headaches and nausea and depression, and maybe it's the positive ions in the air or maybe it's that we recognize the howl of the wind as something that lives inside us, a nameless, unhappy thing that rages deep within.

"Where are we going?" Jane asks, her voice cutting into my head.

"To see my grandfather," I answer.

"What?" Jane says, gripping my arm to stop me. "We don't have time to waste visiting an old man."

I yank my arm away from her and glare. "You want my help, then we do this my way. Feel free to find someone else to haunt if you don't like my direction."

Jane scowls back at me. "Are you cranky all the time, or just in the mornings?"

"Stick around and you'll find out," I grumble, starting to walk again. "And quit grabbing at me on the sidewalk; people will think I'm having a seizure."

Jane follows me into the nursing home and I nod at the receptionist on duty today, a stern-looking woman named Grace.

"You're early," she says. "I think they're still finishing breakfast."

"Thanks," I say, and head toward the cafeteria down the hall. "Stay close," I whisper behind me, and Jane nods.

Deda is sitting at a table by himself against the far wall, his tank propped against his chair and his face buried in a newspaper. I grab a banana and a yogurt from the bar and weave through the plastic tables full of ancient people.

"Deda," I say, and he looks up, his eyes warming when he sees me.

"I thought you—" He cuts himself off as he sees Jane behind me. "Alexandra," he says, face closing. "What is the meaning of this?"

Jane glances from Deda to me and realization dawns on her face.

"You could have told me," she says to me softly.

"I'm telling you now," I say. "Deda, meet Jane. Jane, this is my grandfather, Sergei Ivanovich."

"It is nice to meet you," Deda says, giving Jane a deep

nod. "I am sorry for your loss."

Jane's lips tug up at one corner. "I guess it is my loss, isn't it? More than anyone else's."

"Please, sit," Deda says, gesturing to the empty plastic chairs like this is his living room and not a crummy cafeteria lit with too-bright fluorescent lights.

"Thanks," Jane says while I slump into a chair.

"Alexandra, explain yourself," Deda says, his bright eyes narrowing on me.

I peel off the lid of the yogurt and lick it. "You're the one who told me to make friends."

"I meant students and people your own age, not the dead." Deda bows his head briefly to Jane. "I mean no offense."

"None taken," Jane says. "I am dead."

"Deda, I need a favor. I need Carl's number."

He frowns. "What for?"

"I need to talk to him," I say. "It's important."

"Who's Carl?" Jane asks.

I eat a scoop of yogurt and wince at the sweetness. "The coroner."

"Did Urie ask you to do this?" Deda asks.

"He didn't have to ask." I bite my lip and look over at Jane. "Show him," I tell her.

She looks confused for a moment, and then her face clears. Her eyes go unfocused, and then slowly, like tea in hot water, blood starts to drip from her neck and seep into her shirt.

If I wasn't watching him maybe I'd think he didn't care, that he's seen too much, been too close to death for too long. But I am watching and I see the way his gnarled hands tighten around his coffee mug, white knuckles pressing through the thin skin.

"Again, you have my apologies," Deda says stiffly. "No one deserves such an end."

"Maybe one person does," Jane says, and there is nothing living in her voice.

Deda looks at me. "Absolutely not," he says.

"Please, Deda," I tell him. I meet his eyes, eyes like mine, older but no less haunted, and I try to make him understand. I couldn't save her, couldn't save any of them. He knows what it feels like, the blood that doesn't wash away. It's in our pores, under our skin. When you spend so much time close to the darkness, you start to believe you don't deserve the light. "There could be others."

"Alexandra—"

"*Please*," I say. *I need this*, my eyes say.

He sighs and sits back in his chair, his face suddenly

older and grayer. "Very well," he says finally. "I will call Carl for you."

"Thank you," I say, squeezing his hand. "I'll come back tomorrow."

Deda covers my hand for one long moment before pulling away. "Do what you must."

I stand up and wait for Jane to follow. She rises to her feet, then hesitates.

"Mr. Ivanovich?" she says. "Thank you. For helping me. And for—for whatever it is that you gave Lexi."

I cringe inside, but Deda only blinks at her.

"Take care" is all he says.

"Come on," I tell her, my voice harsh.

Jane falls into stride beside me, studying my face. "Did I say something wrong?"

I shake my head, lifting a hand to wave good-bye to Grace. "It's nothing," I say when no one can see my lips moving.

"If it's nothing, then why are you angry?"

I step out into the sunlight, tuck my hands in my pockets. "I'm not angry."

"Really? Because you're acting like you are."

"Were you this pushy when you were alive?" I snap at her, stopping on the sidewalk.

She smiles at me. A real smile, not a cruel one, not a cold one. It's small, and sad, but for a moment her face looks alive, looks like the face of the girl I saw that night.

"Yeah, I was," she says. "So you might as well answer me."

I hesitate, because I don't want that face to disappear.

"He hates it," I say finally. "That he passed this . . . *ability* on to me. I don't blame him, but he blames himself."

Jane presses her lips together, the smile fading, and I feel the loss like an overcast day. "I understand," she says. "But I meant what I said. I'm glad he gave it to you. Maybe that makes me selfish."

"No," I say, starting to walk again before someone sees me talking to myself. "It makes you human."

My phone rings halfway down the block.

"Hey, Carl," I say, answering.

"Lexi," he says, his voice tired but amiable. "Long time, no see. How you been, kid?"

"Oh, you know," I say. "Hanging in there. You?"

"Can't complain. Job security, am I right?" He says that every time.

"Yeah."

"So your grandpa says you need some information?"

114

"Yeah, I'm looking for a John Doe. Teenager, fifteen years old." The police aren't looking for Marcus, but that doesn't mean he hasn't been found. If the same person is responsible, maybe the bodies are close to one another.

"Hmm, I don't think I have anything that matches that description."

"What about stabbing victims?"

"Nothing recently. But I can check around."

"Thanks," I say. "Would I be able to come by later, ask you some questions?"

I hear papers rummaging. "Yeah, let's see . . . three work for you?

"Sounds good. Thanks, Carl, I owe you."

"No problem. See you soon."

I hang up and find Jane watching me with one eyebrow raised.

"So?" she asks.

I shove my phone in my pocket. "Want to see some dead bodies?"

9

FROM THE OUTSIDE, THE LA COUNTY CORONER'S office is a tidy brick building with a cheerful courthouse façade. On the inside, they've given up trying to impress anyone living. Bloody hedge clippers rest to my left and buckets of cheap dish detergent are stacked to my right.

"Jesus," Jane says, her eyes widening at the display. "Is this what they're going to do to me?"

"Try not to think about it," I whisper to Jane, most of my attention focused on trying to breathe through my mouth.

The smell doesn't hit me all at once—first it's licorice, and then something almost floral. But hiding underneath is the thick cloud of rot that even the cold temperature can't cut. Take all the worst smells of the city—open sewer, hot garbage, burning hair—then multiply it by a thousand and add the putrid scent of decay.

That's what this morgue smells like, like dead flowers and astringent. It's suffocating. I cup my hand over my nose and wait for Carl to finish peeling off his latex gloves.

"Lexi! It's been forever," he says, far too cheerfully for the location. "You got taller!"

"Hey, Carl. Am I interrupting?"

"No, no, I'm just about finished. Let's talk in the office."

I nod and follow him through the morgue, my boots echoing on the cold floor and my breathing harsh through my mouth.

"Take a seat," Carl says, collapsing into a chair held together with duct tape. The door snicks shut behind me, cutting off some of the smell at least, and I take a seat across the desk. Jane comes to stand next to me, leaning her back against the wall.

"So. How are you?" Carl asks, and I turn my focus to him. "You look tired."

"Yeah, people keep telling me that."

"Well, this isn't going to help you sleep any better." He nudges a folder on his desk. "All the stabbing victims from the last six months. We haven't had too many this year; it's mostly gunshot wounds and car accidents."

"None of the missing people on the news have shown up?"

"Not yet," Carl says.

I pick up the folder, absently flipping through the photos. Jane moves closer, leaning over my shoulder to look, and I hold my breath as her face comes close to mine.

"God," she says, and blood blossoms on her neck.

Dead faces stare up at me, smooth and bloodless and gray, none of them familiar, none of them with their throat cut. I stop on an autopsy of an older man, examining the picture.

"'Perforated liver,'" I read. "Did they catch the guy that did this?"

"Yeah," Carl says. "Robbery gone bad, he didn't mean to kill him."

"'Diaphragmatic injury, consistent with twelve-centimeter blade,'" I murmur, turning the information over in my head. I shut the folder and drop it back on the desk. Scientific method—to form a hypothesis, begin with the simplest questions.

I look up at Carl. "What size blade would you need to cut someone's throat?"

"You don't need length for that; the carotid is just below the surface. Something short but wide would be your best bet."

I study Jane out of the corner of my eye; the wound

on her neck is slighter deeper and wider at one end.

"Which side of the wound would be deeper?" I ask.

Carl frowns. "Typically the start, where the knife went in."

"So if it's deeper on the right, that suggests a left-handed assailant?"

"Most likely."

"How much strength would you need for an attack like that?"

Carl raises an eyebrow at me.

"Hypothetically," I say.

"*Hypothetically*," Carl repeats, "not much, especially if it's from behind. But if you're talking female murder victim, the odds skew male."

I exchange a brief glance with Jane, who lifts a hand to finger the cut.

"Thanks, Carl," I say, standing up. "Keep an eye out for my John Doe. And let me know if any more stabbing victims pop up, will you?"

"Sure thing," he says. "Do I want to know why you're looking for him?"

"A favor for a friend."

"Uh-huh," Carl says. "This friend in some kind of trouble?"

"Nothing I can't handle. Don't work too hard, yeah?"

"Who, me?" He laughs, but he rubs a hand over a weary face that's just starting to wrinkle. I want to tell him to cut out the cigarettes, to stop working so much, but I don't.

"Take care, Carl."

"So how do you know the coroner?" Jane asks hollowly when we get back to my apartment.

"Deda used to drive for the morgue, back in the day," I say, without going into much detail. Human bone is useful in spells, but hard to get your hands on, unless you know which bodies are being donated to science.

Jane nods, her attention clearly elsewhere.

"Are you okay?" I ask her, tossing the file of dead bodies on top of my books.

"It's just . . . there were so many dead people," she says, touching the bloody cut along her neck.

"It's a big city," I say.

Jane looks down at her fingers, the edges smeared with red. "Shit," she says. "I can't make it stop today." Her shoulders slump, and she turns away from me.

I reach out, years of restraint making me hesitate, but then my hand curls lightly around her shoulder. Her body goes still, and then with a shudder she relaxes and her arms uncross, heat melting into my side.

"Hey, it's okay," I tell her.

Jane pulls away from my arm, and for a moment I miss her warmth.

"Whoever it is could be hurting more people," she says. "Why can't I remember?"

"You didn't remember me until you saw me again," I say gently, "so we figure out who you saw that day. We go over that last day hour by hour, talk to everyone who was with you, spoke to you, even saw you. We know you were at the club. . . ." I trail off, my brain lighting up.

"What? What is it?" Jane asks.

"The tapes from the security cameras at the club. The cops looked at them, but maybe if you watch them, you'll remember. At least we can see who you were with."

I'm already calling Ilia as Jane nods slowly.

"What?" he snaps into the phone.

"How long does Urie keep the footage from the security cameras?"

"Excuse me?"

"I need to see the footage from that night, from every camera."

"Shit," Ilia says, understanding. "The hard drive only keeps it a few days before it records over."

I close my eyes. "So it's gone?"

"Not exactly," Ilia says, "The cops saved the footage, but they took it with them."

"How could you let them take it?"

"Maybe if we had a little *warning* they were coming, we could have done something about it," Ilia says, voice dangerous.

I breathe out hard. "I messed up; I get it," I say. "I'm trying to make it right. Can you get me that footage? I need Jane to watch it."

"Who's Jane?"

"The dead girl, Ilia. Can you get it for me or not?"

Ilia makes a frustrated sound. "Give me a couple days. I need to call in some favors from our people on the force. You owe me, Lex."

"Understood."

I hang up and look at Jane. "We watch those tapes. We talk to everyone. We find *something* to make you remember."

Jane meets my eyes solemnly. "Okay."

"Okay," I say. "Let's work from the beginning. Where would you be in the morning?"

Jane puffs out her cheeks, lets out a sigh. "My house," she says reluctantly. "I'd be at home."

Jane's home is a flat-roofed duplex in El Segundo, the front yard full of gravel and sprinkled with potted succulents. A plastic lawn chair sits by its lonesome, dirt and dust ground into the slats. Jane stares at the front of the house, and a muscle in her cheek tightens.

"So if ghosts are real," Jane says to me from the front seat, "what else is real? Magic?"

I nod.

"Vampires?" I roll my eyes and she shrugs. "What? I don't know; it's possible."

"No, vampires aren't real. Although witches can get weird with blood on full moons."

"Gross," she says.

It doesn't escape me that she's stalling.

"Was it that bad?" I ask. "When you came back?"

Her jaw tightens again. "My mother . . ." She stops. "We don't—didn't—always get along. Being dead doesn't really change that."

It's suddenly hard for me to breathe, a block of ice in my lungs.

"No," I say, my voice tinny in my ears. "It doesn't."

"Let's just get this over with."

I nod and walk up the small path to the screen-covered door and ring the bell. It buzzes inside, and I wait a long minute before trying again.

"Maybe she's not home," I say. "We can wait for her."

"We'll be waiting a long time," Jane says, crossing her arms. "There's a key under the flowerpot."

"I can't just go in," I tell her.

"Why not?" She shrugs. "It's my house. I'm giving you permission."

"Yeah, but that's not exactly going to work if someone calls the cops."

"Look, my computer is connected to my phone. We can check my messages and see if anything weird happened."

"Okay, okay," I say, crouching down by the cactus. "I'm getting it."

I dig under the pot, unlock the door, and step inside.

The hallway is dark and leads into a small and cluttered living room, a futon taking up one side and a yellow armchair on the other. The TV is dusty, the coffee table piled with dirty cups and a half-empty bottle of vodka.

"Home sweet home." Jane paces around the room, her

hand trailing through framed photos of her as a child, a smiling girl with pigtails, a chubby baby with a bow. She stops in front of a stack of "missing" posters with a posed school photo that doesn't look anything like her.

"I hate this one," she mutters. "I look like a shitty lawyer."

"I think you look pretty," I say, but she doesn't respond.

Two cats stretch up from the couch, and the calico one jumps down and tries to rub against Jane's legs.

"Jimmie?" she says, glancing down in astonishment. "You can see me?"

The cat goes through Jane's feet and it makes a disgruntled sound.

"Cats can see me?" Jane repeats, looking up at me.

"Sometimes," I say. "It sort of depends on the cat."

"Depends on what?"

I shrug. "If they feel like it. Is anything coming back to you?"

She shakes her head. "Not yet. Come on," she says, "my room is this way."

Jane leads me down another hallway and stops in front of a closed door, her hand going through the knob when she tries to open it.

"Oh," she says, letting her arm drop. "Right. You better do this part."

I reach forward and open the door, stepping aside so she can go in first. The room is bright with color, the walls a cheerful yellow and covered in frames of bold artwork. Jane's bed is unmade, a pink and turquoise quilt shoved to one side.

"Sorry it's a mess," she says. She tries to straighten the blanket and her hands melt through it. "Dammit."

"It's okay; I like it," I say, and I'm being honest.

"Well, here," Jane says, going to the small white desk in the corner. It's covered in stickers and photographs, snapshots of Jane with her tongue sticking out, with her arm around a girl with dark hair. "Get the laptop."

I pull out the chair and sit at the desk, moving a notebook out of the way. I stop, taking a closer look at the sketch it's open to.

"Did you do this?" I ask. It's a long-haired girl sitting cross-legged inside a fish bowl, the lines sure and dark.

"Yeah," Jane says, ducking her head. "It's just a sketch."

I look up at the art on the walls, the paintings in a similar style.

"You're an artist?"

"I guess," she says. "I mean, I like to draw."

"You're good," I say. "Really."

"Thanks," Jane says, clearly uncomfortable with my praise. "It's just a hobby."

"If you say so," I tell her, looking down at the sketch-book. "Can I have this one?"

Jane blinks at me. "Why?"

"Because I like it. And I don't have any art in my place."

"I mean, sure. If you want it."

"Thanks," I say, carefully peeling the page out.

"Can we do this now?"

"Yeah, hold on." I fold up the picture carefully and put it in my largest pocket, then open the laptop. "Password?"

Jane clears her throat. "Baby Jane, one word."

I turn to look at her and she scowls.

"What? It's a good movie. Bette Davis was nominated for an Oscar."

I shake my head and type the password and the computer lights up.

"Do you have Find My Phone? Maybe it's still with your body."

"Shit," Jane says. "No."

Of course. Why would any of this be easy?

"What am I looking for?"

"Messages," Jane says, pointing at the blue bubble. "There's a lot of them."

I click on the messages and scroll through them.

Text me when you get home ok

Jane?

Hello?

Call me in the morning

Jane call me please! I'm starting to freak out!

JANE WHERE ARE YOU

"They're mostly from Macy," I tell her. "Some from your mom. Some from Delilah. Looks like she e-mailed you, too."

Jane leans over me, bracing one hand on the desk. "Nothing from Isaac?"

I look back at the messages. "No. Who's Isaac?"

"My boyfriend."

"Oh," I say, and my voice sounds too loud. "I didn't—you have a boyfriend?"

Jane rubs one arm, staring at the computer. "Not anymore, I guess. Being dead kind of creates a problem for the relationship."

"Right," I say.

"What about earlier messages?" Jane asks. "Go back."

Her arm brushes against my cheek, and I instinctively shift away before realizing it won't hurt me.

"This one from Macy is at three. *I'm by the courtyard.*"

"That's when school gets out," Jane says.

"The last exchange with Isaac is from the morning," I say, scrolling back. "You wrote *What time is the concert tonight?*"

Jane leans in to read Isaac's response. "*8:00. Can you meet me in the music room?*"

"Do you remember meeting him?" I ask.

Jane shakes her head. "The concert must have been his. He's a cellist."

"If you were supposed to be at a concert, how did you end up at a club downtown? And why didn't he text you after that?"

"I don't know," Jane says, shaking her head. "That doesn't make any—"

We both hear the car pull up at the same time, and I slam the computer shut.

"Back door," Jane says quickly. "Hurry."

She runs through the living room and into the kitchen, pushing me toward the door near the washer and dryer. I unlock it and slip outside, shutting it behind me as quietly as I can.

"This way," Jane says, motioning me to the side of the house. "We can go around to the front."

"Hold on," I say, carefully using the key to relock the back door.

"She won't even notice either way," Jane says, her hands on her hips.

"Okay, okay, I'm coming," I say, my pulse jumping. I follow Jane along the side of the house and we pop out by a car parked in the driveway. A woman is getting out of the driver's side, struggling with a paper grocery bag.

"She always forgets the cloth bags," Jane says.

The woman stands up and seems to feel my eyes on her; she turns around and I get a good look at her face.

She has Jane's eyes, big and brown, but paler, tired, with deep lines at the edges. Her mouth is different, smaller and harsher, but the cheeks are the same.

"Can I help you?" she asks, her tone slightly hostile.

"Mrs. Morris?" I ask.

"Yes?"

"My name is Lexi. I'm a friend of Jane's."

Silence, and then she hurries toward me.

"Have you seen her?" she asks anxiously. "Did you talk to her?"

"No," I say quickly. "I'm sorry, I haven't. I just wanted to talk to you."

She searches my face, dark circles under her eyes.

"Come in," she says, turning into the house. I follow her, step back into the living room.

"Sit," she says, carrying the bag into the kitchen. "You want something to drink?"

Jane makes a noise in her throat and I glance at her.

"I'm all right," I say. I clear a spot on the futon, pushing aside magazines and a sweatshirt covered in cat hair, and sit down. A cat immediately jumps up and butts its head against me.

"You sure? Water? Soda? Iced tea?"

"Um, okay, iced tea," I say, trying to move her along.

I hear cupboards opening and the tinkle of ice cubes, and after a moment Mrs. Morris is back with two tall glasses. She places one in front of me on the wicker coffee table and sinks down into the yellow chair with her own. Watching me, she opens the bottle of vodka and pours a good portion of it into her glass.

"You want any?" she asks.

"Jesus, Mom," Jane says, rolling her head back.

"No, thank you," I say, taking a sip of the tea. It's bitter, and the ice cubes have that old freezer taste.

"You're a friend from school?"

I nod. "We have pre-calc together."

"So what do you want?"

"Mrs. Morris—"

"Amanda," she interrupts.

"Amanda. I was hoping I could ask you some questions."

"About Janie? Why?"

"I'm a reporter," I lie, "for the school newspaper. I thought I could write a piece about Jane, get her picture out there. I thought it might help."

Amanda looks at me, taking a long drink. "The police asked me all kinds of awful questions. Does Jane do drugs, does she disappear often." She swallows hard, a slight tremor in her hand. "My daughter didn't run away. She wouldn't. She has her whole life ahead of her."

"I don't think she did, either," I tell her.

"That's worse, isn't it?" Amanda asks, her eyes shining. "They told me there are other missing people. They haven't found any of them, not alive, not dead. They're just . . . gone."

"When was the last time you saw her?"

"That morning," Amanda says. "She left for school just like any other day. Left the coffee on for me." She gives a sad, wet laugh. "She's always trying to take care of me."

"Somebody has to," Jane says quietly.

"Were you worried when she didn't come home?" I ask.

Amanda won't meet my eyes. "I was asleep. I thought she'd come home late or spend the night with a friend. I guess she got separated from them somehow. I didn't even know she was missing until the next day."

She takes another long pull from her glass, and when she sets it down I catch a glimpse of red marks on the inside of her arm.

"What happened to your arm?" I ask.

Amanda looks down at her wrist, blinking a few times.

"Oh. I don't know," she says, her voice slightly thick. "I think it was the cats."

I glance at Jane, and her face darkens.

"My mother wouldn't hurt me," she says. "She's a sad drunk, not a violent one."

"We fought that morning," Amanda says suddenly, and I look over at her.

"About what?"

Amanda shakes her empty drink and I understand.

"I didn't want to get up. She yelled at me that I was going to be late for work."

"Wait. I remember this," Jane says slowly. "Oh, god. I told her I wouldn't always be around to wake her up."

"I thought she was trying to teach me a lesson," Amanda whispers. "I thought that's why Janie didn't come home at first."

The air in a normal-sized room weighs a hundred pounds. I swear the air in this room is heavier; I can feel every pound pressing down on me. Maybe it's the faint scent of cigarette smoke, maybe it's Jane, or maybe it's the choking weight of guilt that makes it hard to breathe.

"Can we go?" Jane asks tightly. "I remember that morning. We fought; I left for school. I don't want to be here anymore, Lexi."

"Okay," I say out loud. "Thank you for talking to me."

Amanda nods, her eyes glassy. I get up to leave as she reaches for the vodka bottle again.

"I'm sorry," I say as I shut the door behind us.

"What are *you* sorry for?" Jane asks.

"Janie, your mom—"

"Don't call me Janie," Jane snaps.

"Okay," I say, holding up my hands. "Look, we need

to figure out why you went to the club and who was with you. If people are going missing from the same areas, then maybe whoever brought you down there is involved."

"I don't know why I went there," Jane says. "I'd never been there before."

"Maybe your boyfriend knows? Maybe the concert was canceled and you went dancing with him instead?"

"*I don't know,*" Jane repeats. "I don't have any answers for you, all right? My memory is like Swiss cheese and I can't stop *bleeding.*" She wipes at her neck angrily. "Why can't I fix it?"

I don't answer, because I don't know. She's a powerful ghost, or at least she should be. Maybe she isn't concentrating hard enough.

"It isn't real," I remind her.

"Yeah," she says, huffing out a bitter laugh. "But it was." She wipes her fingers on her shirt, leaving long trails of red, like a claw over her heart.

10

"I HAVE TO GO TO WORK SOON. WE CAN FIGURE
out a plan to talk to your boyfriend when I get back."

We've been driving in silence for almost twenty minutes as I head back home. Jane stares straight ahead, her
back rigid, mouth tight at the corners.

"Jane?" I turn onto my street, glance over at her. "I
said—"

"I heard you the first time," she says.

I park the car and turn to face her.

"Are you going to be okay?"

"I think I passed *okay* a while back, don't you?" She
doesn't wait for me, gliding through the car door and
out the other side. The hair on my arms raises, an electric current pulsing in the air. I know they *can* do that,
but it's one thing to know and another to watch a body
seep through a wall like grease.

I climb up the stairs slowly and Jane's already inside
when I open the door, spreading out on my bed.

"I didn't mean it like that, and you know it," I tell her, pulling the sketch out of my pocket. I unfold it and lay it on my dresser, smoothing out the creases. I open the drawer and pull out a clean black T-shirt to change into.

Jane sighs. "Fine, I'll be *okay*."

"Are you sure? Because you seem a little . . ."

"A little what?" Jane asks. "Upset? Why would I be upset? Because my alcoholic mother is falling apart?"

I tug the shirt on, a tremor running through my hands. "You think you're the first person to have mommy issues? She's falling apart because she cares. At least you can still see her. Not everyone comes back, even if you want them to."

Even if you beg them to.

"Are you saying I'm lucky?" Jane growls at me. "I'm *dead*."

"So are a lot of people," I snap. "Cut it with the self-pity, because I'm not interested. You don't have a corner on shit luck."

Jane's eyes narrow and heat rolls off her from across the room. She sits up, her teeth bared, and then a body flickers in front of my face.

"Dammit, Trevor," I yell, pushing him away from me. "Stop *doing* that."

"It's not my fault," he says, holding up his hands. "You're always in the way." He glances from me to Jane, taking in her eyes and the sweat beading my forehead. "So, what's up?"

"Nothing," Jane says, her jaw flexing.

"I talked to Jane's mother today," I tell him, my voice too light.

"Oh," he says. "That bad, huh?"

"It's none of your business," Jane hisses at him. "Or Lexi's. So both of you can just *back off*."

"Hey," Trevor protests. "Back off yourself. Lexi's trying to help you. It isn't easy for her to meet people, you know."

A rush of panic hits my lungs.

"Oh, I'm sorry, is my murder getting in the way of your social anxiety or whatever?" Jane asks me.

"What?" Trevor frowns. "No, I mean—"

"That's enough," I interrupt, before he can clarify why I don't like to touch people. "I have to go to work."

Trevor blinks at me. "Aw, right now?"

"Yeah." I shrug on a hoodie. "Don't break anything."

"Very funny," he huffs, and turns to Jane. "Well. Guess it's just you and me, baby doll."

"Keep an eye on her," I tell him quietly.

"I don't need a baby-sitter," Jane says, her voice cool. "And take that thing out of here." She points at the sketch on my dresser.

"What is that?" Trevor asks.

"One of Jane's sketches," I tell him while she glowers.

"I like it," Trevor says, leaning over the paper. "I didn't know you could draw."

"Not anymore," Jane says curtly. "I can't hold a fucking pencil now, can I?"

"You said I could have it," I tell her.

"You can have it, but I don't want to see it."

There's a spike of heat, and if I keep fighting I'm going to be late. "Fine," I say, teeth gritted, and I grab the picture and leave, slamming the door behind me.

"Lexi!"

I turn around in the hallway, find Trevor running after me.

"She doesn't know, does she?" he asks, his eyes troubled. "Everything you can do."

I go still, and then with a sigh the tension bleeds out, my back softening. "Don't tell her. Please."

He stares at me, pity blooming across his face. "You touched her, didn't you? You saw what was going to happen."

"I have to go." I go to turn away, but his hand on my arm stops me.

"Is that why you're doing this?" he asks. "You're trying to make it up to her?"

"No," I say, stepping out of his reach. "I know I can't."

"Maybe she would understand."

"Would you?"

Trevor's eyes are pained, and I nod.

"Yeah. That's what I thought." I start back down the hall.

"Wait, Lex—"

"I have to go, Trevor," I say, not stopping.

"I know," he calls after me. "Just . . . don't get rid of the picture, okay?"

I tuck it more firmly under my arm.

"Wasn't planning on it."

Nicole gives me a bright smile when I finally show up to work.

"Hey," she says, wiping water rings from the bar. "Listen, thanks for the other night. I probably shouldn't have made you come all the way out here for something so silly."

"It wasn't silly," I tell her.

She huffs out her cheeks. "I never know how much of it is real, you know? How much is true and how much is me wanting it to be true."

I take my hoodie off and hold out my hand for a towel. She tosses one to me and I start cleaning the other end of the bar.

"You should trust yourself," I tell her. "I do. How many times have you saved me from breaking my fingers on some guy's face?"

Nicole laughs, and it rings out like a bell. "Yeah, well, I wouldn't want you getting arrested." Her face turns serious. "But I'm not like some of the others here. I can't do what Theo does with the tattoos; I don't see ghosts like you."

I turn before my face gives away anything I don't want to tell. I don't want Nicole looking at me the way my mother did, the way Jane would if I told her the truth.

"I wish things were clearer, you know?" she says. "Like, my aunt, she's the strongest psychic I know. She's been working with me, but it's still just feelings, nothing concrete."

"You're young," I say, even though she's two years older than me. But I've never been young. "And maybe they're just feelings, but you've never been wrong. You'll get stronger the more—" Nicole's eyes go wide and unfocused and I stop. "Nicole? What is it?"

"Something's wrong," she says, her face draining of color.

"Where?"

"Stockroom," she says. She blinks and her eyes snap to me, wide with fear. "Someone's hurt."

"I'll go." I drop my towel on the bar. "You stay here and call Ilia."

She reaches for me but pulls her hand back at the last second.

"Be careful, Lexi," she says, and I can feel her watching me as I head toward the door.

I keep pressing the button for the basement, even though I know it won't make the elevator go any faster. When it finally dings open, I burst out into the stockroom. I can hear a voice, low and frantic, coming from behind the rows of wooden shelves stacked with wine and liquor. The room is huge, with cement floors, and I shiver at the clammy chill in the air and zip my hoodie.

"Hello?" I call out, heading toward the rows. "Who's there?"

There's a scrape of movement, and then Ilia steps out

from behind a shelf, his skin pale under the fluorescent lights.

"Lexi?" he asks, eyes wild.

"What's going on, Ilia?"

He opens his mouth like he's about to say something, then closes it.

"Ilia?" I prompt.

"Over here," he says, snapping into movement. "I need your help."

He runs over to the wall lined with heavy wooden crates of beer, and I suck in a breath when I see what's waiting for us.

"Ilia, what the hell? Who is that?"

The man is slumped against the wall, his face so bruised and swollen it's hard to make out the features.

"Jordan," Ilia says through gritted teeth, looking like he wants to smash something. "I just came down to get mixers."

I glance back at the man, try to rearrange the face into the rangy features of the man usually outside Urie's office.

"Here, help me move him," Ilia says.

"What?" I shake my head. "Ilia, no. Let me get Theo—"

"Just help me," Ilia snarls. "Get his feet, okay? He's got boots on; you don't have to touch him much."

"Shit," I say, moving closer to Jordan. His eyes open a slit, and a soft moan comes out of his mouth.

"Jordan, are you okay?"

"Of course he's not okay," Ilia says. "He's beat half to hell."

"So how did he end up here?" I ask.

Ilia meets my eyes. "I don't know; I just found him down here, looking like this. Feet, Lexi."

I set my jaw and go toward Jordan's feet while Ilia crouches next to his face.

"Jordan, we need to get you off the floor, okay?"

Jordan opens one eye and mumbles something.

"It's gonna hurt," Ilia says. "I'm sorry." He looks up and waits until I nod.

"Go," I say, and I wrap my hands around Jordan's thick boots while Ilia takes his shoulders. His death whispers against my senses, tugging at the edge of mind. I grind my teeth and try to shut it out as we shuffle Jordan over to the stack of crates.

"Here," Ilia says, and I let go, breathing hard. I only caught a glimpse, but it's enough. Jordan's death has blood, and pain, and a bullet. Not yet, but soon.

Jordan grunts as Ilia releases him, his eyes closing as he settles against the crates. I rub my hands against my pants, wait for the images to trickle out of my mind.

"You still with me, buddy?" Ilia asks, leaning over Jordan's face.

"Ilia, he needs to go to the hospital."

"No." The word is garbled but clear coming out of Jordan's lips. "No hospital."

Ilia's mouth goes flat, but he doesn't argue. "I'll call Phillip," he says, glancing at me. "Stay with him."

I nod, bending down so my face is close to Jordan's.

"Hey," I say. "Jordan, it's Lexi. Can you hear me?"

"No hospital," he says again.

"We got that," I tell him. "No one's taking you anywhere, okay? Relax."

"Just hurry," Ilia says into his phone, coming back over. He hangs up and runs a hand over his face. The lines around his eyes are deeper than I remember, his eyes shadowed. He looks scared—scared and angry. "Phillip's coming down."

"Good," I say.

"Jordan?" Ilia says. "Can you tell us what happened? Who did this to you?"

Jordan takes in a rattling breath. "Don't know," he mumbles. "Spell."

He coughs, his whole body shaking, and Ilia braces him across the chest.

"Easy, man," he says. "Try not to move. What spell?"

Jordan blinks his eyes open and focuses on Ilia. "Protection spell," he says slowly. "Someone tried to break through."

"Do you know who?" I ask him, my heart pounding.

His gaze flickers to me. "No. I tried a trace, but it went wrong."

"Wrong how?" Ilia asks.

"They're concealed," Jordan says. "Spell rebounded on me. Too strong."

I meet Ilia's eyes over Jordan.

"Blinding magic?" he whispers, horrified. "A conceal-ment spell?"

"It's one of us," I say, dread hammering at my spine. "The killer is a witch."

"Why?" Ilia asks, looking as sick as I feel. "Why would anyone do this? Is this some sort of fucked-up witch sacrifice thing?"

"Don't do that kind of shit," Jordan says, struggling to breathe. "Not anymore. Not even the old-timers."

"Then why?" Ilia asks harshly. "Just to scare us?"

"Don't. Know," Jordan says, his voice getting weaker. "Ilia?"

"Oh thank god," Ilia says, closing his eyes for a brief second. "Phillip, over here."

Phillip comes around the shelf, and the smile he has for me drops off his face when he sees Jordan.

"What the hell?" He doesn't ask for an explanation; he just runs forward and puts both of his palms down on Jordan's chest. "Get me water and bandages," he orders, not sounding like the Phillip I know at all. "Ilia, call my mother and get her down here."

"No," Jordan groans. "No one else."

Phillip's mouth goes thin and he looks at Ilia. "I can't fix this all by myself; I'm not strong enough."

"Just do what you can for now," Ilia says. "I'll get the bandages." He looks over at me, jerking his head toward the stairs. I follow him, crossing my arms tight across my chest.

"How did you know?" he asks me quietly.

"Nicole," I say. "Ilia, we can't break through a spell this strong. Not if that's what it did to Jordan." I don't know much about witchcraft, but I do know blinding spells are notoriously hard to break. "And if we can't trace them—"

"We'll keep trying," he says. "Or we'll figure out another way to find them."

"And if we can't?"

He swallows hard. "Then I need you to make that girl remember."

For a moment I wish Jane were here beside me, her heat driving away the chill.

"I'll try," I say. "But I can't force her memories out. I need you to get me that footage."

"I'm working on it," he says.

"What do we do, Ilia?" I ask softly. "If we can't stop it?"

"We watch each other's backs," he says. "And we hope the protection holds."

I nod once, but a shiver creeps down my spine.

"What did you see?" he asks me. "When you touched him?"

We're the same height, and it's easy to turn my head and meet his eyes. He's just starting to get lines around the edges, but mine will always be older.

"Don't ask me that," I tell him. "Unless you're willing to carry the answer."

Ilia blinks first, ducking his head down.

"Just go, Lexi," he says, and I go.

11

PYROCLASTIC FLOWS CAN REACH SPEEDS OF FOUR hundred miles per hour and temperatures of a thousand degrees Celsius. When Mount Vesuvius erupted, hot gas and volcanic ash descended onto Pompeii with the thermal energy of a nuclear weapon, incinerating people where they stood. Some fates can change in an instant; some ends can't be outrun.

"Jane?"

I'm barely inside my apartment, but something is wrong. It's hot as hell and Jane is lying facedown on the floor, not moving. I drop to my knees, and as I start to turn her over she shudders in my arms.

"Jane?"

Her mouth opens wide in a silent scream, her eyes huge and white and blood dripping down her neck.

"Shit!" I grab her shoulders and shake, her body stiff and frozen.

"Jane," I say, putting my face close to hers. "Look at me."

Her mouth is still wide, but her eyes at least start to focus on my face.

"Look at me," I order. "You're okay. It's Lexi. You're okay."

Her body jerks in my arms and she makes a small choking sound.

"That's it," I say, making my voice stay low and calm. "Keep looking at me. You're in my room. You're okay."

Jane goes completely limp beneath me, but I don't let go. She blinks up at me, once, twice.

"Lexi?" she asks, her voice raw.

"Yeah," I say, releasing her. "Yeah, it's me."

I move back and Jane slowly pushes herself up until she's sitting. She looks around the room, her eyes still white and dazed.

"Are you all right?" I ask.

"I—I think so." She shudders suddenly, her body curving in on itself. "What . . . what was that?"

She looks small and fragile, blood thick around her neck. She scoots closer to me; I go stiff for a moment and then lean toward her, pressing against her side.

"I have no idea," I tell her. "What happened?"

"Trevor left to go to a movie," she says. "I was practicing, trying to make my clothes change . . .

and then I was back in the alley."

I reach one arm out and almost stop, then let it slip around her shoulders.

"Did you remember anything?"

"I . . . I couldn't move. No matter how much I fought, I couldn't move."

"It's okay," I tell her, but I don't know if it is. Jane isn't acting the way ghosts are supposed to act. She doesn't remember her death, she can't hold her form, and whatever this is. But she doesn't need to hear that right now.

"Whatever it was," I say, "it's over."

I can feel Jane shiver even as her heat seeps through my shirt. I'm not good at this, at giving comfort, at being kind, but I try. I press my cheek against her hair, her face tucked under my chin.

"I'm going to get blood on you," she says quietly, but she doesn't move away.

"No, you won't," I tell her. "I told you, it isn't real."

Jane goes still, her body loose against me. "Am I real?" she asks, so softly I barely hear it, like she doesn't want to know the answer.

"You're real enough to me," I say, my thumb making small circles on her shoulder.

"But I'm not . . . what I was."

I try to think of the right way to say it, to make her understand.

"Sound waves can travel through water and air, even walls and furniture," I say. "But if the waves hit a big-enough obstacle, they bounce back and return to the sender."

Jane twists her head up to look up at me. "I'm a sound wave?"

I shake my head. "You're an echo."

Her forehead creases as she considers it. "An echo."

"You're not less. Just not the same." And I don't want to tell her, but I owe her the truth. Or *a* truth, at least. "You don't have to be, if you don't want to." I say it softly, almost afraid of the words.

"What?"

"You don't have to . . . stay here. On this side. If you don't want to."

She pushes her head away from me and my arm wants to tighten.

"You think I should go?" she asks.

"No," I say quickly. "No, of course not. I just want you to have options."

Jane shudders suddenly, her body vibrating under my arm. I know she isn't cold, not when I can feel sweat collecting at the nape of my neck.

"I used to think it would be like going to sleep," she says. "Dying, I mean."

"Sleep is the sibling of death," I mutter.

"What?"

I shake my head. "It's just something Deda says. It sounds better in Russian."

"But it's not like sleeping at all," she says. "And now I'm afraid of what will happen if I close my eyes."

I look down at her, find her eyes wide open and clouded.

"Do you know what it is?" she asks. "Whatever is on the other side?"

"I don't think any of us are supposed to know."

"Do you think it's bad?"

I press my lips together, lick them wet. "Maybe it's not good, or bad. Maybe it's . . . different."

"I know I'm not alive," she says quietly. "But I still think. I still feel."

I should tell her about Jordan, that Ilia and I think it's a witch killing people, but I'm afraid if I start talking she'll move away. She leans back against me, rests her head on my shoulder. Something dormant starts to prickle inside me, something sharp and cold and lonely.

"I'm an echo," she says. "Maybe that's enough for now."

Heat creeps into my arms, into my chest, but it doesn't burn. I've never held someone like this before, never let anyone get this close to me. Never had anyone want to get this close. It feels strange, like using a muscle I didn't know existed, uncomfortable but not painful.

I fall asleep sometime in the night and wake up alone and cold, curled up on my side on the floor.

"Jane?"

Nothing but silence answers me, the light streaming in from the window telling me it's long past morning. I take a hot shower to get the kinks out of my back, and she's still not there when I get out, still not there when I leave for Deda's.

"Where is your friend?" he asks me when I show up. He takes one look at my face and pours me a large cup of coffee.

"I don't know," I say, wincing as I sit across from him. I definitely pulled something in my neck sleeping on the floor. "I'm not her chaperone."

Deda makes a noncommittal noise and pushes the coffee toward me. I dump in as much sugar as my stomach can handle and enough cream to turn it almost white.

Deda frowns at me and I shrug.

"It's breakfast," I tell him.

"You need to take better care of yourself," Deda tells me. "You are not getting enough sleep; you are not eating enough."

"I'm fine, Deda, you don't have to worry."

"Yes, I do," Deda snaps, and I look up, surprised. "They will consume you if you let them."

"That's not—"

"Listen to me, Alexandra," he says, leaning forward. "They are not like us. They do not have cake or wine or cigars. They will take your attention, your time, they will take and take until you have nothing left to give. And still they ask for more."

I look away from him, feeling acid bubble in my chest. "Jane isn't like that."

"Then why do you look like death warmed over?"

I rub at my eyes, trying to rub his words out of my head. "That has nothing to do with her. You don't even know her."

"Do you? She is not what she was in life."

"So what? Maybe I like who she is now." I shove back

my chair and stand up. "And none of this is Jane's fault. You want to blame someone, blame the monster who killed her. It's one of us. One of *us* did this, Deda, not Jane. And I'm leaving."

"You just got here."

"Yeah, well, that was before you said I look like shit."

"Alexandra—"

"I'll come back soon, okay? You're right, I need to get some more sleep."

I walk away from the table, but I can feel his eyes watching me leave, burning angry, worried holes into my back.

Jane is still gone when I get home, and my stomach twists strangely as I stare at my empty apartment. I haven't seen Trevor since yesterday. It's not like they can get hurt, I remind myself, but it doesn't fix the hollow feeling in my center.

I pick up the dirty clothes on my floor, throw them into a larger, dirtier pile that I thrust into a corner. I think about making the bed, but instead I flop back onto it and stare at the ceiling, lying to myself about the pit in my stomach.

It shouldn't hurt anymore; I thought I made my

peace with this a long time ago. But it's loneliness that's scraping out my organs, ancient and unmistakable. I shouldn't have let them in, shouldn't have gotten used to the warmth at my back, a voice at my ear. It hurts worse now, because I know what I've lost.

I curl up on my side, press my legs to my chest. I let the loneliness take me, let it creep through my veins and settle into my bones, let it become part of me. It will always be a part of me.

"Lexi?"

I sit up, my eyes blurry; I don't remember falling asleep.

"Where have you been?" I ask her, and it comes out angry.

"I went home."

That knocks the air out of me, and I sink back onto the bed. "Oh."

"I wanted to check on my mom," Jane says, coming closer. "I used to make her hangover cures on mornings like this. Never really helped."

I study her for a moment. "You're not bleeding."

A little smile plays at the corner of her mouth as she runs her hands over her clean shirt. "It's working today. As long as I really concentrate."

She stands at the foot of the bed, and there's an awkward silence as we stare at each other.

"Thank you for . . . helping me last night," she says finally. "For talking to me."

"Sure," I tell her, shrugging. Hurt flashes across her face for a moment, but I can't drop anchor here, can't get used to having her around. She'll leave eventually, like everyone does, and I'll still be here, curled up with my loneliness.

"Look, you were upset yesterday, so I didn't mention it. . . ."

"What?"

I rub one arm awkwardly. "Someone tried to break through the protection spells on the club last night."

Jane's shoulders stiffen. "What?"

"Don't worry," I say quickly, "they didn't get through. Urie has it under control."

"But how?"

"Whoever killed you has power." I blanch, remembering Jordan's face. "A lot of power, going by what I saw."

A line appears across Jane's neck, and her eyes start to go milky. "What does that mean?"

"It means you crossed paths with a witch at some

point. And if you can't remember who or when, then we need to figure out what made you go to the club and who saw you there. I think we should talk to your boyfriend and see why you didn't go to his concert."

Jane nods, her movements jerky. "Fine," she says. "He'll be at school right now."

She turns away, and it bruises something inside me.

"Jane," I say. "I'm sorry. That it was someone like me that . . . did this to you."

When she looks back, her eyes are white and empty. "It's all the same to me," she says. "Dead is still dead."

I forget sometimes that most people my age are in school during the day. I drive us to Culver City and park in the back lot of the high school. A bell rings in the distance, and for a moment we sit in the car, waiting while the clumps of teenagers trickle out of the building in fits and bursts.

"Go Centaurs," Jane mutters under her breath.

"You okay?" I ask her, looking over.

"Yes. No. I don't know," she says. "A week ago I didn't think witches were real. Now I'm dead, and you're telling me one of them killed me. It's like a really fucked-up fairy tale."

"Fairy tales *are* fucked-up when you read the original versions," I tell her. "You should hear the Russian ones. Baba Yaga eats children."

"Yummy," Jane says dryly, staring out the window. I watch the line of her throat move as she swallows. "It feels different, from this side. Watching them. I used to be a part of that, you know?"

"Not really," I say. "I was never a part of it."

Jane slides through the door and I follow, making our way along the football field. Boys in jerseys are starting to wander onto the grass, slapping at one another and laughing. I watch them for a moment, and it's like a movie with the sound slightly off, their lives so separate from mine that they feel unnatural.

"Did you play any sports?" I ask, and Jane scoffs.

"I'm not the sporting type." She shoulders ahead, past the football players toward the school. "What type were you?"

I lift one shoulder. "I liked science, I guess."

Jane grimaces. "I'm terrible at science. History, too— I can never remember the dates. The only class I got A's in is art, and you have to be a real a fuckup *not* to make an A in art."

No one stops me as I open the heavy door to the

building. A group of kids lounge around the hallway, looking young enough to still need baby-sitters. I hunch my shoulders up and glare, and they move out of my way in a hurry. None of them meets my eyes as I walk by, flattening themselves against the lockers.

"Why do you do that?" Jane asks, keeping pace with me, one of her shoulders melting through the row of lockers.

"What?"

"Glare at people like that, pretend to be all mean. You're not mean."

I shove my hands in my pockets, give a slight shrug instead of answering. "Which way?"

"Take a left," Jane says, and I don't like the way she's watching me, like she knows what I'm thinking.

We walk down an empty hallway, fluorescent lights bouncing off the linoleum floor. This place could be my high school—the same look, the same scent of tedious misery. It lingers, seeps into the walls with the grease and the disinfectant.

"There." Jane points to a row of shut doors along our left. "Music rooms," she says, her voice flat. "He'll be practicing."

I look through the glass on the doors, but the first

two rooms are empty. The third one is occupied by a tall, thin boy playing a cello. The room is soundproofed, but I can imagine the notes as the bow draws across the strings. His head is bent over the instrument, and I get a glimpse of brown skin and hair that's not much longer than mine. He certainly doesn't look capable of hurting anyone. I look again, closely; he's playing the bow with his right hand.

"That's him," Jane says, watching him with a look of regret on her face.

I rap sharply on the door. His head whips up, eyes dark, lips pursed in concentration. He frowns as he tries to place my face, but I don't move from the window. Finally he stands up and carefully leans the cello against his chair before coming to the door.

He opens it a crack and looks out.

"Can I help you?" His voice is polite but suspicious.

"My name is Lexi," I tell him. "I'm a friend of Jane's."

I don't catch everything that flits across his face; there's anger, and anxiety, and something like dread. It finally settles on resignation, and he opens the door wider.

"Thanks."

The room is small, chairs and music stands stacked

in one corner and a chalkboard on the other. Isaac nods to the chairs and I pull one out and sit facing him as he rearranges himself with the cello.

We stare at each other for a long moment and the room feels too small to contain the both of us. Both of us, and the presence at my side.

"He looks thin," Jane says, her eyes roving over his face.

"I don't know you," Isaac says to me.

"No," I agree. "But I know Jane."

"Have you seen her?" he asks softly, like he's afraid of my answer.

"No," I say. "I'm sorry."

He closes his eyes for a moment, and when he opens them he looks at me more sharply.

"You don't go here," he says. "And you don't look like a friend of hers."

For some reason that irks me. "Why not?"

Isaac lifts one shoulder. "Jane's friends are mostly boho types. You look a little, I dunno, rougher. Older. No offense."

I suppose that's fair. "We grew up together," I lie. "I already graduated."

"So what do you want from me?"

"I just wanted to talk to you."

"About what?"

"About what happened that day. The day she went missing."

Isaac narrows his eyes at me. "I didn't hurt her," he says. "If that's why you're here."

"You think she's hurt?" I ask.

"He didn't say that," Jane protests.

"No," Isaac says. "I don't know. I don't know what I think. But I know I wasn't with her that night, and the police already searched my car."

I frown. "The police think she ran away, why would they search your car?"

Isaac stares at me for a long moment and I grimace.

"Oh. Right. Good old LAPD."

"Yeah," he says flatly, leaning back in his chair. He has an easy grace about him, his long arms draped casually over the neck of the cello. I can see what drew Jane to him; he's beautiful, in a languid, romantic way.

"Sorry," I say awkwardly. "Look, I'm not here to . . . Jane's mom is getting really worried. I know she was supposed to go to your concert that night. I'm just trying to figure out how she ended up at that club."

"I don't know," he says. "You should probably ask one of her friends."

"You don't know?" I repeat. "Well, did she cancel on you? You're her boyfriend, aren't you?"

He doesn't answer, his lips pressed together.

"Aren't you?" Jane asks sharply.

"I'm not . . . her boyfriend anymore," Isaac says awkwardly.

"What?" Jane snaps.

My eyes flick in her direction but I stay still.

"What happened?" I ask.

"Look, Jane . . ." Isaac rubs the back of his neck. "She's what my dad calls a spark plug. She's fun, energetic. I feel happier just being around her. But . . ." He pauses, chewing on his bottom lip. "She doesn't feel the same way about me."

Jane lets out a cry. "You broke up with me!" She steps closer to him, her hands on her hips. "I remember. You said I didn't care about you. I can't *believe* this!"

I let out a sigh. "You broke up with her."

Isaac glances up, looking miserable. "I met her here and said I was tired of feeling like an afterthought. And she didn't even argue with me. She just left. The last time I saw her, she was getting into Macy's car."

Jane swears, low and harsh.

"She went to that club because of me," Isaac says, his voice thick. "If I hadn't broken up with her that day . . ."

"It's not your fault," Jane says with a sigh. "You're an ass, but it's not your fault. I must've called Macy and wanted to go out to blow off steam."

"The thing is," Isaac says, "I still care about her. I'm still worried. Jane is tough, but she should have called someone by now."

I don't want to meet his eyes, afraid he'll see the truth in mine.

"Will you let me know?" he asks. "If you hear anything?"

"Sure," I tell him.

"Thanks," he says. "I appreciate it."

He holds out his hand then, and everything inside me cringes. I stare too long at the slight dusting of resin on his fingers, and I know I have to take it but I don't want to.

"Lexi," Jane says impatiently, and she nudges me forward.

I clasp his hand, my arm rigid and angry, and let the nausea roll through my body. His grip is stronger than I expected, and he doesn't release my hand right away. I bite my cheek, resisting the instinct to yank myself back, tear my skin away from him, do whatever it takes to stop the pain.

"I'll see you around," he says, and I nod back, tight-lipped, not trusting my stomach to stay still.

When he lets go of my hand, I spin around and leave the room, letting the door shut behind me with a soft click. I walk stiff-legged down the hallway until I find a water fountain and use it as an excuse to lean over and wait for the acid to wash from my gut. I take short, gasping breaths and splash a handful of water on my face, the cold shocking me back to my senses.

"What's wrong?" Jane asks, but her attention is still on the closed door of the music room.

"Nothing," I say, my voice harsh. "Let's go."

I walk quickly down the hallway, my body somehow remembering the turns. He lives a long life. That's more than what some people get. But I still can't erase the images of his body getting thinner and thinner, until there's nothing but bones.

12

"TELL ME ABOUT MACY," I ORDER JANE WHEN WE'RE back in the car.

She frowns. "She's my friend. My best friend, I guess."

"We talk to her next," I say. The hollow feeling is creeping back into the pit of my stomach, grasping for my attention. "You think she's the one who suggested the club?"

Jane shrugs. "Possibly. She likes to go dancing."

"Then maybe she saw something that can help us."

"Maybe," Jane says quietly, staring out the window. "He broke up with me." Her voice is tinged with disbelief.

"What, were you planning on marrying him?" I ask, and it comes out harsher than I meant it.

"No," Jane says, her forehead scrunching up. "But I thought . . . I don't know, I thought things were going well."

"That isn't always enough."

"Has anyone ever told you that you're a real fucking downer?" Jane snaps at me.

"Yes," I say. "A number of times."

Jane glares at me and the corner of her mouth twitches. It spreads across her lips and she starts to laugh. If there's an edge of hysteria to it, I pretend not to notice.

"God," she says when she finally quiets down. "I needed that."

"Feel better?" I ask, rolling my eyes.

"I do, actually. You should try it sometime. Laughing. Or you know, even smiling. Any expression, really."

"I have expressions."

"Sure," Jane says. "There's scowling, glaring, and staring blankly. Truly a rich tapestry. Oh, and half the time you look like you're about to throw up. That one's my personal favorite."

I don't say anything, and it doesn't help that I know I'm glaring. I try to school my face into something smoother, and Jane giggles again. Her laugh does something to me, makes me feel tight and loose all at once.

"Shut up," I say.

"Oh, anger!" she says. "That's something, at least."

"Would you cut it out and focus?" I say, annoyed with

her and myself. "I'm trying to help you, remember?"

"Yeah, yeah," she says, falling quiet. She turns and stares out the window, and a fist curls up in my chest. I'm mad, but I don't want her to look away. I don't want her to stop laughing.

"I really thought he liked me," Jane says after a long moment.

"He did," I tell her. "He does. Too much, I think."

"That person he was describing," Jane says slowly, "I don't think I'm that person anymore. I don't have that . . . spark inside me." She presses a hand to her stomach, like she can feel where it used to be. "It's gone. Now there's just this *anger*. This darkness."

I pull up outside my apartment, but I don't get out of the car.

"You're not the only one," I say, turning to her, "who knows the darkness."

I don't tell her I'm glad she's different. I don't tell her that the living Jane would never tease me, smile at me. I don't tell her that something inside me recognizes her darkness as my own.

"Where does—dammit," I say.

There's a flicker in the rearview mirror and suddenly Trevor is in the backseat.

"What the—"

"Whatcha talking about?" Trevor asks, leaning forward.

"Boyfriends," Jane says.

"Oh?" Trevor says, waggling his eyebrows. "Is Lexi finally spilling about Phillip?"

"Who's Phillip?" Jane asks, pursing her lips at me.

"Nobody," I say crossly. "Trevor, you couldn't wait till we get inside to bother us?"

"Don't tell me you didn't hear?" Trevor asks, his eyes going wide.

"Hear what?" I ask.

"It's all over the news."

I get a sinking feeling as I stare at him.

"Trevor? What happened?"

"They found a body."

It isn't her. Jane paces the apartment while I read every article I can find in the news.

"Twenty-four years old," I say, my eyes scanning my phone. "Last seen at MacArthur Park." I swear harshly; that's right inside our boundaries. "They found her body in the lake."

"What was her name?" Jane asks, voice tight.

"Veronica Lourden."

"She has a nice smile," Trevor says, peering over my shoulder.

"This wasn't supposed to happen," Jane says angrily. "I thought you said your boss had it under control."

"We don't know if this is even related," I tell her. "No other bodies have been found."

"Come on," Trevor says, pointing at the picture on my phone. "It's the same area, she's young, and she was stabbed. What are the odds?"

"Then why was she dumped and not Jane?" I ask.

"Interrupted, maybe?" Trevor says.

"I guess that's possible," I say.

"Find her," Jane orders. "Find her ghost and bring her here so we can talk to her."

I shake my head. "It's not that simple. I would need to be at her house, or someplace she remembers. I have to have a connection, either to a place or an object."

"Then let's go," Jane says, gesturing to the door. "Take me to where she died; that's a connection."

"Would you stop pacing?" I say. "The place is still a crime scene; I can't just walk in looking for a ghost. It's probably swarming with cops."

"Who cares about the cops?" Jane yells.

"You don't understand," I say. "Even if I go, she might not show up. I couldn't find Marcus, and I *knew* him. If you just calm down—"

"Don't tell me to calm down," she yells, whirling on me. Her eyes have been filmed over since we got the news. "Another girl is dead because we did *nothing*, and you want to keep doing *nothing*."

"That's not what I'm saying," I tell her, stung. "Carl will call when he's done with the autopsy, but there's nothing we can do right now but wait."

"Well, I'm not waiting," Jane says, storming toward the door. "You want to sit on your ass, fine, but I won't."

"Jane—" I call, but she's melting through the door and leaving me staring at nothing. "Dammit." I look back at Trevor. "I have to go to work. What am I supposed to do now?"

"Let her go," Trevor says, giving my shoulder a squeeze. "I'll follow and keep an eye on her."

"Will you talk to her?"

"I don't think talking's going to help," he says. "She's a ghost, Lex. She can't touch or communicate or do any of the things she used to do. Anger is all she has to focus on right now, all that's getting her through the days."

"So how do I help her? How do we get past the anger?"

"I don't know," he says. "Find a way to distract her? What did she like to do before she died?"

I pause, think back to Jane's room and the pictures on the wall. "Art," I say. "She liked to draw."

Trevor winces. "Afraid we're shit out of luck with that one."

"Yeah," I say, chewing on my lip. "I guess so."

"Look, don't worry," he says. "We'll find ways to help her. And in the meantime, I'll make sure she doesn't get into any trouble."

"Thanks," I say. "Be careful, okay?"

"I will." He heads toward the door and looks back. "Oh. If the new girl does show up?"

I nod at him. "Bring her back here."

I make a quick stop before work, turning down a street lined with taco trucks and secondhand shops. A few dollars and ten minutes and I'm back in the car with a paper bag on the seat next to me.

"You're late," Ilia says when I show up at the club. "And Urie's in a bad mood. Like, really bad."

"What the hell happened?" I ask. "How did someone get past the protection spells? I thought we strengthened them?"

"I have no idea. The cops are canvassing the whole area again. Everyone's on edge."

I swear under my breath. A number of people here had run-ins with the cops before Urie took them in. Forging isn't exactly a skill you can put to use in an office.

"Did we try tracing back the attack again?"

Ilia shakes his head. "We didn't know in time. And I don't know if I can ask anyone to risk what Jordan went through. Does the girl remember anything?"

"Still working on it," I say. "What else can we do?"

"Keep our heads down," Ilia says. "Keep everyone calm, and—"

"Ilia," a voice calls out.

We both look over to see Theo practically running down the hallway.

"What is it?" Ilia asks.

"We got a problem," Theo says.

Ilia and I exchange a worried glance. If Theo, steady-handed *Theo*, thinks we have a problem? We move forward to meet him halfway.

"What happened?" I ask hurriedly.

"Jordan's been rotating the witches responsible for upholding the protection spell so no one gets drained," Theo says, voice grim. "Adam was in charge tonight.

Something happened, and he let the spell lapse."

"Shit," Ilia says, speeding up. "Of all the damn times . . ."

We turn the corner, headed for the office, when I hear the muffled cry from behind the door.

Ilia lunges forward and twists the handle, and Adam falls back into the hallway. Urie is framed in the doorway, shoulders wide, his face a dark storm. Smoke curls from his right hand and I smell burnt hair and something worse.

"I'm sorry," Adam says. I don't know him well; he mainly works the first floor, a jittery chain-smoker with deep-set eyes.

"Get your things and leave," Urie tells him. "Don't bother coming back."

Ilia heaves Adam to his feet, and I catch a glimpse of the angry red burn at the back of his neck, right where a tattoo used to be.

"Ilia," Adam begs. "It was a mistake."

"I know," Ilia says, face set.

Urie finally notices the rest of us, and he gives Theo and me a quick scan with his eyes.

"Get him out of here," he says calmly. "Make sure everyone knows he's no longer one of us."

"Please, no," Adam says. "I didn't mean to fall asleep. I don't know how it happened."

Urie ignores him, turning back to his office.

"Uncle, wait," Ilia says. "It might be time to consider closing the club. Just temporarily."

Urie looks back over his shoulder, and I take a step back.

"You think I can't protect our people?" he asks, his voice deadly quiet.

Ilia swallows. "No, sir. That's not what I meant. I just think—"

"I don't need you to think," Urie says. "I need you to do your job. So do it, Ilia."

Ilia nods sharply as Urie steps into his office and shuts the door. It would be better if he slammed it, but he closes it gently, with an awful finality.

Adam looks up at Ilia, desperate.

"Ilia, please," he says. "I don't have anywhere else to go."

"I'm sorry, Adam," Ilia says. "I'll ... I'll make sure you have something to keep you going. Lexi?"

I blink and look away from Adam. "Yeah?"

"Get Nicole on the main floor tonight. I need her watching the crowd and I need you watching her back.

Any hint of a disturbance, you call me. Got it?"

"Yeah. I got it."

"I'll be back."

Adam starts to cry as Ilia helps him down the hall-way, a lamb being led to the slaughter.

Theo watches the retreating forms, a frown wrinkling his usually smooth face. I wonder if he feels it when his spells are destroyed. If it hurts him like the ghosts can hurt me.

"Ilia's right," I say quietly. "We shouldn't stay open."

"What else are we going to do?" Theo asks. "Stay inside and hide? This is our home. At least here we can protect one another."

"Like we protected Adam?"

Theo lifts one shoulder. "He fell asleep—"

"Bullshit," I say. "I don't believe that for a minute. Someone did this to him."

Theo stays quiet for a long moment, then lets out a breath.

"Nothing we can do now," he says. "Someone's out there killing, and Urie needs to show a strong front to our people."

"Adam's one of our people," I tell him. "We're supposed to keep him safe, not throw him to the wolves.

One of *us* is doing this, Theo, and it's not going to stop."

"It will," he says. "I'm not psychic, but even I can feel it."

"Feel it?" I repeat.

"Have you ever been sailing?" he asks.

"Do I *look* like someone who goes sailing?"

"There's a moment when everything goes quiet. The waves, the wind, the sky. You learn to watch for it—the calm before the storm." Theo turns to face me. "Things are coming to a head. It *will* stop, Lexi."

"When?"

Theo gives me a wry smile. "After the storm hits."

The protection spell is patched up, but too many faces are grim, too many people checking over their shoulders. Fear is an oily residue on my skin, sinking into my pores. If we can't trust the people in this club, we can't trust anyone. *Is it you?* The question is on my lips for every face that passes.

I work my shift like an automaton, going through the motions of pouring and swiping, my brain in another place entirely. The apartment is dark when I get home, carrying my paper bag under one arm. I flick on the lamp by my bed, but it barely makes a difference, the light muted and dull.

"What makes someone stay on this side?"

I jump and the bag falls to the floor; Jane's voice came out of the dim corner of the room.

"Jesus," I mutter. "When did you get back?"

"When I realized Veronica's ghost wasn't going to show up and I got tired of yelling. Answer the question."

I can see her now, her outline pale and almost glowing. She looks like a cliché of a ghost in this light, floating and insubstantial.

"It's different for each ghost," I say, rubbing my eyes. "For the murdered, your energy carries over after you die. At least, that's how it's supposed to work. But Marcus's ghost never appeared. Maybe Veronica's won't, either."

Nothing about these deaths makes any sense. Jane's lost control of her form again, the blood on her neck black in the gloom. I sink down along the wall until our knees are brushing. I'm still learning how to touch, learning this new language that has words I can't translate.

"What are we supposed to do next?" she asks, light making her eyes shiny and flat. The skin beneath them looks so delicate, almost translucent, the veins showing through. I wonder if I lean closer if I could see what color they are.

"We keep going," I say. "We don't stop until it's over."

Jane nods slowly. "Okay." She blinks, and seems to finally see me. "Lexi?"

"Yes?"

"What's in the bag?" She nods at where it rests on the floor.

"Oh," I say, suddenly feeling embarrassed. "I, uh, I got something for you."

Jane turns so she can see my face. "Really? What is it?"

"It's . . . well, it's nothing." It seems silly now, after everything, another clumsy attempt at comfort.

"Show me," she says.

I reluctantly tug the bag to me and pull out its contents, spreading them on the floor: a blank sketchbook and two black pens.

"They're cheap," I say, not meeting her eyes. "Probably not what you're used to. I don't have much money. I'm sorry."

She doesn't say anything and the silence cuts into me until I finally can't take it. I look up and find her staring at the pens, a sad, starved gleam in her eyes.

"Jane?"

"I can't," she says, her voice rigid. She clears her throat and tries again. "I can't touch them, remember?"

"I know," I say. "But I can. And you can touch me. I thought I could hold the pen and you could, sort of, direct my hand."

"Like a Ouija board?"

"It's stupid," I say quickly. "Never mind. I shouldn't have bought—"

"No," Jane interrupts. "It's not. It's . . . can we try it?"

I nod, releasing a breath. "Yeah. Sure."

I flip open the sketchbook, the paper creamy white and slightly rough under my fingertips. I grab both pens and hold them out for Jane to see.

"I don't know much about drawing," I say. "One's thinner and one's thicker. I can get different ones if you want."

"This one's perfect," Jane says, pointing at the thinner one.

I pull off the cap and fold my legs up, sitting in front of the sketchbook. I position the pen in my hand and look at Jane expectantly.

"Go ahead," I say.

She scoots closer and reaches for my hand, then pulls back, hesitating.

"What should I draw?" she asks, almost shyly.

"Anything you want," I say.

"It might take a while."

I shrug. "I have nowhere to be. Just ignore me and pretend I'm part of the pen."

She reaches for me again and this time her hand curls around mine. I keep my hand loose, letting her direct the movement. She makes a few cautious strokes, but after a minute her lines become firmer, more defined. Slowly a face begins to take shape on the paper, eyes wide and lips pouting, and I recognize Trevor staring back at me.

"Lexi," Jane says softly, shadowing Trevor's hair with small crosshatching strokes. "Thank you for this."

"You're welcome," I say.

Jane keeps drawing until the page is filled and I have to flip to a blank one. I sneak glances at her while she draws, lips pursed in concentration. Slowly her eyes go warm brown, the blood receding from her neck. The light bulb starts to glow hotter from her focus, casting shadows in the peaks and valleys of her cheekbones. She keeps drawing and it burns even brighter, until everything is light and warm, until it feels like every pocket of darkness has been chased away. I don't move my hand away, even when my arm goes numb, even when my fingers cramp; I let her keep drawing, unwilling to be the first one to let go.

I don't sleep well, my dreams full of red storms. I wake up sometime past dawn, cold and alone in my bed. I roll over, find myself reaching for something that's not there. I try to fall back asleep, but the gray light steadily grows brighter and my limbs feel twitchy and hot.

I give up, kicking the blanket off me and throwing my feet to the ground.

"You're awake," Jane says, looking up at me with clear eyes. She's sitting cross-legged on the floor, examining one of the sketches from last night.

"Unfortunately, yes," I say, yawning.

"You don't sleep much, do you?"

"Not always." I shrug.

"I think this one could use more shading," she says, looking down at the paper.

I flex the fingers on my right hand; they're still a little sore.

"Okay," I say.

"Not now," she says quickly. "It's Wednesday."

I frown; I have to work again tonight. "What does that mean?"

"Macy will be at work after school. We need to talk to her next."

"Right," I say, nodding. "We've got a couple hours. Want to get something to eat?"

The diner around the corner is just opening when I walk up and the waitress gives me a tired nod and waves me inside.

"Anywhere you want," she says, so I sit down at a booth with bright red upholstery and maps glued under the plastic tabletop. Jane sits across from me, sliding onto the seat with a small smile on her face.

"Something to drink?" the waitress asks.

"Coffee, please."

"You can't really talk to me," Jane says as the waitress walks away. "She'll think you've lost your mind."

"Most likely," I say softly. "But I have a plan."

I take my phone out and hold it to my ear.

"So," I say in a normal tone of voice. "How's it going?"

Jane gives me a startled grin. "Oh, you know. Murdered, haunting some chick, looking for my killer, same old, same old."

"*Some chick?*" I repeat. "This is how you refer to me?"

"Well, to be fair, I barely know you."

The waitress brings me coffee with a bowl of creamer and puts a laminated menu down on the table.

"Thanks," I say.

"See, now," Jane says, pointing, "I don't even know how you take your coffee."

"Well, all that's about to change."

I grab two sugar packets and dump in two creamers, turning the coffee almost blond.

"Okay, you like your coffee like a child does," Jane says.

"How do you take it?"

"Black."

"Oh, you mean bad and bitter."

Jane laughs, and the sound rolls over my skin.

"Tell me something else about yourself," she says.

I look down at the menu, my eyes skipping down to the cheapest option on the breakfast menu. "I don't like runny yolks."

"Not that," she says. "Something real."

"Like what?" I ask, meeting her eyes.

"Where did you grow up?"

"Here," I say. "In a different crappy apartment."

"Where are your parents?"

Icy fingers grip my heart, and I feel my throat close up. I take a long sip of coffee that sits on my tongue, turning bitter in my mouth.

"My mom died," I say when I can talk again.

"Oh," Jane says, her face going slack. "I'm so sorry, Lexi."

"It was a long time ago," I say, feeling a cry rattle in my chest. "And I never knew my dad. I think they were together for a couple months, but the only thing I know about him is he must have been tall." Ivanoviches have pretty terrible track records when it comes to relationships, even the ones who can touch people.

"What about you?" I ask, desperate to stop trawling my memories.

"Well, you met my mom," Jane says, shrugging. "Although she was better when my dad was around. They got divorced when I was eight and he moved to Toronto. He got remarried and had other kids, so . . . he doesn't really keep in touch."

"That's shitty," I tell her.

"Yeah," she says. "Parents kind of suck sometimes, don't they?"

"People," I correct. "People kind of suck sometimes."

"Okay, new topic," Jane says, clearing her throat. "Umm, let's see. Have you ever been in love?"

I almost spit out my coffee. "Me? No. God, no."

I feel guilty as I say it, even though it's the truth. I care about Phillip, but love is something else entirely. At least, I think it is.

"Me, neither," Jane says. "That's unfair. Everyone should get to be in love before they die."

"Well, maybe you still can," I say.

Shit, that was stupid. Why did I say that? Jane looks up at me askance and I rush to try and fix it.

"In quantum mechanics, objects exist in cloud of probability; they have a chance of existing at point a, a chance at point b, on and on and on. Maybe you still exist somewhere else, in a different form, in a different universe, and *that* you still has a chance to fall in love."

Jane blinks at me and doesn't say anything, and then the waitress is at my elbow.

"Have you decided?" she asks.

I glance down at the menu, feeling my face flush, the phone still glued to my ear. I order the pancakes because it's the first thing I see and my brain doesn't want to work anymore.

"I hate pancakes," Jane says quietly as the waitress leaves.

"Really?" I say, and she gives me a wry smile. "Me, too."

Cold Rose Creamery is in a small shopping center in Santa Monica, next to the kind of clothing store I know I can't afford because there's only a single rack of shirts inside. Jane and I wait in the car until the after-school rush has come and gone, the bell over the door finally silent.

It jangles once more as I enter the shop, the air-conditioning and the smell of vanilla hitting me at the same time. There's a boy and girl behind the counter and one girl sitting at a table with a computer, all of them young and pretty in an indistinct way. There are so many people in this city, so many lovely girls with white teeth and fresh cheeks, so many beautiful boys with soft smiles and dimples. They blur together after a while, every face starting to look like the next. They never change, never get older, each face replaced with the newest crop of hopefuls that move here every year, an endless churning of the gorgeous and disposable.

"Delilah's here, too," Jane says, glancing at the girl

with the computer, her hair a shiny, shellacked blond.

"Hi there," says the girl behind the counter. She has a mass of curly black hair and freckles on her brown skin, a pink apron tied around her front. "What can I get for you?"

"That's her," Jane says sadly.

I clear my throat and take my hands out of my pockets. "You're Macy, right?"

She blinks at me. "Yeah?"

"I need to talk to you. It's about Jane."

Her mouth goes slack for a moment, and then she's coming out from behind the counter.

"Have you seen her? Did someone find her?"

The girl with the computer looks up, her eyes wide.

"No," I say, before anyone gets too worked up. "But I'm helping her mom, trying to figure out what happened."

"This is about Jane?" the blonde says, coming over.

"Brian, will you be okay if I take a break?" Macy asks the boy behind the counter with black hair and tattoos.

"Yeah, sure," he says, giving me an appreciative look that I do not return.

"Here," Macy says, pointing to a larger table by the window. I slide into a seat, Jane next to me, and the two girls sit across.

For a moment we just stare at one another; Macy looks tired, the skin under her eyes dark.

"This is Delilah," she says, motioning to the blonde.

"I'm Lexi," I say. "I . . . grew up with Jane."

"She never mentioned you," Delilah says, frowning, and I decide I don't like her much.

"We weren't close anymore," I say.

Macy narrows her eyes at me. "Look, if you're some kind of reporter just trying to get quotes—"

"No," I say quickly. "I'm not, I swear."

"Tell them I told you about spring break when we went camping," Jane says.

"The last time I talked to her she said you guys went camping for spring break," I say.

Macy's face clears slightly. "Yeah. Damn, that was miserable."

"Probably would have helped if we knew how to camp," Delilah says.

Jane laughs, and for a second my heart hurts, because I'm not a part of this.

"Jane has the *worst* ideas," Macy says, smiling. "Remember when she made us go rock climbing? Or when she tried to make macarons?"

Delilah mock shudders, but her laugh dies quickly.

"God, she's a terrible cook," she says softly.

"You still ate them," Jane says. "Even the burnt ones."

"You were friends for a long time?" I ask, trying to bury my jealousy.

"Since freshman year," Macy says. "Del and I have known each other forever, and then Jane popped up in our homeroom. The three of us just clicked. Sometimes you can tell about a person, you know?"

Delilah nods. "She just came over and started talking. She wasn't shy, didn't seem nervous about starting high school like the rest of us."

"Yes, I was," Jane says. "I just hid it better."

"I only want to help," I tell them. "That's all. I'm worried about her. I know Isaac broke up with her that day."

"Jerk," Macy says angrily. "What kind of bullshit is that?"

"Whose idea was the club?" I ask.

"Mine," Macy says.

I focus on her, wondering what's hiding beneath the pretty exterior. "Why *that* club?" I ask sharply.

"She wanted to go dancing," Macy says. "And they have a big floor."

"You've been there before?"

Macy shrugs. "A couple times. They don't card you,

and the drinks are really good."

I frown; was Jane being at the club just bad luck? Wrong place, wrong time? She has no magical ability, so why did someone pick her? There has to be something that connects the victims; it can't just be random, can it?

"Did you see anything that night?" I ask, thoughts tumbling over in my head. "Anything suspicious when you left?"

"We were drinking," Delilah says guiltily. "I got tired and I wanted to leave."

"We both wanted to leave," Macy says soothingly.

Delilah's eyes grow wet, and her bottom lip wobbles. "Maybe if we'd just stayed—"

"Del, it's okay," Macy says. She rubs a hand over her face. "The police are looking for her, remember?"

"Yeah," Delilah says, but her voice shakes.

Macy glances at me and then back to her friend. "Look, I need a smoke."

Delilah wrinkles her nose. "Oh, Macy—"

"You don't have to come," she says. "Lexi will keep me company. Why don't you go tell Brian to make you a milkshake."

Delilah nods, and Macy gestures to me. "Come on."

Jane and I follow her out onto the patio, a large

umbrella blocking the worst of the sun.

"You want one?" Macy asks, holding out a crumpled pack of cigarettes.

I've only smoked once before, when Ilia practically dared me to. But something about the way she's eyeing me makes me agree.

"Sure," I say, and pull a cigarette from the pack.

"You don't smoke," Jane says, crossing her arms. She stands next to Macy, scowling at me. "You know how bad that is for you, right?"

I ignore her and let Macy hold her lighter to the tip of the cigarette. I breathe the smoke in, tar and heat and something bitter. It almost tastes the way death tastes.

"Thanks," I say, letting smoke trickle out of my mouth. I feel light-headed, like I stood up too fast.

"No problem," Macy says, lighting her own cigarette. "Sorry about Delilah. She's not dealing with this well. I figure it's kinder to lie to her."

I go still, not bothering to pretend to smoke anymore.

"Jane's dead," Macy says, her voice rough. "But I think you already know that."

"Shit," Jane says.

I look at Macy, *really* look at Macy. She licks her lips and flicks the ash from her cigarette, but her eyes never leave my face, tracking every small movement I make. *Shit* is right; nothing is getting past this girl.

"Why do you say that?" I ask, not bothering with a lie.

"Jane would never take off without telling anyone."

"They haven't found a body."

"It doesn't matter," Macy says, one foot tapping on the ground in an anxious pattern. "I know she's dead. As soon as I woke up that morning, I knew."

"How?"

Her foot stills, and she chews on one side of her mouth, debating whether to trust me. Finally she shrugs, taking another drag. "I know it sounds crazy, but I get these . . . hunches sometimes. I woke up with a sore throat and a really bad feeling in the pit of my stomach." Macy rubs a hand across her neck absent-mindedly. "And it was like I knew something terrible had happened. I tried texting her, calling, but I knew it was too late. She's gone."

"Damn," Jane mutters. "I had no idea."

Now it makes more sense; if she has psychic affinity, I'm not surprised she's the one who suggested the club. The place draws people like her, like calling to like.

"You're right," I say, looking at Macy with a newfound

curiosity. "It does sound crazy. But I believe you."

Macy smiles at me, and she lets me see a lot of teeth. "I also have a hunch that you're not who you say you are," she says. And I think if I met her under different circumstances, maybe we could have been friends. "'Cause there's no way Jane had a friend I didn't know. So who are you really? Informant? Are you working for the cops?"

"None of the above." I toss my cigarette on the ground and crush it beneath my boot. "I meant what I said; I only want to help. Believe me when I say I'm just trying to figure out what happened that night."

Macy meets my eyes and nods slowly. "Well, you can't do worse than the cops, I guess."

"Was there anyone watching her?" I ask.

She exhales and smoke billows out from between her lips. "Yeah, people were watching her," she says. "Jane's the life of the party, always has been. But I wasn't keeping track."

"Was anyone acting odd?"

"I don't know," Macy says. "We danced with boys, mostly. Some girls. But they were just . . . people. The same kind of people you see every day."

Jane sighs, and I share her frustration.

"Look, if anyone had been creeping on her, she would have told me," Macy insists. "We would have left. It was a normal night, right up to the end."

"So what happened at the end?"

"Del got tired and we finally left, at around one. But outside the club, Jane said she forgot something. We were taking separate rides anyway, so she said she'd just see me the next day."

I don't say anything, and Macy's face twists.

"I know I shouldn't have left her. I *know* that. But we've done it a hundred times before, and our Uber was there."

"You can't blame yourself," Jane says firmly, but I don't know if I believe those words. We make choices, and consequences result from those choices. Shouldn't we feel guilty for that? Shouldn't that keep us up at night?

"You didn't do this," I say, but I don't tell her she's faultless.

Macy shakes her head. "Yeah. It's not that simple, though, is it?"

"No, it isn't."

Macy meets my eyes and nods slowly, and I think we understand each other. We don't get redemption for this.

"What did Jane say she forgot?" I ask.

She frowns, takes a drag of her cigarette. "Her jacket, she said. She had to get her jacket from the coat check."

I go still. "She brought a jacket with her?"

Macy shrugs. "I guess."

"Do you remember her having it earlier that evening?"

She frowns. "I don't know. But she must have, if she had to go get it."

"What is it?" Jane asks, staring at me.

I tilt my head at her, just a fraction, enough to say *later.*

No one uses the coat check; we don't even have someone there at night. Which means Jane lied. Something else brought her back to the club.

"That was the last time I saw her," Macy says hollowly. "I could see her back as my car drove off. And that was it."

She swallows hard, wipes at her eyes angrily. I give her a moment, let her get herself under control.

"Thank you," I say, my pulse rapid in my ears.

"Sure," Macy says. She stabs out her cigarette against the palm tree and flicks it to the ground. "I have to get back to work."

"Okay." I start to walk back toward the car, but

hesitate. "Listen," I say, turning back around. "I know people who can help you. If you get any more of your hunches . . ."

I trail off, but Macy looks up, a spark of interest in her eyes. "Really?"

"Yeah," I say. "I'll give you my number."

I rattle it off for her and she puts it into her phone.

"Just give me a call," I say. "If you get a feeling, or you ever want to talk to someone about it."

"Thanks," Macy says. "But, um . . . what if I don't want to talk about my hunches? Can I still call?"

I blink, and one side of her mouth quirks up in a small smile.

"Oh," I say. "Well. I guess that's up to you."

Macy's grin gets bigger, and Jane clears her throat loudly.

"Are you finished?" she asks, her eyes narrow.

"I'll, uh, see you around," I tell Macy, and she raises her hand and watches me walk away.

"What do I you mean I lied?" Jane asks from the front seat of my car. She's angry, her eyes going back and forth between white and brown.

"We don't have a coat check," I say again.

"That doesn't mean it was a lie," Jane protests. "Maybe I was confused."

"Or maybe you lied."

Jane glares at me, the silence between us hanging heavy and dark.

"Why would I lie?" Jane finally says.

"I don't know," I say. "Maybe . . . maybe you wanted to meet someone."

"I wouldn't do that."

"You don't know that. You don't remember." I try to say it gently, but it sounds wrong, hanging harshly in the emptiness.

I need the footage from that night. I need to see what happened when she came back in.

"I know me," Jane says, her voice tight. "And I know you're wrong. And *what* was with giving Macy your number?"

"She's showing signs of psychic ability," I say. "That doesn't just go away if you ignore it. She needs someone to teach her control."

"That doesn't have to be *you*, though," Jane argues. "You get she's going to ask you out, right?"

"So what if she does?" I ask, tension buzzing under my skin.

"What about Phillip?" she asks, narrowing her eyes. "I didn't even know you liked girls."

"You didn't ask," I say. "All you asked was if I've ever been in love. And what difference does it make?"

"None," Jane snaps. "Not a damn bit."

And then she's gone, too, and I'm alone in the car with nothing but the smell of copper and wires to keep me company.

13

THERE ARE POLICE CARS PARKED DOWN THE BLOCK from the club, and the air feels tense and electric as I dodge people on the sidewalk.

"I need that footage," I say to Ilia when I finally get in the building. He's in the hallway, slick hair mussed up, a pen dangling out of his mouth while he looks over a delivery list.

"You're late," he says.

"Did you hear me? I need the footage, and I also need whatever police files you can get me on the other missing people."

There has to be something that connects all of them, something the killer is drawn to.

Ilia takes the pen out of his mouth, strain in every line of his body. "Yeah, I heard you. I'm working on it, Lexi, but things aren't easy right now. We have cops parked outside, Urie's gonna have an aneurysm, everyone is jumpy as hell—"

"Ilia, I'm serious."

"So am I." His eyes travel over my face, and the lines around his mouth deepen. "I'm doing the best I can, Lexi." He rubs the bridge of his nose, and I can almost see what he's going to look like as an old man.

"I know you are," I say, feeling guilty. "Everyone knows you're doing everything you can, Ilia."

He gives me a tired smile. "Look, I'll have it for you soon, I promise. I talked to one of our guys on the force; they should release it in the next couple of days. I'll ask about the files."

"Just keep me posted."

Ilia nods. "I'll call you if anything changes."

"Thanks." I head for the floor, but pause. "Any more attacks on the protection spell?"

"No. Maybe it's finally—"

"Ilia! Dad wants to know—"

Phillip cuts himself off as he appears in the hallway, and I close my eyes. Perfect. Just perfect.

"Well," Ilia says, glancing from me to Phillip and back again, and a spark of humor comes back into his face. He's enjoying this far too much. "I'll just go see what dear old uncle wants, won't I?"

He winks at me as he walks away and I bare my teeth

at him. But then he's gone, and I'm left standing in the hallway, trying not to make eye contact.

"Hey," Phillip says.

"Hey."

"You left without saying good-bye the other night."

"You were . . . busy." That's one way to describe it, I suppose. I angle my body toward the door, away from him. "How's Jordan doing?"

Phillip winces. "Not great. But better. He's healing, just slowly."

"Good. I should get to work."

"Okay."

I frown at him, suspicious. He doesn't usually give up this easy. "Okay?"

"Yeah," he says, and I realize he's taken a step toward me, his bright eyes on my lips. "I won't keep you." Another step.

"Good. Because I'm already late."

And now he's standing right in front me, close enough to touch.

"Then you better hurry," he says, and I can feel his breath on my face. I could turn, I could leave, but my feet don't move from this spot.

"Goddammit," I mutter, and then of course we're kissing.

I open my mouth even as my brain screams at me that this is stupid. But it feels good, and who cares if I'm not really in love with him; Jane's never been in love, either. Suddenly I'm thinking about the dip above her lips and the way it moved when she teased me about the pancakes.

"No," I say, tearing my lips away. Phillip reaches for me, his eyes worried, but I twist out of the circle of his arms.

"Lexi, wait," he says, but I'm already halfway down the hallway.

"I'm sorry," I say over my shoulder, but it's meaningless. I'm always running from him, too selfish to end it and too spineless to stay. Eventually he'll get tired of watching me walk away.

I work my shift, serving up drink after drink to beautiful people without really seeing any of them. We're busier than usual, the edge of danger a compelling draw for a certain kind of customer. The mood is jittery, fear and lust bleeding into the air and mixing into something unpleasant and potent. Nicole smiles and slides coasters under glasses, spreading her calm while I sink deeper into myself, my hands by my sides and my mind on the dead.

My shift doesn't end until well after midnight, and my eyes are hot with fatigue as I drive the dark streets. I pull up to the curb by my apartment, and even before I get out of the car I can hear the deep thump of bass coming from the building.

I sigh and press my head against the steering wheel, hard enough to hurt. I'm tired enough that I doubt any amount of noise will keep me up long.

The music gets louder as I walk up the stairs, a snaking, shimmery beat that echoes off the walls and vibrates in my chest. Someone's laughing loudly somewhere, the tang of cheap beer permeating the hallway and mixing with the smell of stale smoke. I don't know which of the units is throwing the party, but it doesn't matter. This isn't the kind of place where you knock on your neighbors' doors.

I shove inside my apartment, half ready to drop into bed with my boots on, when I pull up short.

"What are you doing?" I ask before I can stop myself, straining to be heard over the blare of the music.

Jane and Trevor come to a stop and she laughs, a full-bodied, throaty sound.

"We're dancing," Trevor yells at me. "What does it look like we're doing?"

I don't know what to say to that. It looks like two ghosts are spinning each other around in my studio apartment.

Trevor grabs Jane again and starts to twirl her, over and over until she finally stumbles. He catches her and tilts her back in a mockery of an elegant dip.

"Mademoiselle," he says, flourishing a hand.

"Monsieur." She giggles back.

Trevor releases her and Jane staggers forward, clutching at my arms.

"Lexi," she says, her eyes fever bright. "If you spin enough, it's almost like being drunk!"

"That doesn't make any sense," I say. "You get dizzy because of inertia and endolymph fluid in your inner ear; if you're a ghost—"

"Would you just shut up and dance with us," Lexi says, tugging at my hand.

"Yeah, come on," Trevor says, his grin a wicked thing. "Live a little."

All I really want to do is go to bed, but the beat is pounding through the walls and Jane is pulling me forward and my body is alive and can still move, still breathe, still dance.

I close my eyes, let the sound of the bass fill up and

swallow the pressure inside me, let my limbs go loose and easy. Lexi is on one side and Trevor on the other and we're spinning and they're laughing and their bodies press against me. The music swells and my lips curve up, drunk on contact and the taste of iron under my tongue.

"Oh, my god, you're smiling," Jane says, her own face lit up with a grin.

"So?"

"So I've never seen you smile."

"That's not true," I tell her, shaking my head.

"Trevor?" Jane asks.

He nods in agreement. "She's right; you never smile."

"See?" Jane laughs, spinning me around.

"You're both wrong," I say.

"Oh, a scowl!" Jane says, wagging a finger in my direction. "Now that, I'm used to."

I fight it, but not hard enough, and the smile creeps back onto my face. And then a laugh, dredged up from the place the scream lives inside me. I open my lips and it escapes, tumbling across my tongue, rough as sandpaper.

Jane claps, delighted, and Trevor slings an arm around both of our waists. And then just as suddenly, the pumping bass stops, and we're left in silence.

"Damn. Fun time's over," Trevor says as we come to a halt. His voice sounds strange in the quiet, like I'm hearing him from underwater.

"Lexi can put some music on," Jane says, staring into my face hopefully.

"Some other time," Trevor says, running a hand through his floppy hair. "Party's over; that means the bars are out. If you'll excuse me ladies, WeHo is calling my name."

I roll my eyes at him. "Voyeur."

Trevor elbows me as he moves toward the door. "Prude!"

"Perv!" I call after him, and he gives me the finger as he glides through the wall.

"Where is he going?" Jane asks, her eyes trailing after him.

I make a noise in the back of my throat. "The bars are closing, which means boys will be making out on the sidewalk."

"Oh." Jane blinks. "Does that, uh, do something for him?"

I shrug. "I don't know. I guess it's better than your imagination?"

"No, I mean . . . he can still do that? As a ghost? We can still do that?"

"That?"

Jane tilts her chin and I suddenly understand.

"Oh, *that*," I say. "Yeah, I think it's like the clothes or the chair. If it's real in your head, it's real to you."

"Huh."

I rub my arms, trying to shake off the spell of the music.

"I should get some sleep."

Jane starts to nod and then stops, biting her lip. "Can we . . . can we dance for just a little bit longer?"

I look wistfully at my bed, but the longing in Jane's eyes is much greater than my own.

"Sure," I say.

I don't have any kind of stereo, but I turn my phone up as far as it will go and play what pops up first. It's a slower song, the singer's voice clear and sweet, and my pulse stutters.

"Sorry, I can change it," I say, starting to turn back.

"No, don't," Jane says. "It's pretty." She smiles at me and offers out her arms.

I swallow, my mouth suddenly dry, and step closer. Jane closes the distance between us and wraps her hands around my waist. She's smaller than me, only coming up to my chin, and her hair tickles my nose as we start to sway.

"I asked Ilia about the footage," I tell her softly. "He said he'll get it, and the files on the other missing people."

Jane's head nods, but she doesn't say anything. Is she anxious? Am I doing this wrong? I don't know how to dance like this, with my body pressed against someone.

"It won't be long," I say, to reassure her. "A day or two, maybe."

"I don't want to talk about that," she says, her voice muffled.

I stop dancing, slowly push her shoulders away.

"I thought you wanted answers," I say.

Jane hugs her arms to herself, like she's trying to keep something inside. "I did."

"And?"

She won't meet my eyes. "And maybe now I don't."

"What happened to 'I have to do something'? What happened to 'you have to help me'?"

She shakes her head.

"Jane," I say gently. "What is it?"

Finally she looks up, her face almost translucent in the moonlight.

"What if . . ." Her voice catches in her throat. "What if I lied because I wanted to meet someone? What if— god, what if I went to *be* with whoever killed me?"

I step closer, grab her by the shoulders to make sure she hears this. "No. No matter what happened, you didn't ask to be murdered. This is not your fault, Jane. It could never be your fault."

Slowly, so slowly, she looks up at me, her eyes half-lidded, and somehow part of me knows what she's going to do before she does it. *Wants* her to do it, but never even dared to hope that she would. Tilting her head up, she balances on her toes and presses her lips against mine.

Time moves slower around large objects due to their gravitational pull. Fractions of seconds pile up around the bases of the pyramids. Jane is like that. I swear time moves differently around her.

I go completely still, locking my muscles in place; if I'm still, she won't know how much I've wanted this, how my body is screaming out for more touch. If I'm still, she won't know how desperately I want to crush myself against her, twist my fingers in her hair, bury my face into the hollow of her neck until all I can smell is hot metal.

The lamp flickers on and off, strobe lights behind my closed eyes. Her lips are soft beneath mine, her arms too warm beneath my fingertips, but it's nothing compared to the rush of heat in my blood. All I can taste is copper and all I can think is how loud my heartbeat pounds in my ears, and I wonder if Jane can hear it, if it sounds like it's taunting her.

It's only when the kiss breaks that I can move again, coming up for air with a noiseless gasp. We stare at each other, Jane's eyes wide and glazed, her lips still parted. It takes everything in me not to reach back out, not to grab her hips and press her to me.

"Jane—"

"I'm lonely," she says, her voice ragged.

A stone hits my stomach and I drop my hands, curling my fingers into tight fists as the heat leaves my veins.

"That's not," I say, stepping away from her, "a good reason to kiss somebody." The words are sticky in my throat. "Trust me on this."

The silence is thick between us, and that feeling of chance, of a beginning, dies without a sound.

"I'm sorry," Jane whispers, staring at the ground. "I shouldn't have done that. I just . . . I miss being able to touch. To be touched."

I swallow hard, something in my chest cracking painfully. "It's okay. It's nothing."

I get it, I do; the need inside is a greedy, grasping

force. But she doesn't want *me*, not the way that I want her. I shove my heartache down as far as it will go, seal it and cauterize it. And because there's nothing more to say, I sit on the bed and start to tug my boots off.

"Should . . . should I leave?" Jane asks, one hand gripped in the other. It's the first time I've seen her look awkward, like she doesn't know what to do with her arms. This must be how I look when I'm with Phillip.

"You don't have to do that."

"It's fine," she says. "If you want me to leave, I will."

She's hiding it well, the despair. But I've heard it too often in my own voice to mistake it. That awful dread that you'll be turned away again, outcast and mocked. It always happens, when they finally figure out what I am; I'm always waiting for that sudden look of fear and disgust.

"No," I say, "I don't want you to leave."

Jane's mouth goes slack with relief, but she keeps her chin firm.

"But I do need to get some sleep."

"Right. Of course," she says, nodding too quickly.

I pull on a pair of sweatpants and brush my teeth, washing away the tang of hot metal that's still on my lips. I pause over the sink, catching my reflection in the mirror. My eyes are dark holes in my head, my cheek-bones razor sharp and flushed. I close my eyes, press my forehead against the cold glass. It's too much, everything inside me twisting and needy, the trapped scream pounding against the cage I keep it in.

I'm lonely, she said. As if a few days as a ghost can compare with the endless want that lives inside me. And I can't even tell her.

I push away from the mirror and grab my sleeping pills from the counter. I don't want to dream tonight.

My phone wakes me up, pulling me out of a sweaty, foggy sleep. The drugs make my limbs heavy, and it feels like I'm swimming through the air as I reach to answer.

"Hello?" I mumble, my tongue too big for my mouth.

"Oh, hey, Lex. Did I wake you?"

"'Sfine."

"I finished the autopsy. Did you still want to come by?"

I fight to clear the cobwebs from my head and check the name on the phone. Carl. Autopsy. Right.

"Yeah," I say, kicking my blanket off my legs. "Yeah, I do."

"Well, come anytime after noon and I'll give you what I have."

"Okay. Thanks, Carl."

I hang up the phone and struggle to sit up. My mouth tastes sickly sweet, like I downed a liter of cream soda. My eyes roam around the mess of my apartment and settle on Jane curled up in my chair. She's awake but unmoving, her eyes tracking me in bed. She looks so small, her knees tucked under her chin. Small, and vulnerable, like she's still waiting for me to make her leave. There's a knot in my chest that wasn't there yesterday.

"Hey," I say.

"Hi."

"Veronica's autopsy is finished. I'm going to go see Carl."

"Oh," she says. "Okay."

"Do you want to come?"

"Yeah," she says, relief flitting across her features when she realizes I'm not going to talk about last night. It stings more than it should. "Yeah, I really do."

The car ride is strained, both of us too polite, and I'm almost grateful for the stench of decomposition and licorice because at least I have an excuse for the pit in my stomach.

"Lexi! Good to see you again," Carl says, like there

isn't a corpse with a gaping hole in its chest behind him. I can see the wet, red shine of organs filling the cavity, looking more like chunky soup than body parts. Or maybe I'm thinking that because there's a ladle sticking out of the goop.

"Hey, Carl. How's it going?"

"Can't complain," he says, smiling. "Job security, am I right?"

"Yeah." That joke gets less funny the more I hear it. "So what do you have for me?"

Carl peels off his red-slicked gloves.

"Not much, I'm afraid. There's no usable DNA," he says wearily. "All the blood we found is from the victim. This killer is precise, probably wore gloves, took precautions."

"So they're smart," I say. "They came prepared."

Carl motions me toward his office, where he picks up a folder from his desk and hands it over to me.

"Multiple stab wounds consistent with a single-edged blade," he says.

"Multiple?" I repeat, flipping through the pages.

Carl nods. "Single cut to the neck, multiple injuries to the chest and abdomen. That's what the cops call overkill."

"What does that mean, the killer was angry?" I ask. Why stab this girl so many times and Jane only once?

"I don't do the why," Carl says, "only the how. Official cause of death is massive blood loss, and I'm ruling it a homicide."

Jane scoffs softly. "No shit," she says.

"Do the cops have any leads?" I ask.

"Not yet," Carl says. "They're gonna be pissed about the DNA. No blood, and we didn't find any skin under her fingernails, so she didn't get to put up much of a fight. No defensive wounds at all, in fact. He must've been strong, or was able to get close to her."

"Come on, Carl, there's got to be something you can tell me," I say, frustrated.

"Sorry, Lex, this one's looking like a real dead end," he says wearily. "There's not much more to tell. Unless you want to see her."

"See her?"

"Yeah," he says. "See the body."

I swallow hard. No, god, no, I don't want to see her. But this isn't my decision to make. I tilt my head until I can see Jane's face. She looks pained, her mouth twisted tight and her eyes flickering white.

"I don't think—" I start to say, but Jane cuts me off.

"Yes," she says. "I want to see her. I want to see."

"Uh, actually, yes," I correct myself, stomach sinking. "I'd like to see her."

"This way," Carl says, unflappable as ever. He leads me out of the office and toward the wall of small metal doors that each house what used to be a person.

He stops in front of one row and opens a door, reaching inside. I brace myself for what's coming.

The table rolls out almost silently and the white of the sheet is too bright under the fluorescent lights. I blink and then Carl is peeling back the sheet and something mean and vengeful peels back my lips.

The girl on the table isn't that much older than Jane or me. She's bloated from the water, her skin pale and blue against the dark of her hair. I keep my eyes on her face, refusing to look at the rest. I've never given much thought to my body, even when it's under someone else's. I'm reckless with it; I forget to feed it, don't rest it, carve into it with needles and ink. I never think about how it's keeping me alive, how my heart is beating, how my lungs are breathing. How easy it is to lose everything you've always taken for granted.

"Veronica," Jane says next to me. "That was her name."

There's a ringing in my ears, and it takes me a moment to realize it's a telephone.

"I'll be right back," Carl says. "Stay put."

He disappears back into the office, and Jane takes his place on the other side of the table.

"She looks so cold," Jane says, running ghostly fingers down the girl's face.

"I know. But that's not her anymore."

"He was right, she didn't fight," Jane says, frowning over the body. "Look. Her nails are still perfect."

I don't want to see, but I force myself to look, to pretend this is a picture in one of my textbooks, all the yellowed bones diagramed and labeled. Here is the clavicle. Here is the manubrium. Here is where it joins with the sternum.

There's an ugly Y shape stapled down her chest and stomach that doesn't obscure the few dark, deep cuts. But her arms are unmarked, nothing but sallow, waxy skin all the way down. Her fingernails are painted a dark, shiny blue with tiny white stars.

Jane looks down at her own hands, the skin creamy and unblemished. "I didn't fight back, either."

"Then you were surprised by the attack," I tell her. "I've spent the last week with you, and there's no way you would go quietly."

"But why dump her body and not mine?"

"I don't know," I say. "Maybe it's not the same person. Maybe Trevor's right and they got spooked?" Without thinking, I lift one of her fingers to look closer, and to my horror the nail falls off into my hand.

"Shit!"

I stare at the nail in my palm until I hear a snort. I look up at Jane and she has a hand clamped to her mouth.

"Acrylic," she says, and then tries to stop her laughter again.

"It's not funny!" I hiss at her.

"It's a little funny," she says, and I'm freaking out but at least her eyes are back to brown.

"This is evidence."

"He said they already did the DNA; it's just a fake fingernail now. It's not like she'll miss it."

"Carl!" I yell, turning toward the office.

Carl ducks his head out of the door, the phone still tucked under his chin. "Yeah?"

I hold out my hand like an offering. "I touched her, I'm so sorry, but one of her nails came off."

He covers the mouthpiece with his hand and shrugs.

"No harm done," he says. "Just toss it."

"In the garbage? But . . ."

"She's going straight to Woodlawn. Talking to them right now," he says, turning back into his office.

"Oh." I turn around.

"What's Woodlawn?" Jane asks.

"Crematorium," I tell her. I look down at the nail in my palm and wonder how much she paid for it. If she got them done for a special occasion. Maybe she just liked stars. I wonder how fast the polish will burn.

"Let's go," I say, pulling the sheet back up over Veronica. She deserves better than this, to be open and displayed for us.

"Lexi."

"We got all we can."

"*Lexi.*"

I look up, and we're no longer alone.

Veronica's ghost is wearing a low-cut, cream-colored dress that's soaked through with blood, a sticky red cross plastered to her neck. Her stomach is a mess of skin and fabric and wet meat, and I raise my eyes until I'm looking at her wide-eyed face.

"I thought it was just me," she says, staring at Jane.

"Veronica," I breathe.

The ghost's eyes flicker away from Jane to me.

"You're not one of us," she says, frowning.

"No."

"She can see us, though," Jane says. "Even touch us. See?" She threads her fingers through mine, holds our hands up so Veronica can see.

"How?" she asks.

"It's a long story," I say. I look behind me anxiously, but Carl is still in his office.

"We can explain it to you," Jane says. "Come with us back to Lexi's place; we'll tell you everything. There's another ghost there, too, Trevor; he can teach you." She's talking too quickly, her voice high-pitched.

She's excited, I realize, to have another ghost around. Someone just like her, maybe killed by the same person, a violent bond that ties them. I untangle my hand from hers, and she doesn't even notice.

"I don't—I don't think I'm supposed to be here," Veronica says.

"No kidding," Jane says. "But it gets easier, I promise."

"No," Veronica says, taking a step back. "I mean I'm not supposed to be *here*. Like this," she says, gesturing at her body. "I don't understand. I'm dead. Why am I still here?"

"You were murdered," I tell her. "It almost always creates an echo—a ghost."

"But I don't want this," Veronica says. Her body flickers out, then back in, like someone turning a switch. "I don't want to be a ghost."

"Someone killed us," Jane says. "Don't you want to find out who?"

Veronica shakes her head. "The dead should stay dead. This isn't right." Her hand goes to her neck, fingers gripping the cross.

"Lexi?" Jane says, looking at me anxiously. "Make her understand."

"You don't have to stay on this side," I tell her, looking back and forth between the office and the ghost. "I can help you, if that's what you want."

"What?" Jane says, spinning to me. "No, that's not what I meant. What are you doing?"

"Please," Veronica says. "I just want to go where I'm supposed to go. Where my grandma is waiting for me."

"But—no!" Jane says. "Veronica, please, you don't have to go right now. Just stay for a while; maybe you'll like it."

"It's her choice, Jane," I say quietly.

"Goddammit, Lexi," she yells at me, but I look past her to Veronica.

"Can I ask you a few questions first? I'll be quick."

Veronica swallows hard, then nods.

"Did you see who did this?"

She shakes her head. "I just remember lying on the ground. I couldn't move. And then the pain."

"You couldn't move?" Jane repeats.

Veronica nods. "I tried. It's like my arms and legs were frozen. I couldn't even open my eyes." She flickers out again, and Jane makes a frustrated sound.

"What's wrong with her?" Jane asks me.

"I'm not sure," I say, frowning. "I think she's weakening."

Veronica flickers back in, her form blurry at the edges.

"Was there anything else?" I ask quickly. "A voice, a smell, a sound?"

Her face goes small and scrunched. "I could smell gasoline. On the ground. And someone said 'no.' They were angry, and they said 'no.' Now please. Help me."

"You understand—I don't know what's out there," I say. "I can't promise anything. I don't know what's waiting for you."

"I know what's waiting for me," Veronica says. "And I'm not afraid."

"Lexi, don't," Jane pleads one last time, but I move past her and stand in front of Veronica.

"Okay," I tell her. "Don't fight it."

She nods, and squares her shoulders back. "I'm ready," she says.

I reach out with my magic and start to push. I see Veronica's lips start to move, a whisper of prayer in my ears.

"... should walk in the valley in the shadow of death ..."

She doesn't resist me, doesn't try to stay. I push, gently, until her ghost slips into whatever is waiting on the other side.

"I didn't know," I say, breathing hard. "That it could be like that."

"Like what?"

"Peaceful," I say. "Something they don't need to fight. A good thing, not a threat I make."

"Well, I'm glad you're happy," Jane says bitterly.

"It's not about me," I say. "It's what she wanted."

"You didn't even try," Jane says, blood pooling under her chin.

I rub a hand over my head and turn back toward the office.

"Where are you going?" Jane demands.

"She said she couldn't move," I say, and open the door wide. "Carl?"

He's still on the phone, but he covers the mouthpiece. "Yeah?"

"Could she have been drugged?" I ask.

"We checked, toxicology tests didn't show anything suspicious," he says.

"Any chance it missed something?"

He shakes his head. "No way. We ran them twice; first time came back inconclusive, so we did it again to be sure."

"Inconclusive?" Blood rushes to my head.

"Yeah, pretty sure that was just the cancer drugs, though."

I stare at him. "What?"

"Didn't you see that? It's in the report," he says. "Poor girl didn't have long to live, anyway. Stage four lung cancer."

Jane swears loudly behind me.

"Anyway, the first time the readings were wonky, measurements all over the place. We just assumed it was a computer malfunction and ran it again and it came out with normal levels. No drugs except the cancer ones."

I nod, anger a hot pulse under my skin. "Thanks for everything, Carl," I say. "I owe you."

"Hey, Lex?" he says, lowering the phone. "Be careful out there, okay?"

"Yeah. I will." I turn away from him, and Jane sees my face.

"What?" she asks. "What is it?"

I wait until we're outside the building to answer. Spells mess with your body, mess with you on a molecular level. That test wasn't inconclusive.

"You were spelled," I say through gritted teeth. "The bastard spelled you so you couldn't move. Son of a *bitch*."

I want to smash something, want to let my screams out until my throat is ravaged.

"Lexi," Jane says, grabbing my shoulders. "Calm down. It's okay."

"It's *not* okay," I say. "You were alone, and you were in pain, and I—" My voice chokes off, and Jane steps forward, wrapping her arms around me. Even though she's angry with me, even though I should be the one comforting her.

"It's over, Lexi," she says. "I don't even remember that part. I'm right here, and I'm fine. Come on, let's go before someone sees you hugging the air."

I pull away from her reluctantly, and I realize I'm still holding the fake nail in my hand. I tuck it into the pocket of my jeans, though I don't know why. It wasn't even a part of Veronica, not really.

"Are you going to throw that away?" Jane asks me.

"No," I say, taking a shaky breath.

"Why not?"

I don't have an answer, other than it feels wrong.

"Because," I finally say, "it's not garbage."

14

A HARVEST MOON HANGS HUGE AND YELLOW AND fat, dwarfing the million pinpricks of light from the city. It's a fire moon, a devil wind moon, the kind that demands a sacrifice. The witches will be out in full force tonight, getting their hands sticky with lamb's blood. Or maybe something thicker.

I don't mess with their pentagrams and chicken bone nonsense, but even I feel the pull. It's hot out tonight, the air dry and charged with intent. I roll down my window, let the air buffet my face, let the light from the moon spill across the dashboard. There's almost no atmosphere on the moon, only infinitesimal amounts of sodium and potassium. The footprints the astronauts left will take a hundred million years to fade. Imagine that kind of permanence. When the sun finally sputters out, the ghosts will be the only things left.

Jane's face swims in my mind, her eyes cloudy white when I left her at the apartment. Even now, part of me wants to go back, wants to sit and smooth her hair back until the blood stops dripping. I'm in too deep, even I can tell that. Did I know this would happen? I only wanted to make things right, to give her some peace and ease my conscience. I never meant to let her get so close, never meant to let her kiss me. I didn't think she'd dig herself into my mind, into the empty pockets inside me. Deda was right; I am consumed by her, by this ghost of a girl. But he didn't realize that I would want to consume her, too, want her bare skin to rub against mine until it smooths all the rough parts of me.

I find a parking spot and shut off the car, lean my forehead against the smooth plastic of the steering wheel. I made a mistake. I never should have started this, but now I need to finish it; the longer it goes on, the harder it will be when it ends. And it has to end, even though the thought makes the rage scream inside of me.

A rap on the window makes me flinch, and Theo holds up a hand in apology.

"Sorry," he says. "You coming in? We're supposed to walk in pairs. Urie doesn't want anyone caught alone."

I nod and slide out of the car, slamming the door shut with a finality that feels symbolic.

"Yeah," I say, "I'm coming."

We walk toward the club, our silence easy and usual. Theo and I understand each other, our friendship a surface one based on mutual recognition. I trust him with my skin and he trusts me with his gifts, and nothing else needs to be said between us. I don't ask him questions, and he doesn't pry at me. Not like some people, who push when they shouldn't and slip under your guard while you're looking the other way—

Enough, I tell myself. I dig my fingernails into my palms and welcome the pain, a Pavlovian response.

"You doing okay?" Theo asks me, his eyes on my curled fists.

"Fine," I lie, and make an effort to relax my hands. "You?"

Theo shrugs. "Not bad. Considering there's a murderer out there."

"Are you scared?" I ask him.

"Not so much for myself," he says. "But for the others, yes. Are you?"

"Yeah," I say. "I'm scared. But not of dying."

"Of what?"

I'm scared of failing. Scared of letting Jane down. And scared that the end will come before I'm ready.

"A lot of things," I finally say.

Theo nods, and doesn't press me. "Found a new design I want to try out if you're game."

"Sure," I say. "What is it?"

"Something to do with light, I think," he says, frowning. "I don't know exactly. They come into my head, but I'm never sure what they mean until I start to ink them."

"Well, I'm running out of room on my arms." I give Theo free rein over my skin, let him work out the details like I'm scratch paper. Half the time they don't work, like the clock frozen at midnight on my shoulder, or the raven on my forearm.

"That's what legs are for," he says. "You working with Nic tonight?"

I shake my head. "She's off." I give him a sidelong glance. "Why do you ask?"

If I wasn't looking at him, I would miss the slight flush that turns his cheeks darker.

"No reason," he says, and quickly changes the subject. "How's your ghost situation?"

I chew the inside of my cheek. "I'm working on it."

"Sounds complicated."

"You have no idea."

"Be careful," he says. "Those tattoos will only go so far."

"Is this where you tell me the storm is coming?" I ask. "Or some other cryptic bullshit?"

"No," he says, shaking his head. "It's where I tell you to call me if you need help."

We reach the door, and Theo opens it for me.

"Thanks," I mutter, stomping inside. "I'll keep that in mind."

"You know where to find me," Theo says. "I don't know the rules to this game, but I know you're on the board."

"Yeah?" I ask, heading down the hallway. "Well, some of us didn't ask to play."

Nic is off tonight, and part of me is grateful I don't have to even pretend to be cordial. Lila usually works the main floor and barely makes eye contact with me all night. I don't know if she can sense my sour mood or if she's angry about the lack of customers and tips up here, but either way I'm not complaining.

"Can I get a gin and tonic?"

I nod at the man across the bar and splash some gin into a glass. At least I think it's gin; it's clear; that's close enough.

"I'm David," the man says, grinning wide at me. He's

not unattractive; he has dark, soft-looking hair and slightly crooked front teeth. But I don't care what his name is, and he's getting close enough for my hands to graze. I set his drink down and stare back stone-faced.

"Thanks," he says, the drink spilling over the side when he grabs it.

"So is this what you do all night?" a familiar voice asks. "Glare at people?"

I suck in a breath, lock my muscles in place so I don't jump when a hand thrusts through David's chest and wiggles its fingers at me.

"He can't feel me, can he?" Jane asks, her head poking around him. She waves her hand back and forth. "Hi, I'm David," she says in a deep voice. "I'm thirty but I still hit on teenagers; want to read my screenplay?"

I bend over and cough loudly until David's smile slips and he hastily retreats. Lila gives me a disgusted look that I pretend not to see, then goes back to ignoring me while Jane slips through the bar.

"What are you *doing* here?" I whisper, trying not to move my lips.

"I wasn't on this level that night," Jane says, leaning back against the ice bin. "Macy liked the dance floor.

I thought I'd try walking around, see if I remember anything."

"And?" I glance around the room, but no one is paying close attention to me. Maybe they'll think I'm just singing along with the music.

"Nada. Your guy's not that old, is he?" She cocks her head at the disappearing David, something reckless and bright in her eyes. "The one Trevor mentioned? Phillip?" She makes his name sound like a cut.

Lila has her back to me, so I make a face at Jane. "No."

"Well, which one is he then? Is he here?" She leans over the bar, propping her arms on the wet counter. It distracts me, the smooth skin of her forearms, the dusting of freckles on top.

"Why do you want to know so bad?" I ask, and I can't resist leaning next to her, letting our shoulders brush.

She looks down at my inked arms, the opposite of her own.

"How many tattoos do you have?" she asks.

I blink. "Oh. I don't know, actually. I stopped counting after a while. I let Theo practice on me."

"What do they mean?"

I shrug. "Different things."

Jane makes an annoyed sound. "That one," she says,

pointing at the compass on my shoulder. "What does that one mean?"

"That's in case I get lost. It directs me toward the club."

"What about this one?" she says, poking at the circle near my elbow. "It looks like a wheel."

"That's a ward against coercive spells."

"And this one?" she asks, pressing a finger to the shield knot at the inside of my wrist, the lines oddly broken in places.

"That one's for protection," I say, looking away.

"Protection from what?"

"It's hard to explain." That was one of the first tattoos I got. I asked Theo for something that would block my powers, to keep me from seeing death, to hide the ghosts from my sight. It burned going into my skin, and no matter how much power Theo tried to channel, the ink wouldn't stay connected.

"You keep a lot of secrets, don't you?" Jane asks, tilting her head.

"I have to. It's another kind of protection."

"Lexi," a voice calls, and I jump, my elbow slamming into something warm.

"Watch it," Ilia says, stepping back.

I flinch away from him, cursing myself for getting distracted.

"Uh, sorry," I stammer out, shaking out the tension and the images inundating my mind.

Ilia frowns at me as I curl my arms around my center.

"You okay?" he asks slowly, like I'm a wild animal he's trying to soothe.

"Fine," I snap back, but he doesn't look convinced. I almost never bump into people; I always look where I'm going, always try to minimize the chance of touching.

"Is *that* Phillip?" Jane asks, her tone disapproving.

"What do you want, Ilia?" I stress his name just slightly.

His face goes serious. "Our folks came through. I got the footage back."

My pulse speeds up until I can feel it in my throat.

"Think you can get your little friend down here?" Ilia asks, raising one eyebrow.

"Guess it's our lucky day," I tell him, glancing at Jane.

"Wait, she's here? Right now?" Ilia eyes dart around the bar like he's looking for her.

"He's not that bright, is he?" Jane says.

"He does his best," I tell her. "Ilia, meet Jane. Jane, Ilia."

Ilia chooses to focus on a spot to Jane's left. "Um. Nice to meet you?"

"Likewise," she says wryly.

"So, are we doing this?" he asks.

"Yeah," I say. "Let's go."

Ilia heads toward the hallway and I follow a step later. Even without turning around, I can sense Jane behind me, feel the gravitational pull of her. I can't escape it; she's like my compass, like a lodestone. I always know where Jane is.

Ilia opens the door to Urie's office, shutting and locking it behind me. Jane seeps through the wood and slowly spins, taking in the large room with its wall of TVs. All the lights are off, but the flash of illumination from the screens plays across Ilia's face, leaching all the color from his skin.

"Give me one sec to load it up," Ilia says, plugging a flash drive into the control. "Are you ready?"

Jane's face is tense, and she jumps when I touch her shoulder.

"Jane? You okay to do this?"

She nods, lips tight. "Yeah. I want to see it. I need to see it."

Her voice is even, but her eyes are starting to get milky and the TV flickers.

"Keep it together," I order. "Jane—"

"I'm fine," she snaps, closing her eyes. When she opens them, they're brown again. "I can do this."

Ilia turns back to us. "I'm sorry about what happened to you," he says, talking to a spot over my shoulder. "But we really need your help. We can't trace whoever's doing this, so anything you can remember, no matter how small. . . ."

"Yeah," Jane says, swallowing hard. "I get it."

"She knows," I tell him. "Go ahead and play it."

Ilia nods, and he presses a button and the TVs skip and start to play. I watch the footage of the club, the bodies pressed close together, swaying to a silent beat. Lights flash overhead, the blues and greens slightly muted and grainy.

"I'll start it at midnight and go forward," Ilia says. He fiddles with some knob and the footage skips choppily, going from day to night, faces disappearing and reappearing in different places. He stops and the video starts to play, four screens filled with different angles of the same room. I glue my eyes to the screens, but it looks like every other night in the club, beautiful people packed in as tight as they'll go. I move closer, until I'm directly in front of the TVs, searching through the mass of the crowd for the face that's right at my shoulder.

We don't talk while the scene plays, the reality of that night too heavy, too full of memories for the both of us. Every movement someone makes feels like a choice leading to the inevitable finish. Maybe if this DJ had played a different song. Maybe if this drink hadn't been spilled on the floor. I watch the night spool out in front of me, a movie I've watched a hundred times but still hoping for a different ending.

"There," Jane says finally, and I shake myself out of the guilt. She points at a group of people on the left screen, filing into the club, and I catch Delilah's shiny blond hair first. Then I see Macy, in a bright red dress, and then Jane. She's laughing, her head thrown back, revealing a long expanse of neck. Jane, alive and whole, and happy. I glance at the girl next to me, and I would never mistake her for the girl on the screen. They may look the same, but my Jane is not this Jane. My Jane has never looked this carefree, this innocent. My Jane is angry and wild and a little cruel. I know which one I prefer.

"I think . . . I think I remember this part," Jane says

softly. "I remember feeling light. I remember music."

She touches herself on the screen, her fingers melting through the glass. There's an aching hunger on her face, raw and vulnerable. The picture goes static for a millisecond, and she snatches her hand away.

"Sorry," she murmurs.

"That's her, isn't it?" Ilia asks. "That's Jane?"

"Yeah," I say curtly.

Ilia sighs heavily as I watch as the girls dance with one another in a small circle, drinks in hand. A boy joins in, spinning Macy around until she laughs and clutches at him. Eventually his friend calls him over and he leaves. Another boy joins in, then a girl with bangs, but none of them stay long. I pause on each face, commit them to memory and take a grainy picture with my phone. Each of them is clean-shaven, cheeks still round with youth. None of them look like killers.

"I remember dancing," Jane says slowly. "My shoes were pinching my toes."

I don't know how long we watch the girls dance and drink and giggle. I see some of our people in the corners; Lila and Theo are behind the bar, serving drinks as fast as they can pour them. Adam and Jordan push through the crowd, brushing past the girls with stoic security faces on. I'm afraid to skip forward, afraid I'll miss the split second that will finally give us an answer. Another boy comes to dance, this time looping an arm around Jane's waist. I try to pause on his face and frown; he's wearing a black ball cap, tugged down low. I can't get a good look, so I go to a different angle and look again, but in this one his head is turned the wrong way. In every view, his face is blocked, almost like he knew where the cameras were. Almost like he'd been scoping out the club.

"Him," I say, my voice somewhere below a whisper. Jane moves closer to the screen, her eyes filming over as she stares at the man. I very gently lay a hand on her arm, my fingers just touching the fuzz of her hair.

"It's okay," I breathe.

"What?" Ilia asks, and I drop my hand. "The ball cap?"

"Maybe," I say.

"I don't recognize him," Ilia says, squinting at the screen. "He *could* be one of ours."

"He could be anybody," I say.

When he's done dancing with Jane, the man whispers something in her ear and then walks away. I try to track his movements, but he loses himself in the crowd, disappearing between one breath and the next. Is this the man who killed her? Or is this just some stranger, trying to hit on a pretty girl?

"He spoke to me," Jane says, her rage a wounded animal. "He said something to me. I let him *speak* to me. I let him *dance* with me."

"Do you remember?" I ask, almost begging. "Was that him?"

"I—I can't say for sure," Jane grinds out. "But he said something to me. And why is he hiding his face?"

"We don't know it's him," I say, for Ilia's benefit.

"We don't know it's *not* him," Jane counters.

The girls dance for another song, until Delilah puts a hand on Macy's shoulder. From the stifled yawn and the jerk of her head, I can guess what she's saying. Macy pouts for a moment, but Delilah pulls at her, fanning herself, and the girls start to make their way through the dance floor. It takes them a while to weave through the crowd, their hands linked. I follow their progress from one screen to another as they push through the throngs of dancers and drinkers, until they finally hit the door and spill out into the night.

"Here we come," Ilia says.

I look paler on the screen, gaunter, like a skeleton

given flesh. I don't want to watch this part, but I can't make myself look away.

"This is when we met," Jane says. "Or when you met who I used to be. The before me."

My memories mix with the footage, making everything sharper. I remember the sound my boots made on the pavement, the smell of cigarette smoke and perfume from the club. The sour churning of my stomach, Ilia calling for me to wait. If only I had listened.

I know it's coming, but I still flinch as Jane runs into me. It doesn't feel right that there isn't any sound; it should boom, it should echo, this cataclysmic moment.

"You look so scared," Jane says, frowning at my stricken face on the TV. I watch myself stumble back, desperate to get away from the doomed girl. Poor fools, the both of them.

"What was it?" Jane finally looks over at me. "What were you so afraid of?"

I clamp my lips together. I can't tell her. I won't ever tell her.

"And there you go," Ilia says, watching me lurch past Jane and run into the building.

"Yeah," I say, my voice cracking on the word. I swallow some moisture into my mouth and turn my attention back to Jane, standing in the parking lot with her friends. She's arguing with them, her hands gesturing widely. Lying to them.

Delilah yawns and plants her hands on her hips, and Macy throws her arms up in the air in surrender. Delilah hugs Jane quickly and lets her go, and Macy points a bossy finger at her. Jane laughs and waves goodbye as the two climb into a waiting car.

"I told them to leave me," Jane says, watching her friends drive away. "They didn't want to, but I must have told them to go."

When the car is out of sight, the smile falls from Jane's face. Without another look back, she turns and marches back through the parking lot toward the club. I check the next camera angle, searching for whoever's waiting for her inside. It has to be the boy in the hat, it has to be, but I don't see him anywhere.

And then, just before she gets to the door, Jane jerks left and heads down the alley.

"Wait, what?" Jane sputters. "Where the hell am I going?"

I look from TV to TV, searching for a car, for another person, but we don't have cameras down the alley. All I see is Jane's back as she recedes from view, walking like she knows exactly where she's going.

"Pause it," I snap at Ilia, and he freezes the footage.

I study the screen, looking for something, *anything* hiding in the darkness around Jane.

"I went to meet him, didn't I?" Jane asks, but I don't think she's asking me. "It's bad enough I didn't fight back. But I walked into the arms of the person who killed me."

She gazes at me, her eyes horrified, her mouth half-open.

"More?" Ilia asks.

There's nothing on the screen. Nothing but the flickering streetlamps, the wet pavement, and the slim figure of a girl headed to her death. What did she meet there? The man in the hat? A stranger? And why is Jane's body missing when Veronica's was found right away?

"I don't know," I say quietly. "Jane, what do you remember after the dancing?"

"Nothing," she says, her fingers curling up. "It's like it all goes black."

"When? When exactly does it go black?"

She screws up her face, and I can almost hear how hard she's thinking.

"Right before I danced with the boy in the hat," she

says. "I don't remember him. The only thing I remember after that . . . is you."

"Shit." I have too many questions and not enough information. I'm reaching into a dark chasm, rooting blindly for a rope I don't even know is there.

"You want me to run it again?" Ilia asks.

"I don't think it will help," Jane says.

I shake my head. "I—"

A rap at the door makes me jump so hard my ribs hurt. Ilia strides to open it, and the face peeking in doesn't calm my nerves any.

"Oh," Phillip says. "Hey. Ivan was looking for you, Ilia, he needs to go over the schedule."

"It's fine," I say. "We—I was just leaving."

"The files," Ilia says, pointing to a folder on the desk. "Of the other missing people."

I pick up the folder and tuck it under my arm while Ilia pulls the flash drive out and holds it up. "Take it," he says. "Just in case."

I nod, and he tosses it to me; I catch it in one hand and bury it in my pocket.

"Thanks," I say, trying not to make eye contact with Phillip. I follow Ilia out of the office, and he shuts and locks the door behind us.

"Lexi, call me if anything comes up, okay? Any detail we can use."

"I will."

"I'll go find Ivan," Ilia says. "Thanks, Phillip."

Jane gives a small intake of breath when she hears his name, and panic flutters in my mouth.

"Yeah, no problem," Phillip says, nodding at his cousin.

Ilia leaves, and Phillip and I regard each other for a long moment. I open my mouth to say something, I'm not sure what, but before I get the words out Phillip steps forward.

"You look serious," he says. "What were you doing in there?"

"Watching security footage." I look back at Jane, but I can't read her face. I swallow and close the distance to Phillip.

"Sounds interesting." I look away, afraid of the emotion in his eyes.

"Phillip—"

"Is this the part where you run away from me?" he asks, giving me a small smile. I hear a scoff from behind me that I ignore.

"No," I say, meeting his eyes. "Not this time."

He searches my face, and his smile falls away.

"I'm sorry," I tell him, and I am. Phillip deserves better than what I'm willing to give. "We don't want the same things. And I can't keep pretending."

"You never pretended," he says softly. "I just didn't like listening."

I shrug. "I didn't want you to listen."

He laughs quietly.

"Please," Jane mutters under her breath.

"I should go," I say awkwardly, sidling back.

"You know you can always talk to me, right? That's what friends do, Lex. They talk to each other."

I frown. "Friends? Is that what we are?"

Phillip shrugs, but his eyes are sincere. "If we can't be more, then yes. At least I'd like to be."

I risk a glance at Jane; her face is carefully blank, and I wonder what she's hiding under that mask.

"I'd like that, too," I tell Phillip.

He reaches out and I keep myself from cringing as he takes my hand, presses it to his lips.

"Good," he says, letting my fingers drop. "Call me if you ever get lonely."

I raise an eyebrow. "I thought you wanted to be friends."

"I didn't say what kind," he says, grinning. "I'll see you later, Lex."

"I'll be around," I tell him, and for once he leaves while I stand in place.

"So," Jane says, her voice too light. "That's Phillip."

15

THE CLOCK ON MY DASHBOARD TELLS ME IT'S AFTER three in the morning. Anywhere else, the freeway would be empty, people cycling through REM to slow-wave sleep, but LA is always awake. I pass other cars on the road, wondering what misfortune brought them out in the middle of the night. Airport trip? Out drinking? Or are they like me, and only seem to really live in the in-between times, the pockets the world ignores, the devil's and the witching hours?

"So what's his deal?" Jane's voice cuts through the quiet of the car as I drive us back home.

"Who?" I ask, even though I know who she's referring to.

"Phillip. Is he boring? Sloppy kisser? Bad tipper?"

My hands flex on the steering wheel, tattoos stretching over my knuckles.

"He's none of those things and he's also none of your business," I say. "And we need to talk about what was on those tapes."

"Oh, you mean how I served myself up on a silver platter to my killer?" Jane asks, crossing her arms. "See, I don't want to talk about that. I don't even want to *think* about that. I'd rather talk about how your ex-boyfriend is still in love with you, whereas mine couldn't wait to get rid of me."

"That's not what happened with Isaac," I tell her. "And Phillip was never my boyfriend."

"Well, why not? He clearly wanted to be. Hell, he *still* wants to be."

I can feel my jaw clenching, my back teeth grinding. "It's complicated."

"He's cute and he's into you," Jane says, and there's a mocking ring to her voice that's rubbing me wrong. "What's the problem?"

I don't like this version of Jane. I'd rather have her furious and bitter, I'd rather have her sad, anything but this scornful, spiteful ghost sneering at me across the seat.

"We are not having this conversation. Just leave it alone, Jane."

"Was it the chemistry?" she asks, plowing ahead anyway. "No spark?"

"I said leave it," I snap at her, the words loud and harsh in the close space. "Why are you acting like this? Why do you have to push at *everything?*"

"Because it's not *fair*," Jane snaps. "You were talking to him like I wasn't even there."

I sigh, steering us north, the smell of citronella candles through the open window warring with the copper scent of Jane.

"Jane, you do realize I can *hear* you, right? I knew you were there."

"But I wasn't. Not really." She turns her head away, but I can still feel the warmth she's giving off. "You have your whole life ahead of you, Lexi. You'll get older, you'll change, you'll fall in love. And I'll still be the same. I'll still be stuck in place."

"You won't be," I tell her, feeling bitter. "Stuck, I mean. Once this is done, there's nothing keeping you here. You can go anywhere you want, anywhere in the world. You can go to the Louvre after hours, you can sit on top of the Burj Khalifa. You can cross to the other side, find out what's waiting for us all. *I'm* the one who's stuck; I'll be living in this shitty apartment until I die, still working for Urie, still broke and hungry."

Still empty, still alone. And she'll be long gone by

then, but she doesn't even realize it yet.

"Why?" she asks crossly. "You're smart, Lexi; you could do anything you want. Why don't you go to college?"

Because I couldn't even make it through high school, I want to say. Because I can't be around people without wanting to vomit.

"College isn't free," I say instead. "And I can't quit my job to go to school."

"Well, take some classes online then."

"You need a computer for those. And computers cost money. And textbooks cost money. And—"

"Okay, okay, I get it," Jane says, holding up her hands. "Fine."

I pull my car alongside the curb, then look over at her. "I guess we're both stuck, then."

There's no music tonight, only the smell of cigarette smoke and grilled meat in the stairwell. My stomach growls, and I can't remember the last time I ate. I'll go see Deda tomorrow, fill up on coffee and stale cereal. There should be a few boxes left from the last time I ransacked the cafeteria.

I unlock the door and rummage around in my single cabinet, finding two small boxes of bran flakes. I don't have any milk, so I eat the cereal dry, shoveling fistfuls into my mouth.

"God, you're a mess," Trevor tells me, spread-eagled on my bed. "Why don't you buy some real food?"

"Are you paying for it?" I ask him, washing the flakes down with a glass of water.

"With my ghost money?" he asks, waving around imaginary bills.

Jane settles herself into the chair and Trevor turns his attention to her, sitting up.

"How did it go tonight?" he asks in a gentler tone.

Jane shrugs. "Not great."

"That's not true," I say. "We got more information, at least."

I sit down next to Trevor and flip open the folder, spreading the files out. Pictures stare back at me accusingly, all of them different, all of them somehow connected. A girl smiling with her dog, a boy on a skateboard, a young woman holding a diploma.

"These are the others?" Jane asks from over my shoulder. "What are we looking for?"

"Anything," I say. "Anything that connects you. None of you went to the same schools, you're different genders, Marcus had magical abilities but as far as we know the rest of you didn't. But there has to be a *reason* you were targeted. Something the killer noticed about you, wanted from you."

"We're young," Jane suggests. "No one over twenty-five."

"Most people at the club are under twenty-five," I say. "It has to be more specific than that."

"Maybe he's just a psycho," Trevor says. "One of those guys who wears people's skin. He probably ate the other bodies or something."

"Trevor, cut it out," I say. "He's using spells to incapacitate; he must have some sort of goal."

It's not hard to kill people. You don't need a spell to shoot someone, to cut their throat, to cause massive brain injury. But you do need a spell to keep someone immobile if you're killing them for a purpose. I bring up the picture of the man in the hat on my phone, set it next to the files like I can force a link to appear.

"Who's that?" Trevor asks.

"Suspect," I say. "He's the only guy whose face you can't see on the security footage."

"I let him dance with me," Jane says, wrapping her hands around her middle. "I let him *touch* me."

"Hey," I say gently. "We don't know that he's the killer for sure."

"Yeah, maybe he just wanted to dance with you," Trevor says, taking one of Jane's hands and prying her arms open. He raises their hands up, spinning her around. "I would ask you to dance."

"Thanks." Jane's mouth tilts just a little. "What about Lexi?"

Trevor dips Jane and wags his eyebrows at me. I cross my arms and stare back.

"Hmm, I don't think she's in the mood," he says dryly.

"Maybe *Phillip* would put her in the mood," Jane teases. "He seemed pretty eager to dance with you, if that's what you want to call it."

Trevor bounces up, his eyes widening. "No way! You met Phillip? What did he look like? Tell me *everything.*"

"All right, give it a rest, both of you," I growl at them.

"This is so unfair," Trevor says. "You won't show me a picture; I don't even know if he's hot."

"He's okay," Jane says, her voice hardening a little. "Comes on a little strong. And Lexi won't tell me what's wrong with him."

"There's nothing wrong with him," I yell, my voice muffled by bran flakes.

"Then why aren't you into him?"

Trevor laughs. "Uh, probably because she can't touch

him without seeing him die. That's gotta kill the mood."

My blood goes cold and Trevor stops laughing immediately.

"I—I'm sorry," he says to me, his eyes pained.

"What?" Jane asks, frowning. "What are you talking about?"

She doesn't sound mad, only confused. I should say something. But I can't make my mouth move. I'm rooted to the spot, every muscle tight, my blood vessels constricting.

"I didn't mean that," Trevor tells her. "Just ignore me."

"Lexi?" Jane asks. She walks toward me, until her face is inches from mine. "What does he mean, you saw Phillip die? He's not a ghost."

"I should go," Trevor says.

"Can somebody tell me what the hell is going on?" Jane says, annoyed.

My mouth opens, but nothing comes out. I don't know how to tell her.

"Hey, whatever it is," she says softly, "it'll be okay."

"No," I finally say. "It won't."

Jane eases a step toward me. "What did he mean, you saw Phillip die?"

"Not just him," I say, my throat thick. "I can tell when

people are going to die. It's part of . . . it's part what I am. What I can do."

"You can tell when someone's going to die?" Jane repeats, staring at me. "Jesus, Lexi, that's awful."

I nod, hoping she'll leave it. Please, let her leave it alone.

"So, how does it work?" she asks. "You just know? Is it everyone?"

I glance at Trevor, and he shakes his head, looking at me with pity. My breath is coming faster now, my heartbeat an incessant buzz in my ears. The fight or flight response starts in the amygdala, which triggers the hypothalamus and—

"Lexi!" Jane grips my shoulders, her face worried. She's worried for *me*. It breaks something inside, something I didn't know was holding me together; the words build up in my mouth, until it feels like I'm choking on the truth.

"No." It tears out of me, razors across my tongue. "I don't just know. I have to be close. I have to touch someone."

"Why didn't you tell me? You've never said anything. . . . " She stops talking and I close my eyes. But not soon enough. I still see it, the fraction of a second where her face twists with the knowledge.

"That night," she whispers. "The night I died. You touched me."

I swallow, and my throat is tight and painful. "Jane."

"Did you see it? Did you know?" Her voice is desperate, like she's begging me to deny it.

But I tell her. "Yes."

She drops my shoulders, and the cold air on my face snaps my eyes open. Jane steps away from me, her face slack and horrified.

"That's why you looked so scared." Blood starts to well up from her neck and her shirt blooms red.

"Jane," Trevor says, getting up from the bed. "Are you okay?"

"I'm sorry," I tell her, and it's pitifully inadequate. "I'm so sorry."

"You *knew*," she says again, and her mouth curls with disgust. "And you did nothing. You let me die."

"It's not that simple."

"Then explain it to me." She storms forward, and I can feel the rage barely contained under her skin. "Tell me why you didn't stop it."

I try to move away, but she grabs my arms, yanking

me close. Her eyes film over pure white, blood bubbling from her throat.

"Jane, please." I try to tug away, but she only digs her fingers farther into my wrists.

"Did you see him cut me?" she growls. "Did you see me bleeding?"

Her hands are hot on my skin, too hot, crossing over into pain. I don't fight; I let her hurt me, let her anger roar past the spells in my skin.

"Tell me," she yells, shaking me. "Tell me!"

My arms are burning under her hands and I grit my teeth to keep from crying out. My mind stops working, screaming at me to stop the agony by any means necessary. And there's only one way left.

"Jane, stop," Trevor says, pulling at her hands, but they're fastened around me like manacles.

"Stay out of this," Jane hisses at him.

My skin starts to blister, the stink of burning hair filling my nose.

"If you don't stop, she'll have to push you out," Trevor yells. "Do you hear me? She'll make you *leave*, Jane. Permanently. Is that what you want?"

She knows that I won't. I don't even try. It feels like my skin is being charred to the bone, and still I don't do the one thing that would stop the pain.

"Don't do this," Trevor begs. "Please don't make her hurt you."

My vision is starting to darken at the edges. I focus on Jane's face, pale and bloody and twisted with hate. The pain starts to recede, and that's a bad thing, but I'm grateful for the relief. Everything is moving very slowly, and Trevor's voice comes to me muffled and muted. I can see his lips moving, but I can't quite make out the words.

There's a loud crack, and then I'm falling backward, landing hard on the floor. I cry out when my arms hit the wood, the pain snapping me back into consciousness.

I look up and see Trevor looming over Jane, his hand still clenched in a fist. He looks back at me, and I suck in a breath. His eyes are black holes, bruises and cuts mottling his angular face. Blood drips down his neck, his arms, pools in places beneath his shirt.

"Go," he says to me. "I've got this."

I stare at him, barely recognizing the boy in front of me. He turns his face away like he doesn't want me to see it. Like he can hide the fact that he, too, died violently and painfully. That his anger might not match Jane's, but it's far older, a cold burn instead of a fire.

Jane makes a horrible screeching sound and tries to

run past him, but he catches her around the waist and pulls her back.

"Go," he yells at me, and I scramble to my feet, my arms screaming. I run to the door, my legs unsteady, and I throw it open.

I take one last look back, and too late I wish I hadn't. She'll never forgive me; she'll never want to see me again. This will be my last memory of Jane, this shrieking, clawing creature in Trevor's grasp. I shut the door behind me, and I shut everything I wanted with it.

I move in fits and starts, my body not responding properly to my commands. I head for my car, then realize I don't have my keys. So I start walking, my feet stumbling along the sidewalk, somehow propelling me forward. I don't know where I'm going until I'm pounding on the locked door and Nancy is frowning at me from the other side of the glass.

"Lexi?" she asks, reaching down to unlock the bolt. "It's the middle of the night."

"Deda," I say, my voice echoing strangely in my ears.

"He's sleeping, what's going—" She stops, halfway through opening the door, staring down. "Lexi, what on earth happened?"

I look down and catch sight of my arms. The skin around my wrists is bright red and blistered, peeling away in places to show pink, wet spots underneath.

"Come in," Nancy says urgently. "The on-call nurse can look at you."

She opens the door wide and I pause in place. I'm tired; I'm so, so tired.

"Lexi," Nancy says sharply, reaching a hand out. Then her tone gentles, goes coaxing. "I'll wake up your grandfather. He can sit with you."

I stare at her hand like a threat, think of the nurse's fingers on my wrists. I can't take it, not tonight. What am I even doing here? Deda warned me, and he was right. This was my mistake, and I won't lay it on his doorstep.

"No," I say, taking a step back, and then another.

"Lexi, you need medical attention," Nancy says warningly.

I shake my head. "Tell him—tell him I called. I'm taking a break, but I'll come see him soon."

"Lexi—"

"Don't tell him I was here," I say, still backing away. "Don't tell him any of this."

Nancy yells after me, but I'm already running. My

legs don't carry me far. I barely make it two blocks before my knees lock up and I have to stop. It's okay; I know where I'm headed now. I wait at the bus stop, and no one else is there to stare at my arms or ask any questions. I don't know what time it is; the buses start running at four a.m. and it has to be close to that. I left my phone at home, along with everything else I thought I cared about.

My arms are throbbing and I focus on the pain, anything to keep me from thinking about what just happened. I don't know how deep the burns go, how many layers of skin I've lost, only that it feels like I've been seared to the bone.

I sink into the pain, let it fill me up, until my body becomes one large ache. I can feel my pulse in the raw skin of my arms, the blood rushing beneath the wounds. Each beat sings to me that this pain is earned, and I welcome it. If this is my punishment, I'll take it. I deserve worse.

The stink of exhaust hits me before the groan of the bus. In the darkness, the driver barely glances in my direction as I get onboard and pick a seat in the shadows. I close my eyes and lean my head against the grimy window; I'm in too much pain to fall asleep, but

I let the lurch and tug of the wheels lull me into kind of stupor.

My stop isn't far, but it takes every ounce of energy I have to get back on my feet. When I climb off the bus and stumble outside, I'm running on nothing but delirium and the certainty that this is where I belong.

The doors of the clinic's psychiatric ward slide open and I stagger inside, almost weeping when I see the familiar green tile and the nurses' station.

"Can I help you?" asks the orderly behind the glass, but I barely hear him.

"Lexi?" Someone takes my elbow gently. "Are you all right?"

I look at the white-haired man hovering over me with concern.

"Hi, Dr. Ted," I say, his face swimming in and out of focus. "I need some rest again."

"Who are you talking to?" the orderly asks.

I blink, and it takes forever for my eyelids to open up again.

"No one," I say. "It's no one."

And then my bones can no longer hold up my body.

16

THE NURSE THINKS I BURNED MYSELF. I DON'T correct her; it's easier than the truth. She doesn't ask me how I did it, or why, but she makes small, disapproving sounds as she dabs ointment on my blisters. I flinch each time, for once more from pain than what lives in my head. Not that I can unsee it. Ironic, really, for a woman who works in a psych ward to kill herself. Physician, heal thyself.

I hiss as she starts to bandage me, the gauze scraping across raw skin. I wish I was still unconscious, but I only collapsed for a few minutes. The Vicodin should be kicking in soon, but right now it's only making me nauseous.

"Don't pop the blisters yourself," the nurse says, fixing the gauze in place. "Keep applying the antibiotic and keep it clean."

I only nod and her mouth purses.

"The new skin will be sensitive to the sun, so take precautions. There will be some scarring."

I pull my arms away and fold my tattooed fingers together. Do I look like the kind of person who cares about scarring? I'm only worried whether the lines of ink on my wrists will need to be retouched, if Theo's magic has been broken. I guess I'll find out if I catch a cold.

The nurse sighs and peels off her gloves, tossing them into a bin.

"You're done," she says, her voice heavy with resignation. "I'll check the bandages tomorrow."

Maybe it's not so ironic. Maybe what she sees every day would be enough to break anyone.

"Thank you," I say, sliding off the table.

I could tell her to get help. I could tell her to talk to someone, that I know what it's like to feel the darkness closing over your head. But of course I don't. Instead I cross my thickly wrapped arms and leave the room. I'll always have this reminder of how I didn't save Jane. Scars tell a story, and mine is a cautionary tale. Get too close and get burned.

The Vicodin is almost better than the sleeping pills. It hits me like a hammer wrapped in cotton, and it takes me long minutes to undo my shoes and climb into bed, my fingers clumsy from the burns and the drugs.

I curl up on my side, half convinced the bed is rocking on waves, and let the movement ease me to sleep. I try not to think about her, but I can't seem to stop. I shouldn't have let her kiss me. I shouldn't have kissed her back. Maybe she could have forgiven me, at one point. But I let her die and then I let her kiss me. There's no forgiving that kind of betrayal. I never should have left this hospital bed.

I sleep, and sleep, waking only when the nurses come to do their checks, and sometimes not even then. The light is low when I finally open my eyes and keep them open, late afternoon at least. The drugs have worn off and my arms are stinging, but I still don't get out of bed. The stiff hospital sheets smell like bleach and powder as I burrow my face into the pillow. They'll make me get up to eat something eventually, or I would stay in this bed for the entire seventy-two hours.

"Are you ready to tell me what happened?"

I open one bleary eye to stare at Dr. Ted. He's in his therapist pose, legs crossed, thoughtful expression.

"No," I say, and turn my face back to the pillow.

"I can't help you if you don't talk to me."

"You can't help me at all," I say, my voice muffled. "You're dead."

Dr. Ted sniffs. "I don't see what difference that makes."

I sigh and roll onto my back. "You can't fix what's wrong with me, doc. There's no point in trying."

"I don't 'fix' people, Lexi. But why don't you tell me what *you* think is wrong with you?"

"God, do you have to be such a . . . a *shrink?*"

Dr. Ted laughs a little. "Why else would you come here?"

I frown. "I come here to rest, that's all. It's quiet here."

"There are lots of quiet places, Lexi. Libraries. Hotels."

"You don't understand."

Dr. Ted leans back and presses his hands together. "What I understand is that for the past two years, you've come here more and more often. Out of all the places you could go, you choose a clinic full of doctors whose job it is to help people who need help. Now maybe the living doctors haven't figured it out, but I don't have other patients to distract me. So I'll ask again: Why do you come here?"

I press my head back into the pillow, staring up at the ceiling and the water stain spreading at the corner. It was smaller the last time I stayed in this room, barely more than a handprint. Now it's like a beach ball with strange tentacles growing out of it. Has it really been so long? Have many hours have I spent staring at these ceilings, sleeping in these scratchy sheets? And for what?

Twenty-six thousand light years from us, at the very center of our galaxy, is a supermassive black hole. It is the heaviest object in the Milky Way, the mass of millions of suns condensed into a single point. The closer you get to it, the stronger the gravitational pull. Get close enough, and nothing can escape. Not even light.

"There's this . . . scream inside of me," I say finally. "I can feel it *here*." I press a fist to my chest, just where my rib cage ends. "Sometimes it's weightless. And sometimes it feels like it's packed with cement, like it's a cinder block pressing down on me."

"How long have you felt it?" Ted asks.

"All my life," I say. "Ever since I knew what I was."

"What do you think it is?"

"I think it's where things were supposed to go," I say. "Normal things. Like having your mom hug you when you scrape your knee. Or having a secret with your best friend. Or holding hands with someone when the lights go off at a movie. I think those things were meant to be there, but I never got them. Instead I got . . ."

I pause, and Dr. Ted nods at me. "Go on."

"Guilt," I say. "Every time I didn't save someone. Loneliness, when I had to push everyone away. Because it hurts to have them near. Anger, because it isn't fair. And when my mom died . . ." I swallow past the lump in my throat. "I knew if I let it out, I would never stop screaming. So I buried it. I let it rot and calcify and I chained it beneath my rib cage."

"And you never let it out?"

I don't want to think about Jane. Not here, not yet.

"I tried," I say. "Just a little. I thought it was safe. I was wrong."

Dr. Ted leans forward. "Why do you say that?"

"Look what happened." I hold up my bandaged arms. "I thought I could control it, but I can't. I think I'm supposed to be like this. Not just the ghosts, not just the death. I'm meant to be . . . trapped."

I look over at Dr. Ted and he gazes back at me a little sadly. "I don't have an easy answer for you, Lexi. I doubt you'd trust one, anyway. You and I both know there's no such thing. But I will ask you consider this: the scream you say is inside you? Maybe it's not about learning to live *without* it. Maybe it's about learning to live *despite* it."

I curl up on my side, exhausted again though I haven't left my bed. I don't know if he's right, if there's a way to live like this. But if there's no fixing what's wrong with me, then what choice do I have?

"You know, you don't have to wait until you're ready to break before you come here," he says. "You could come see me every week, have someone to talk things through with. There's a cafeteria on the bottom level that's usually empty."

I blink at him, unsure.

"Just think about it," Dr. Ted says, standing up. "It's not like I have a busy schedule."

"Yeah," I say, pulling the covers up to my chin. "Maybe."

"Get some rest," he says, patting my foot.

"Hey, doc," I say before he turns around. "How did you die?"

He smiles down at me. "Old age," he says. "Went to sleep at my desk and never woke up."

I nod, wearily. "I think I would have liked you in life. It wouldn't have hurt much to know you."

Maybe he says, "I would have liked that, too," but I can't remember if I'm awake or if I'm dreaming.

I get up for dinner. For Dr. Ted's sake. I don't think he can help me, not really, but he's trying, and so I will, too.

I put my boots on, rinse my face, pull myself into something resembling a human being.

They sit us around a Formica table to eat and we avoid making eye contact with one another. It reminds me of high school; I hated eating there, too. At least in this place, I don't have to pretend to fit in. We're all outcasts here.

The food isn't bad, considering, not any worse than the stuff they serve at Deda's. The spaghetti is too soft and the sauce is too sweet and they don't let us have knives, but the meatballs are decent and I'm hungry enough to not care about the rest.

I glance around the table while I drink from the small carton of milk. There's a woman in a pink sweatshirt, a young man with a patchy beard. Everyone is quiet, focused on their food, focused on their minds. No one looks like they belong here. They look just like me—tired. Like they've been fighting something for a long time, something no one else can see. I told myself I was different, I was just coming here to rest; it turns out that's all anyone here wants. A place where you don't have to hide how hard it is. How much it takes out of you to just *be* every day.

"There you are."

I look up and the fork slips from my fingers. It hits the edge of my tray, bounces off the table, and clatters to the ground. In the silence, the noise is deafening, and every face turns toward me, but all I can see is her standing in front of me.

Her eyes are still white, her shirt soaked through with blood.

"Jane," I whisper through numb lips.

"I'm not here to hurt you," she says.

My eyes flick down to my arms resting on the table, and she blanches.

"Again," she says, swallowing. "I'm not here to hurt you again."

All I can do is stare, so sure that if I blink I'll find she's not real.

"Can we talk?" she asks, glancing around the table. "Maybe somewhere else?"

I stand up too fast, knocking my tray to one side. Suddenly the food is sitting wrong in my stomach and I wish I hadn't eaten so fast. I head for my room, ignoring the orderly who shadows me for the few seconds it takes to get back.

Jane follows me and I pause, seeing the room through her eyes: hospital bed, plastic table, toothbrush, a small bottle of light green liquid that's body wash and shampoo and doesn't really get anything clean. *I can't take care of myself* is what this place says. I keep my back straight, defiant as I sit on the bed and face her. This is me, the real me, for Jane to finally see. Maybe I'm fucked up and messy, but at least I'm being honest.

"Why are you here, Jane?" I ask.

She takes a deep breath. "What I did to you . . . I didn't mean to. I didn't mean to burn you like that."

"I know." Does she think I blame her for this? This is my fault, all of it.

"I'm sorry," she says.

"I'm sorry, too."

"Don't," she says, holding out her hand. "Just don't."

"Please," I blurt out, standing up. "Give me a chance to explain."

"Explain?" She whips her hand down, takes a step toward me. "You missed your chance to *explain* every single day we spent together. I can't believe I trusted you. That I liked you. That I—" She closes her eyes. "God, just looking at you makes me want to break something."

"I was afraid that you'd hate me," I tell her, almost begging. "That you'd run, and I'd never see you again."

"You were right to be afraid."

I hug my arms around my middle, until the burns start to sting. "Jane, I was a coward, I know that. I should have told you the truth the moment I saw you in that alley."

"No, you should have saved me *that night*," she yells.

"I *couldn't*," I yell back.

We stare at each other, both of us desperate and bloody and furious.

"Tell me why," Jane says finally, her voice harsh. "You want to explain, well, here's the one and only chance I'll give you. Five minutes. Tell me why you let me die."

I swallow hard, and nod. "Okay. Will you sit?" She doesn't move. "Please?"

Her jaw flexes, but she sits on the bed, as far away from me as she can get. It's still close enough to feel waves of heat blowing off her body.

"The universe . . . tends toward disorder," I say, grasping for a way to explain.

"What?" Jane snaps.

"In thermodynamics, a change in a system that cannot be restored to its original state without expenditure of energy is called an irreversible process," I say, the words memorized from a defunct textbook. "Heat flows from a hot body to a cold body and always will. You can't unscramble an egg. Some things, once done, can never be undone. Once set in motion, can never be stopped. The entropy of the universe is always increasing."

"I don't understand," Jane says.

"Neither did I, for a long time," I tell her. "I just knew I was different. Like how I knew my mom was going to die at sixty-three, from a blood clot. Deda understood. He said the two of us were the same, but we weren't like everyone else. And he made me promise that if I touched someone, never to tell them how they would die. But he didn't tell me what would happen if I did."

There's no mistaking the bitterness in my voice, and Jane sucks in a breath.

"You tried, didn't you?" she whispers.

"I'm not a monster," I tell her, my voice thick. "Whatever you may think of me. I never asked for this."

"What happened?"

I close my eyes against the onslaught of memories, the hole inside me snarling. "Mrs. Kimble was my second-grade teacher. She let me eat lunch at my desk instead of the cafeteria, so I wouldn't have to be around all those other people. She brought me her old *National Geographic*s to read. She taught me the difference between stalagmite and stalactite."

"You tried to save her." It isn't a question.

"I saw it the first time she patted my shoulder," I say. "I knew when it was coming. I made her promise to wear her seat belt that day. I made her *swear* it."

I stop, because I don't want to remember the next part.

"What happened, Lexi?" Jane asks, and I shake myself. She wants the truth, and I owe it to her.

"She made it home in one piece." I try to keep my voice steady. "And at the exact moment she was supposed to wrap her car around a tree, my mom fell over in the kitchen. She never got up."

"Jesus." Jane's lip trembles. "But—you said your mom—"

"It's not how she was supposed to die," I say dully. "I did that to her. I tried to interfere, and she paid the price. Just like my grandma did when Deda tried the same thing."

Jane stares at me, her eyes searching. "What happened to Mrs. Kimble?"

I look down. "I bought her a week. No one escapes death for long. Some things, once set in motion . . ."

"Lexi—"

"I wanted to save you, Jane," I say. "I want to save

everyone. But it doesn't work that way." I meet her eyes, because this part she needs to understand. "You can't outrun death. If you try to cheat it, it only comes back for more. It took my mother. It took my grandmother. Deda is all I have left. I can't stop it. All I can do is get out of its way."

Jane stands up, backing away from me. I watch her retreat, watch her run away from me just like everyone else.

"Why didn't you tell me this before?" she asks.

"Because I didn't want you to look at me like you're looking at me," I say. "Like I'm the one who killed you."

"You're not the one who killed me, Lexi."

"What difference does it make?"

"What do you mean, what *difference* does it make?" Jane says, throwing out her arms. "How can you say that?"

"Because it doesn't *matter*," I yell. "You're still dead, you, Trevor, Mrs. Kimble, all of you are still dead, so what does it matter? What is the point of this fucking *thing* I have if I can't do anything with it? Is it just to make me suffer?"

Jane stops in place, but I'm not watching her anymore.

"I thought I could make it up to you somehow," I say,

more to myself than to her. "That if I helped you, maybe it would make up for not saving you. But I messed it up, didn't I? I just wanted . . ." I sigh, trying to sort out the truth. "I don't know. I just *wanted*."

A pair of black shoes enters my vision, and when I look up, Jane is standing in front of me. Her shirt is still bloody, but her eyes are brown, and they're looking down at me.

"Was that five minutes?" I ask.

She lets out a watery laugh. "I don't know. I wasn't really keeping track."

"Thank you for coming here," I say. "You deserved to know the truth."

She nods, then carefully sits down next to me. Her shoulder brushes mine, a small blast of heat.

"I wasn't sure if I should," she says. "I almost didn't. And I almost turned around, until I saw you. Then I knew. I didn't want to leave things like that between us. I didn't want that to be the last time we saw each other."

"Me, neither." I find myself leaning into her and I have to push away.

"It matters," Jane says softly. "To me. That you helped me."

"Yeah," I say. "I've done a stellar job so far. That's why

your killer is still out there and I'm in a clinic."

"I don't mean about that," Jane says. "I mean the rest of it. You could have left me in that alley, and I would have become something awful. Something twisted. Being with you, talking with you, touching you . . ." She bumps my shoulder. "It means something to me."

"I'm sorry," I say. "That I couldn't save you. That you died like that. No one should have to die like that."

Jane blinks, looking at something I can't see in the distance. "I'm angry," she says. "Not at you, not anymore. But I'm angry. I'll probably always be angry."

"Yeah, well." I shrug. "I'm angry, too."

Jane smiles, almost, and silence stretches between us.

"So what now?" I ask into the quiet.

"Now we get you out of this place," Jane says, glaring at the door to the room.

I frown. "How did you find me, anyway? I never told Trevor where I was."

"Yeah," Jane says with a wry smile. "But you told your grandfather."

I look up in surprise. "You went to see Deda?"

"It took a long time for Trevor to calm me down. I couldn't think straight, I just wanted to . . ." She pauses. "*Hurt* something. Someone. But Trevor wouldn't let me. He held on to me, even when I fought him. I don't want to think about what I would have done if he wasn't there."

Trevor shouldn't be strong enough to stop a murdered ghost, but nothing about Jane has ever been normal.

"You would have stopped," I tell her.

Jane's eyes are on my arms, her mouth tight. "I'm not so sure. That wasn't me; that was that thing you found in the alley. I don't know what she is, but I don't trust her. And neither should you."

"You're here now," I point out. "You came back."

"Only because of Trevor," she says. "I don't even remember what he said. I think it was nonsense mostly, but it was like I was following his voice through the dark. And eventually I found the way out. Only you were long gone by then."

"So you went to Deda?"

"Trevor said you disappeared sometimes, for days at a time. He didn't know where you went, but he thought your grandfather would know. I swear, it was like he was expecting me."

I wince. "Yeah. I kind of made a scene over there."

"So I heard," Jane says dryly. "I sat down and he just looked at me and said, 'She's at County Mental Health.

Tell her not to scare Nancy again.'"

"Sounds like Deda," I say. "Did he say anything else?"

"Yeah," Jane says with a small smile. "He told me I should give you five minutes."

Her smile tugs at something in my chest, and I'm suddenly afraid. I can't go down this road again, trying to fill myself up with Jane, trying to plug the hole with some sort of redemption. It hurts too much to lose it. And I will lose it again, when we find the killer, when Jane decides she's ready to go. I can't keep her forever.

"Come on," Jane says, taking my hand. "Let's go home."

And I realize it doesn't matter how much it's going to hurt. I'll follow her anywhere, because even when I'm burned and in a psych ward, Jane doesn't hesitate when she takes my hand.

"Wait," I tell her as she stands up. "Just give me a minute, I have to take care of something."

17

THE DOCTORS WANT ME TO STAY, BUT NOT ENOUGH to fill out the paperwork required to keep me here. I sign myself out and find Dr. Ted to tell him I'm leaving. He doesn't make a fuss, though, not after I promise to start coming to see him for an hour every week. He even pats me on the back and says we're "making good progress," whatever that means.

"Was it because of me?" Jane asks softly as we wait for the bus to arrive. "That you came here?"

"No," I tell Jane. "Not entirely. I came here long before I met you, and I'll probably be seeing Dr. Ted long after you're gone."

"Gone?" she asks. "Where am I going?"

"I don't know," I say. "Buenos Aires? Paris? Istanbul? Wherever you go when you finally get sick of fires and palm trees. And there's always . . ." I can't bring myself to say it, because I can't imagine a world without Jane, in whatever form.

"Yeah. There's always that." She shakes her head. "But Trevor doesn't leave. Not even LA."

"Trevor's from Midland, Texas," I tell her. "Los Angeles *is* his Paris."

The bus arrives in a cloud of exhaust and I cough as we climb on.

"You know, I've never left California," Jane says, sliding into the window seat.

"Me, neither," I say quietly, the bus loud enough to hide my voice.

"My mom used to take me to the zoo in San Diego for my birthday," Jane says. "And we went to San Francisco for a field trip. They took us to a fortune cookie factory, and they gave us bags of fortune cookies, but none of them had any fortunes in them. They were just these flat, crunchy disks."

The bus lurches forward, rush hour traffic still stopping up the roads.

"We could go somewhere together," Jane says. "Trevor, too. We could take a road trip, see all the places we've never been before."

I can almost picture it, Jane's bare feet on my dashboard, Trevor yelling at me to change the music on the radio. We could go east, find a place where the sun isn't always shining, spilling lies of happiness over everything. Then the bus jerks to a stop and the fantasy breaks apart in my mind. I can't afford a trip, and my car would never make it across state lines.

"Yeah," I say lightly. "Maybe one day."

Trevor's waiting for us inside and gives an exaggerated sigh of relief when he sees us.

"Finally," he says, looping his arms around our necks. "You two kids had me worried sick."

His voice is joking, but the hug goes on long enough to tell me he was scared.

I dip my head a fraction so I can speak directly into his ear. "Thank you," I say.

I don't know if Jane could have really gone through with it, but I know I wouldn't have stopped it. Without Trevor, I would have let her kill me.

He squeezes me hard, then lets me go.

"So the gang's all back together," Trevor announces, gesturing widely with his hands. "First things first. Lexi, we voted and it's two against one; you need to get a TV."

I roll my eyes, but I appreciate what he's doing, trying to act like everything is normal. "Ghost votes only count as half a person," I say.

"That's discriminatory," Trevor argues.

"When you start paying rent, you can start making demands," I counter. "Play rock paper scissors if you need stimulation that badly."

Trevor groans as Jane flops onto the bed and my phone buzzes where I left it on my dresser.

"I swear to god, it's always something," I mutter, answering my phone. "What? I'm not working tonight, Ilia; don't even ask."

"I need a favor," he says, his voice strained.

"Are you kidding me?"

"Who is it?" Jane asks.

"I'm hanging up now," I say.

"You owe me, Lexi," Ilia says. "You know you do."

I grit my teeth and count to three in my head.

"What do you need?" I ask grudgingly.

"A pickup," he says. "Right now."

"Seriously, Ilia? Just call a car."

He gives a hollow laugh. "Not a good idea. You coming or not?"

I sigh and run a hand over my hair. It's getting longer, moving from fuzzy to spiky. I'll need to buzz it again soon.

"Yeah," I say. "I'm coming."

"I'll text you the address," he says. "Come alone."

The phone goes dead, and I resist the urge to throw it against the wall.

"What's up?" Trevor asks, watching the expression on my face.

"I have to go out," I say curtly.

"You just got home," Jane says.

"I know."

I grab a clean shirt from the floor and find a pair of jeans that aren't stained and take them to the bathroom. I don't have time to shower, but I wash off my face and peel off the clothes I'm wearing so I don't smell like hospital anymore.

"Where are you going?" Jane asks through the door.

I bang it open and come out, kicking my dirty clothes aside.

"I don't know," I tell her. "Ilia needs a pickup."

"Can I come?"

I shake my head. "I don't know what the situation is, but it can't be anything good. I'm just gonna pick him up, drop him off; it won't take long."

Jane walks with me to the front door, her brow creased.

"Be careful," she says. "And come right back."

"I will," I say. I turn around at the door to face her and Trevor. "I'll be back soon, okay?"

"Good," Trevor says. "We can talk more about that TV."

I shake my head. "Can't wait."

My phone lights up once I start the car; Ilia's off Wilshire, near the ballroom venue downtown. I head south, rolling up the windows when I hit the freeway and the wind starts to chap my face. It smells wild out tonight, smoke and eucalyptus and gasoline. I still smell like cheap soap and starched sheets, and as soon as this is over I'm taking a shower and sleeping in my own bed.

I pull up in front of a darkened car wash, the parking lot deserted, and check to make sure I'm in the right place. I cut the lights but not the engine, and then a dark figure slips by my window.

"Jesus." I jump as Ilia runs around to open the other door. "Make some noise next time."

"Go," he says, sliding into the seat and slamming the door shut.

I take a sidelong look at him; he's dressed like me, in a black hoodie, and his arms are crossed over his chest as he slouches down. He has his hood pulled down low over his face, so I can only see his mouth and chin.

"Go, Lexi," he says.

I flip the lights back on and pull out of the car wash, back onto the road.

"You want tell me what's going on, Ilia?" I ask.

"No," he says. "Do you want to tell me what happened to your wrists?"

I scowl and tug my sleeves farther down over the gauze. "No."

"Exactly," he says. "Thanks for the ride."

"Yeah, well." I shrug. "We're square now."

"Can you drop me off at the complex?" he asks. "You remember how to get there, right?"

"Yeah, yeah," I mutter. Ilia lives in Echo Park like most of the others, in a boxy apartment not much nicer than mine.

I stop at a red light and take another glance at him. He's still got his arms crossed, his shoulders hunched.

"Are you okay?" I ask. "Are you hurt?"

"I'm fine."

I check his face for injuries, look for any ripped clothes, but he looks clean. Rumpled, tired, but in one piece. The light changes, and in the neon green he shoves his hood farther down his face.

"Green, Lex," Ilia says, nodding at the light. "Drive."

Instead I reach over and tug back his hood. He hisses as the fabric scrapes over the blood-matted hair at the back of his head.

"What happened?" I ask him through clenched teeth.

He doesn't answer, yanking the hood back on.

"Ilia, what *happened*?"

"Nothing," he says. "I'm fine."

I slam on the acceleration, too pissed to care that the light has changed back to red. Ilia's head bumps against the back of the seat and he swears.

"Still fine?" I ask him.

"Dammit, Lexi, that hurt," he snaps.

"Tell me what happened, Ilia, or you're walking home," I order.

Ilia growls something at me, but he pushes the hood back enough for me to see his face.

"I made a mistake, okay?" he says. "I shouldn't have gone."

"Gone where?"

"Since we can't break the concealment spell, I thought maybe we could pinpoint where it's coming from," he says. "I asked some of our psychics to do a targeted search, looking for blind spots. Places they *couldn't* see because something's blocking them."

I blink at him. "That was smart."

"Don't sound so surprised," he says, glaring. "Why does everyone think I'm an idiot?"

"I'm sorry," I say. "I don't think that. What did they find?"

"A black hole around the ballroom where they couldn't focus. I didn't know how long it would last, so I went to check it out right away. I got two steps out of my car and then *wham*." Ilia gestures at his head. "I don't know what hit me. Or who. I woke up in the middle of the street feeling like roadkill. Didn't think it would be a good idea to drive myself home."

"Wait," I say, frowning. "Are you saying you went out there *alone*? You know we're not supposed to go anywhere by ourselves. Urie's going to flay you alive."

Ilia winces. "Not if he doesn't find out."

"Oh, I get it. So now I have to cover for you." I shoot him an angry glance. "Why the *hell* didn't you bring backup?"

"Because I didn't want anyone else getting hurt," he says.

"I take it back," I say. "You *are* an idiot."

"Spare me the lectures," Ilia says. "I fucked up, okay?

At least no one else got ambushed."

My car groans as it spins down the streets at a speed it wasn't built for.

"You should have called someone," I tell him. "Or let someone else go. You shouldn't risk yourself like that."

"Yes, I should," he says. "I'm not like you, or the others. I don't have any gifts. This is what I can do, so I do it."

"That's a load of crap," I say, almost fishtailing as I turn onto the freeway, angry for reasons I can't even name. "You think because you can't see ghosts, your life isn't worth anything? Do you have any idea what I would give to be you?"

Ilia lets out a bitter laugh. "Great, both of our lives are shit," he says. "So why don't you stop trying to kill us and just drive."

I grind my teeth together, feel the scream rattle in its cage.

"It won't always be like this, will it?" I ask, not really expecting an answer. There has to be an end, at some point.

"I don't know, Lexi," Ilia says, exhaustion coating his words. "I don't see the future."

The streets are barren tonight as I coast down the

freeway, changing lanes without signaling. It must be a weeknight, the glare of headlights missing from my mirrors. I drive on autopilot, muscle memory making the exits and turns without conscious thought. Ilia lives in the multiplex Urie owns, the apartments stacked like bricks and surrounded by gates and buzzers. The building is painted a bright orange that looks like rust in the darkness.

"Which one is it again?" I ask.

"Twelve-oh-seven," Ilia says.

I drive around the maze of the parking garage until I hit the right level.

"Thanks for the ride," Ilia says, opening the door as soon as I park.

"Wait," I say as he starts to get out.

"Don't start, Lexi," he says tiredly.

"I'm not," I say. "Are you going to be okay?"

He looks over at me, his eyes flat and a little glazed. "Don't worry about me," he says, trying to smile. "I can take care of myself."

He slams the door shut without a good-bye. I wait for a moment, watching him sway toward the door on unsteady feet, and I let out a long sigh.

"Dammit," I say, and turn off the car. "Wait up, Ilia," I yell after him.

Ilia turns around slowly. "I said I'm fine."

"Well, that's obviously bullshit. You can't even walk straight."

I move closer to him, taking a deep breath before I slip my arm around his waist.

"Lexi, you don't need to do this," he says.

I swallow and move his other arm around my neck, shivering as his hand brushes against my skin.

"Just shut up and let me help you," I say, starting to walk forward.

Ilia grumbles but he leans against me, letting me take some of his weight. He's heavier than he looks, and I sag a little under his arm. Ilia presses his keys against a pad, and the door from the garage opens, leading us into a long hallway.

"Fourth on the left," Ilia says, and I guide him down the carpeted hall. His apartment is the only one without a welcome mat, and when he unlocks the door I can smell old cooking oil and the terrible cologne he wears.

"Thanks," Ilia says, flicking on the lights in the kitchen. It looks like a hotel in here, nothing on the counters, the trash full of paper plates and beer cans. "I got it from here."

"Uh-huh," I say. I pull off my hoodie, the fabric snagging on my bandages, and toss it onto the counter.

I follow Ilia into the living room, where he collapses on a black couch with rips in the fake leather. He turns on the large TV and leans back, letting out a strained grunt.

"Seriously," he says, glancing at me. "You don't have to stay."

"Where's your soap?" I ask.

He frowns. "Uh, there's dish tablets under the sink."

I roll my eyes. "For your head, Ilia. Do you have anything to clean it?"

"I thought you were supposed to use, like, hydrogen peroxide?"

I rub my face with my hands. "No, that kills healthy tissue. What about bandages?"

Ilia just stares at me and I scowl.

"Okay, I guess I can run to the store real quick."

"You don't need—"

There's a loud knock on the door and Ilia goes still. He looks at me, eyes wide, and the knock comes again, more insistent.

"Shit," he whispers.

I look at the door and look back at Ilia. "Did you see

anyone following us?" I ask, voice low.

"*Shit*," he says.

"Ilia—"

"Get in the bedroom," he says, and he winces as he reaches for something underneath the couch. "Shut the door and lock it." And he pulls out a small but very real-looking gun.

"A gun?" I ask, my voice too high in my ears. "A *gun*, Ilia? Are you *insane*?"

"Get in the bedroom," he orders, pointing behind me.

The knocking sounds again, and this time a voice comes with it.

"Hello? Ilia? I know you're in there. Can you open the door, please?"

Ilia freezes with the gun in his hand, a look of disbelief on his face.

"Is . . . is that *Nicole*?" he whispers.

"Put that thing away," I snap at him, motioning to the gun. I stride through the kitchen and throw open the door.

Nicole is standing there, tapping a foot and tucking a lock of freshly dyed red hair behind her ear.

"Finally," she says. "What's the hold up?"

"Nicole, what on earth are you doing here?"

"No idea," she says, lifting up a plastic bag from the pharmacy. "Why don't you tell me. What's the ointment for?"

"You just . . . had a *feeling?*" Ilia says, repeating Nic's explanation.

"Yup," she says, dumping her bag on Ilia's plastic coffee table. "I was on my way home after work, but something kept telling me I had to get this stuff and get over here. You owe me forty dollars and a solid eight hours."

The bag spills open and painkillers roll out, followed by saline solution and cotton balls.

"So, does someone want to tell me what's going on?" Nic asks, glancing from Ilia's bloody hair to the gauze on my wrists.

Ilia's mouth tightens and I shake my head.

"Don't ask," I say. "You really don't want to know."

"Fine, be that way," she grumbles. "You, let me see your head," she orders Ilia.

"I can do it," I tell her. "You don't have to."

"Oh, sure," she says, rolling her eyes. "Treating open wounds is great for healing ones, right? And you're so fond of touching people."

"Someone's cranky when they're tired," I mumble,

and she points at the couch.

"Just sit down and hand me things, okay?"

I hold up my arms in surrender and perch on the end of the couch. Nicole soaks a cotton ball in the saline and hands me the bottle to hold. She turns Ilia's head and gently presses the cotton along the wound. Ilia grimaces, but he doesn't make a sound.

"I'll pay you back," he says.

"Yeah, I know." Nicole sniffs. "To be fair, some of that forty bucks was spent on candy."

I rustle in the plastic bag until I find the package of red licorice.

"Give me one," Nicole says as I tear into the plastic. I carefully place a vine in her mouth and it hangs from her lips like a limp cigarette as she finishes with the saline.

"Ointment," Nicole mumbles around the candy.

I find the tube and drop it in her hand, careful not to brush my fingers against hers. She dabs the cream on Ilia's cut, where the raw pink shines beneath his hair. Nicole's hands are careful, clinical, and I watch her touch Ilia while I chew on my candy, another type of craving aching inside me. I press my fist to the end of my rib cage like I could rub the pressure away, but it's a cage so old and solid, I could never reach inside.

"Okay," Nicole says, wiping her fingers on her jeans. "What's next? Band-Aids?"

The bandages are shaped like thick letter Hs, and I toss the box at Nicole.

"How did you know which ones to get?" I ask her curiously.

"I'm not sure," she says, tearing open the top. "These ones just felt right. Like . . . warmer than the other boxes? I don't know how to explain it."

"Helpful," Ilia says, one corner of his mouth tugging up.

Nicole shrugs. "Not really. Helpful would be knowing these things before they happen, not after the fact. I'm nowhere near as strong as my aunt. She's psychometric, did I tell you that?"

She says it too casually, and I glance at her, but her face is focused on the bandages.

"I think you mentioned something," I say. "And knowing the future is overrated. I'm just grateful you showed up when you did."

"Done," Nicole says, standing up after the Band-Aid is fixed in place. "How's that feel?"

"Better," Ilia says, letting out a sigh of relief. "Thanks."

"You have ice in the freezer?" I ask him.

He nods, and Nicole follows me into the kitchen. We can't find any dish towels, but there's a pile of dirty clothes near the closet, so I fill a T-shirt with ice and twist it up.

"Hey, any chance you can drop me off?" Nicole asks me as she searches the dishwasher for a clean cup. "I took an Uber here."

"Sure," I say. "Maybe you can finally get some sleep now."

"No such luck," she says. "I promised my aunt I'd help her open up today. You can just drop me off there; it's not too far. And it's . . . god, it's almost six in the morning."

I blink at the display on the stove and realize I've been up all night. Shit; I promised Jane I'd be right back, and that was hours ago. I don't even have a way to call her.

"Okay," Nicole says, going back into the living room. "Water. Pills." She hands the plastic bottle and glass to Ilia. "And ice."

I set down my makeshift ice pack on the coffee table. "This should help with the swelling," I tell him.

Ilia nods tiredly, swallowing the pills.

"Sorry, Ilia," Nicole says, wincing in sympathy.

"Don't feel too bad for him," I say shortly. "This is partly his own fault."

"Are you done?" Ilia asks, scowling at me.

"Yeah, I'm done."

"Great. Nicole, I owe you big for this," Ilia says, smiling at her. He flicks his eyes to me and just nods. "Lex. You know the way out."

"Let's go," I say, jerking my head at Nicole.

"Shouldn't we—"

"Nope," I say, already heading toward the door. "We shouldn't. Bye, Ilia."

18

READINGS BY PRISCILLA IS A TINY SHOP ON VENTURA, sandwiched between a kosher deli and a nail salon. The blue overhang has scalloped edges, and promises a life advisor, palm reader, and love expert is just behind the blinds. It doesn't exactly scream "reputable," but I suppose psychics have an image to maintain.

"Here okay?" I ask, pulling to a stop in front of the shop.

Nicole's been quiet on the drive over; I can't tell if she's upset about Ilia or if she's just tired.

"Nic?" I ask again when she doesn't respond.

"Huh?" She looks up through the window and sees where we are. "Oh. Yeah, this is good."

"Thanks again for all your help."

"No problem," she says, but she doesn't get out of the car.

"Is your aunt here?" I ask. "I don't want you to wait outside alone. It's not safe."

"She's always here early," Nic says, her foot tapping at the floor. "Hey, do you want to come in? I'm sure she'd love to meet you."

I'm already hours late and I desperately need a shower. And that's beside the fact that I hate meeting people.

"Maybe some other time," I say.

Nicole shifts in her seat, and I think she's about to open the door when she reaches down by her foot.

"What's this?" she asks, lifting up the folded paper. I forgot about Jane's sketch and I feel a stab of guilt; I meant to put it somewhere safe, but it must have fallen under the seat.

"Oh," I say, clearing my throat. "It's nothing. A friend of mine did it."

"It's good," Nicole says, unfolding the paper. She strokes the drawing with light fingers, almost like she's trying to coax something from it, and my stomach flips as I finally understand.

"You said your aunt does psychometry," I say, my voice flat.

Nicole glances at me, her carefully blank face telling me I'm right. "Yeah."

I sigh and rest my head against the seat. "Nicely played," I tell her.

She keeps her voice light. "I don't know what you're talking about."

"Tonight wasn't really about Ilia, was it?" I say.

Nicole gives me a wry smile. "That was part of it. Just not the most important part."

I grumble something under my breath.

"I'm sorry," Nicole says. "Well, not that sorry. I just wasn't sure you'd come if I told you I had a feeling about *you*. I know you don't like . . . talking about yourself. But I think it's important."

Nicole hands me the picture and I take it from her, the paper warm from her hands. If her aunt is what she claims to be, she might be able to get something from this. It's worth a try, at least.

"All right," I say. "You got me here, so I guess I might as well see this through. Lead the way."

Nicole's face brightens and she finally gets out of the car. "Don't worry," she says excitedly. "Aunt Priscilla is the real deal; you'll like her."

"I don't like anybody," I say.

Nicole's laugh splits the still morning, and I fight the instinct to grin back.

"Come on, Lexi," she says. "We both know that's a lie. You showed up when I needed you, and you were glad to see me tonight. Face it: we're friends."

I stick out my tongue at her and she laughs again, pulling out a set of keys to unlock the shop. A bell tinkles inside as she holds the door open for me. The inside is about what I expected: red twinkling lights dot the walls and cheap silk scarves drape over faux-Victorian chairs. Candles cover every exposed surface, most of them burned to nothing but lumps of wax. A shelf displays charm bracelets and evil eye trinkets for sale, with a discount for returning customers. Everything about this gaudy place screams "scam."

Here's the thing about psychics, real psychics: they like to play at being fake. No one believes what they do is real, even the people who visit them. Maybe they fool themselves and say they believe, but part of them knows they're only paying to hear what they want to hear. So the psychics play at being frauds, mix the truth with some easy lies, and in return they get to do what the rest of us can't: they don't have to hide. Hell, they can advertise their gifts on a storefront if they want. Maybe it's not exactly honest, maybe people mock them, but they're still free. They don't have to live in the shadows. And maybe I hate them a little for it.

"Aunt Priscilla?" Nicole calls into the empty store. "It's me."

A beaded curtain across a door in the back clacks, and a woman emerges through the strings.

"Nicole," she says in a deep voice. "You're early."

"Aunt P, this is my friend Lexi," Nicole says. "She's the one I told you about."

Priscilla cocks her head as she examines me. She's a petite woman with the same perfect golden skin as her niece. She's wearing sandals and a loose white dress, and I can't read her expression as her eyes travel over my face and down to the bandages on my arms and the tattoos on my hands.

"Hmm," she says, pressing her lips together to make the sound. "Nicole didn't tell me you were touched by death."

"What *did* she tell you?" I ask, crossing my arms, but Priscilla only smiles.

I don't like the way she's looking at me, like I'm an insect waiting to be pinned and studied. *Lexicus mortem.* She glides forward and suddenly she's in front of me, reaching for my hand. I stumble back.

"Please," she says, holding out her own hand like an offering.

"I— That's not a good idea," I tell her. "For either of us."

"Lexi doesn't like to be touched," Nicole says.

"Is that what she told you?" Priscilla's lips tug up. "I already know what awaits me, my dear," she says to me. "Can you say the same?"

She lifts her hand a fraction higher and levels her gaze at me. Slowly, keeping my eyes locked with hers, I place my hand palm up in hers.

Electricity shoots up my arm, leaving my fingers numb and my mind reeling. Her death twines around me like a cat, rubs against the inside of my skin. Priscilla glances up at me sharply, her eyes glittering.

"Interesting," she says, trailing her fingers lightly over the lines on my hand. "Not just touched by death. Beloved by him."

"Enough," I say harshly, pulling my hand back before I do something I'll regret. If death loves me, he has a fucked-up way of showing it. "That doesn't help me any."

"I apologize," Priscilla says, gracefully moving away. "Your gift is quite rare, and I admit I'm curious. Have you ever thought of selling your talents?"

I rub my palm on my jeans, trying to make the tingling go away. "No. No one wants what I can do. And

I wouldn't tell them, anyway."

"Not that part," Priscilla says, waving a hand. "But you can talk to them, can't you? The dead? Mediums are always in demand."

My mouth twists. "My ghosts do a lot more than talk."

"But there are others," she says. "Grandmothers who want to know the good china is being used. Husbands who still pine for their widows."

She says it like I could fit into this story, sitting over candles and comforting the bereaved with messages from their loved ones. As if I could offer any kind of comfort.

"That's not why I'm here," I say.

"Of course," she says smoothly. "But should you ever change your mind, please consider this an offer."

The condescension sets my teeth on edge, and Nicole steps between us.

"She has an object she needs you to read," she says.

Priscilla closes her eyes for a moment and makes a humming noise in her throat. "Yes," she says softly. "You brought me something with a death imprinted on it."

"I did."

"It's quite powerful," Priscilla says, opening her eyes.

"Come. This way." She leads me over to the high-backed chairs in the center of the room. She sits down in one of them with a flourish, her small body folding into the chair with the slightest rustle of silk.

I sit across from her, a small round table between us. I'm surprised there isn't a crystal ball on it.

"Now then," Priscilla says, "give me the token."

She holds out her hands, and for a moment I have the strangest urge to hide the picture away, where no one but me can ever see it. I shake myself and take a deep breath before placing the sketch in her palms. She looks down at it and frowns; her face loses its dreamlike expression.

"No," she says. "This isn't right."

"What do you mean?" I ask.

"This one is almost empty. It's lonely and shut away."

She drops the sketch on the table, pulling her hands away.

"Aunt P?" Nicole asks tentatively.

"This isn't the right one," Priscilla says. "This isn't what I'm sensing."

"What are you talking about?" I ask, snatching up the sketch. "I need you to read this; it's important."

"No," she says, shaking her head. "There's nothing

for me to find in that one. There's something else, something that's yelling at me."

"I don't have anything else."

Priscilla makes an angry, frustrated sound. "Stand up," she orders, snapping her fingers at me.

I do, but only because I like this bossy version of her better than the lofty, mystical one.

"Nicole," she says, "take the picture and move to the wall; it's interfering."

I hand the sketch to Nicole, and she scuttles off to lean near the twinkling lights on the wall.

"Now what?" I ask.

"Stand still," Priscilla says. She draws herself up to her full height, which barely clears my chin, and raises her hands. She doesn't touch me, just lets her fingers hover by my face before moving them down near my neck and then shoulders. She circles me, keeping her hands moving, like she's stroking the air around my body. She makes a full turn, checking my chest and stomach, then hunching down when she reaches my legs. That's where she stops, halting right in front of me, her hands going still in front of my right hip.

"There," she says with satisfaction as she straightens. "There's something in there."

Frowning, I reach into the pocket of the dirty jeans I pulled off my floor earlier. My fingers dig into the fabric and close around something small and sharp. As soon as I feel it I remember, and then I pull a dead girl's nail out of my pocket.

Priscilla sucks in a breath. "Can you hear it?" she asks, but I don't think she's really talking to me. "It sounds like drums. Like a heartbeat."

She holds out her hand, and this time I don't hesitate. The nail falls into her open palm and she shudders, stepping back and collapsing into the chair.

"Priscilla?" I ask, but she holds up her empty hand.

"Wait," she says, her voice strained.

"It's okay," Nicole says, coming to stand by her aunt's side. "She always needs a moment at the beginning. Let her work."

A wave of cool air washes over me, like a pocket of cold in the ocean. This magic is different, as unlike mine as oil is from water. It's smoother, thinner, and smells like salt and bleach. My eyes start to water as Priscilla's hand twitches.

"There she is," she whispers, her mouth barely parting.

"What do you see?" I ask, leaning forward.

"Poor girl," she says. "So scared. She couldn't move."

"She was spelled," I tell her. "They all were. Can you see who killed her?"

Priscilla shakes her head. "I can't see what's outside her. Only what's within."

"What else?" I insist. "There has to be more."

"It's muddled." Priscilla frowns. "Everything's dark."

"You need to give me more," I say. "I need to know *who*."

"She never saw his face," Priscilla says. "No, that's not right. She *couldn't* see his face."

I swallow hard. "Was he wearing a hat? A ball cap?"

She presses her lips together. "I can't tell. His face . . . it's like a smudge. Like it's been erased."

My hands curl into fists, anger thrumming in my veins. I want to run, want to scream, want to smash something.

"She felt it," Priscilla says, but I don't want to hear this part. I've already seen it, dreamed of it too many times. I stand up, try to shut my ears.

"She felt the life leave her body, being taken away," Priscilla says. "There wasn't much left. There should have been more. Before the sickness took hold, she was so *full* of life."

I pause, turn back to her.

"What did you say?" I ask.

"That's what everyone always told her," Priscilla breathes. "Veronica. She was full of life. And he took it." She opens her eyes and they look fevered, far too bright for the light of the room. "Or he tried to."

There's a flash of pain in my arms, and I look down and realize I'm digging my nails into my own skin.

"Lexi, what is it?" Nicole asks.

I don't answer, slips of voices running together in my mind. *She had her whole life ahead of her,* Jane's mother says in my head. *She was the life of the party,* Macy tells me. *Spark plug,* Isaac whispers.

"I have to go," I say, not understanding what I need to understand.

I move toward the door, needing to get away from this place and the chlorine smell that's burned into my eyes.

"I'm sorry," I tell Nicole. "I can't explain."

"Wait," Priscilla says, standing up. She holds up her hand, the nail still resting in her palm.

I shake my head. "Keep it."

Her fingers snap around it and she smiles at me, her teeth showing.

"Thanks for your help," I say, my hand on the door.

"Come see me anytime, my girl," Priscilla calls after me. "And think about my offer."

"Yeah," I mutter. "Sure."

The bell sounds like a laugh as I leave.

The scream trapped in my lungs is building. My throat is hot and tight, my breath coming in short pants, like the scream is taking all the air in my body. The sun is just rising, turning the palm trees black against the red light. I roll down the windows and speed, trying to let the wind soothe the ragged noise inside me.

"Where the hell have you been?" Jane yells at me when I finally get home.

"Long story," I say, slamming the door behind me, still feeling raw and wild.

"So start talking," Trevor says.

"Ilia was hurt," I say, stripping off my sweatshirt. "And things got complicated." I glance around the apartment, kick over a pile of laundry. "Where are the files Ilia gave me?"

"What do you mean, 'complicated'?" Trevor asks.

I spot some papers sticking out from the bookshelf and tug them free.

"Lexi, you're freaking me out," Jane says. "Would you just tell us what's going on? What are you looking for?"

I sink to the floor, spreading out the files on the missing people and Veronica's autopsy. "I don't know yet. But there's something here, something we missed."

I start at the beginning, tell them about Ilia, about Priscilla and the reading.

"She was like you," I say, looking at the autopsy. "The way people describe you. Bright, full of life. That has to be the connection. The other missing people, they're young. Vibrant. Look at this kid."

I hold out the paper to Jane, who blinks at me. "Seriously? Ghost, Lexi, remember?" she says, waving her hands at me.

"Sorry, sorry," I say, and slap down the file with a picture of a boy holding a skateboard. "His mom said he was *spirited*. He had 'carpe diem' painted on his skateboard."

"I . . . I don't know, Lexi," Jane says. "It seems like a reach."

"Trevor?" I ask, looking up at him. "You see it."

"I'm not sure," Trevor says, frowning. "Lots of people are described that way."

"So it's just a coincidence?" I crush the papers in my

hand. "Nicole said Marcus was outgoing. That he never stopped talking."

"How would he know?" Jane says, sitting next to me. "I'd never seen the guy before that night; how could he know what I'm like? What any of us were like?"

"I know it doesn't make sense," I say. "But he knew. He must have known something about you, somehow. That's why he didn't want Veronica, because she had cancer. She had the right spirit, but she was dying."

"Lexi, you've been awake all night," Jane says gently. "I think maybe you should get some rest."

"Yeah, that's a good idea," Trevor says. "Why don't you lie down for a while? We'll be quiet."

I shake my head in frustration. The answer is close, but I can't see it yet. It's like a word on the tip of my tongue, like a song I can almost place. I study the file in my hand, Veronica staring back at me, looking different from the ghost that kept blinking in and out. Like she didn't have the energy to stay in one place.

"Lexi? Bed?" Jane prompts.

She felt the life being taken from her, Priscilla whispers in my head. I swear I hear mocking laughter follow. I swallow hard, not sure what to do next. I'm afraid I might be wrong. I'm more afraid I might be right.

Veronica's ghost kept flickering. Jane should be stronger than she is. And Marcus never materialized at all.

"*He took it.*" I stop and clear my throat. "He took your lives. But not because he wanted to kill you."

"I don't understand," Jane says.

"He took something from you when he killed you. Your life force. Energy can never be destroyed, only transferred. That's why you can't hold your form, why Trevor was able to stop you."

"Oh, god." Jane shakes her head, steps away from me. "No, that—no."

We don't do that anymore, Jordan said. *Not even the old-timers.* But maybe he's wrong.

"I need to talk to a witch," I say, looking down at my phone.

"Uh, okay," Trevor says. "So call your friend."

"No," I say. "I need an old witch. Someone with access to much older spells."

The problem is I don't know many witches my age, let alone older ones. In fact, the only person I can even think of—

"Shit," I say.

"Now what?" Jane asks.

"I have to go."

She's already shaking her head. "No way," she says. "Not without me."

"Or me," Trevor says.

"Okay," I say simply.

"Okay?" he repeats, blinking. "Really?"

"Really. I'm going to need help. We're going to see a witch with a ghost problem."

19

THE HOUSE LOOKS EXACTLY AS I REMEMBER IT, THE
bars over the windows in need of repainting, the tiled
roof pale from the sun. I don't know that I expected
it to change, but it's hard to reconcile the unassuming
exterior with what's waiting inside. Nothing ever looks
the way it should—not possible killers, not houses with
darkness living in the walls.

"Is this it?" Jane asks, looking out the window.

"Yeah," I say, but I don't get out of the car.

"Well?" Trevor says. "What are we waiting for?"

I take the keys out and turn toward the back. "Just . . .
prepare yourselves. She doesn't want to go, and it could
get ugly."

"Uglier than what I did to you?" Jane asks.

I tuck my bandaged arms to my chest without meaning to. "That's not what I mean."

"What *do* you mean?" Trevor asks.

"I would never do this to the two of you, okay?" I say,

rubbing my face tiredly. "Remember that."

"We know, Lexi," Jane says.

"Okay, then." I open the car door and step out into the heat of the morning. "Try to stay close to me."

The walk to the door takes too long, each step reluctant. There's silence when I knock; maybe she's not home, and we came all the way here for nothing. Then I hear soft footsteps and I square my shoulders as the door creaks open.

"Oh. You," she says, blinking pale, squinting eyes behind her thick glasses.

"Hello, Mrs. Hallas," I say.

"What do you want?" she asks curiously.

"I need your help. And in return, I can help you."

She's quiet then, her face a shrewd mix of caution and hope.

"Come in," she says finally, opening the door all the way.

I glance at Jane beside me and then follow Mrs. Hallas inside.

It smells even worse than last time, the scent of bitter herbs overlaid with damp earth and mold. There's no warding spell that can keep a determined ghost out, but it smells like she's been trying. Underneath the stench is the bright copper of death, and over it all the cloying presence of despair.

"God, this place is grim," Jane says to me, her voice a whisper even though it doesn't need to be.

"I don't know; it could be okay," Trevor says. "If you got rid of the smell and the ghost, maybe a coat of paint?"

I trudge after Mrs. Hallas into her gloomy living room. The candles can't keep the darkness at bay, the lights burning dim and feeble. The television is still busted, the screen black and charred.

"Why is this time different?" Mrs. Hallas asks, turning to face me without offering a seat. "You couldn't manage last time. You said she was too strong."

There's desperation in her voice, almost enough to make me feel sympathy.

"I have help," I say, Trevor and Jane a solid warmth at my side. "But I want your word. I help you; you answer all my questions. No half-truths, no evasions, no excuses."

Mrs. Hallas rises up to her full height.

"You have my word. If you rid my house of unrest, then by my blood and bones, I will aid you in any way I can."

I nod, but she's not finished.

"And if you attempt to cross me," she says, voice dropping, "then I vow there is nowhere you can hide that my curses will not find you and end you."

"Understood," I say. "I don't want you for an enemy, Mrs. Hallas. I'm not that stupid."

She gives me a thin smile. "Then do what you claim you can do."

I plant my feet in the middle of the room, then glance at Mrs. Hallas.

"When I tell you, release the wards," I say. "And you might want to back up."

She nods and retreats until she's watching from the hallway.

"Ready?" I ask quietly.

"Ready," Trevor's voice comes from my shoulder, and Jane nods.

I let my magic spin out, splaying my hands as black wisps of darkness envelop the room.

"Lexi?" Jane's voice is hesitant, unsure.

"It's okay," I murmur. "It's just me."

I reach through the darkness, hot and electric, let it dive into my pores and spin out with my breath. When I brush against something large and sentient, I curl my hand into a fist.

"Now, Mrs. Hallas," I call, and I feel the spells break with an audible snap.

Emily slams into me and I fall back, my head banging hard against the floor. I open my eyes and everything is blurry, smears of red and pink and orange.

"I told you," she says, heat and rage bearing down on me, "to stay out this house."

"Back off," Jane growls.

There's a thud and then Jane is at my side, helping me sit up. Trevor stands between me and Emily, hands in fists at his sides.

"You okay?" he says, glancing back at me.

I nod, coughing. "Yeah."

"Who the hell are you?" Emily demands.

"Oh, me?" Trevor asks. "I'm Trevor. That's Jane. We're the ones who are going to kick your ass for hurting our friend."

Jane stands up, holding out a hand. I take it and she tugs me up, putting her shoulder next to mine.

"You brought backup?" Emily's eyes flash at me.

"Leave this house," I tell her. "And never come back."

She shakes her head. "You know I can't do that."

"Seriously?" Trevor asks. "You can't leave an old woman alone? What is your problem?"

"I was *murdered*," Emily yells.

"Join the fucking club!" Jane yells back.

"I am death, Emily," I say. "Real, final death. No coming back, no watching from the shadows."

Emily looks at me, something terrible and endless living in her eyes. My gut twists, and I try one last time.

"Just go," I say. "Wherever you want, as long as it isn't here. You can still have a semblance of a life, Emily. Please don't make me do this. Please don't make me end you."

"It's too late," she says, almost sadly. And then she lunges for me.

"No," Jane yells.

Emily's hands reach for my throat but Trevor is there, wrapping his arms around Emily's waist and pulling her back.

"Let me go," Emily yells, struggling. Jane jumps in front of her, bracing her hands on Emily's shoulders and pushing her back.

"Now, Lexi," Trevor says, straining.

I close my eyes, block out the sounds of their fighting, and gather the darkness to me.

"No," Emily cries as I begin to push.

She fights it, and even trapped by the both of them

she's still powerful. She shoves back against my magic, battering at me with everything she has until my ears are ringing, my bones vibrating from the strength of it. I grit my teeth against the ache in my joints and I *force* the darkness into her, pour it into her open mouth, sink it into her nostrils, ears, anywhere it can find purchase. My nose starts to bleed and the taste of copper is heavy on my tongue.

She screams, a formless cry of anguish and rage that rips into me, because I know the same sound lives in me. With a last burst of strength, I thrust the darkness into her, push through it and out the other side, and I tell myself there's no other way before she bursts and scatters into nothing. I brace my hands on my thighs, suck in deep breaths as sweat and blood pools around my mouth.

"Is it over?" Jane looks back at me, her eyes white and haunted.

I nod, too exhausted to answer.

"If that ever happens to me—" She stops, clears her throat. "Don't ever let that happen to me."

"It won't," I gasp out. "I won't."

"Are you okay?" Trevor asks. His hair smells faintly like ozone as he slips a hand around me to help me stand.

"Yeah." I wipe my face with my sleeve. "It's just a bloody nose. I'll be fine."

With that I step away, my legs still shaky, and look down into the darkened hallway.

"Mrs. Hallas," I call harshly. "Time to pay up."

She steps back into the living room, her face drawn behind the large glasses.

"I'll make some tea," she says.

She drags out the process, weighing ingredients and insisting we wait a full five minutes for everything to steep. The result is a sweet combination of linden and elderflower that tastes like summer. I might enjoy it if I wasn't buzzing with adrenaline, but I have to force myself to swallow it, knowing it's meant to soothe me. Mrs. Hallas takes her time sipping her tea, sitting across from me in the living room. Everything looks lighter, the lamps finally shining bright, the candles extinguished.

"She's really gone," Mrs. Hallas says, staring at the lights in wonder.

"I held up my end of the bargain," I say. "Your turn."

"More tea?" she asks, glancing at my cup.

"No," I say. "It's not calming me down anyway."

She exhales sharply through her nostrils and sets her

teacup down with a hard clink.

"Very well," she says. "Ask your questions."

"Is there a spell," I ask slowly, "to find people with a specific quality?"

"If it was specific enough, yes. Possibly."

My hands feel sweaty, and I wipe my palms on my jeans.

"Specific how?" I ask.

"Something with a narrow range. You couldn't find people with blue eyes. That's too broad; you'd never be able to power the spell. But you could find people with blue eyes if they were over a certain age and within a certain radius."

"What if it wasn't physical? What if you wanted to find someone who was, say, full of energy? Who had a strong life force."

"Yes," she says, frowning. "As long as the target is focused, yes. Any altered location spell would work."

Jane's fingers thread through mine as I ask the question I'm dreading the most.

"And is there a spell," I ask carefully, "if you wanted to take that life, that spark? Not kill it, but steal it? Keep it for yourself?"

Mrs. Hallas goes pale, her eyes huge behind her

glasses. "Those spells are forbidden," she says harshly. "We no longer deal in death magic."

"One of you does, Mrs. Hallas. The missing people on the news aren't just missing. They're dead. And whoever is killing them is *taking* something from them."

Mrs. Hallas stands up, faster than I would think someone her age could move.

"You wouldn't understand. A modified location spell," she says, "that would be complicated, but doable. The other, though, no witch would attempt to cast."

"But it's possible?" I ask. "Taking someone's life like that?"

Mrs. Hallas looks down and jerks her head yes. "The spells are very old, and difficult. A life force is not easy to contain, and outside the body it rapidly deteriorates. You would need to keep the body to ensure a successful transfer, keep it secure while you drained it. There are rituals to perform, at the moment of death and after. And you would need a target with strong energy, someone young and in good health. But none of us would risk it."

"Oh, god, that's why he dumped Veronica's body,"

EMMA BERQUIST

Jane says. "She was sick. He couldn't *use* her, so he threw her away."

"Why wouldn't a witch risk it?" I ask.

"Death magic is the darkest of magics. You can't use it without paying a heavy price," she says. "Spells to harm rebound on the caster, always. And their effect is cumulative. One small hex might leave you with nothing more than a headache. But a number of strong curses could break your arm. And death magic? You can only protect yourself for so long. You use that kind of spell more than once, the damage would be extensive. You'd be lucky to survive in one piece."

I shake my head. This can't be right; we would have noticed someone with injuries that severe. How did they hide it? The only person who's been that hurt is Jordan, and only because he was trying to *help*—

Everything goes very quiet, from the sound of Mrs. Hallas breathing to the pounding in my chest. The human brain takes in eleven million bits of information per second but the conscious mind is only able to process about fifty of those. *Lucky to survive in one piece.* My brain is telling me something my mind won't process, doesn't want to believe.

"What—" My voice comes out hoarse, and I try to

332

swallow. "What would happen if you tried to break through a concealment spell? Would it hurt you if you weren't strong enough?"

Mrs. Hallas frowns at me. "Hurt you? No. Concealment spells don't function the way other spells do. They absorb power instead of reflecting it. That's why they're so difficult to break. At most you'd get a headache from the effort."

"Lexi?" Trevor asks, looking at with concern. "What is it?"

I blink, the thought finally forcing its way through. "He lied."

20

I HAVE ONE HAND ON THE WHEEL AND ANOTHER on my phone, each ring vibrating against my ear.

"Pick up, pick *up*," I yell, but all I get is Ilia's voice telling me to leave a message he'll never check.

"Lexi, slow down," Jane says. "Shouldn't we call the police?"

"And tell them what?" Trevor asks from the backseat. "A witch told us how to find the killer?"

Jane goes quiet and I try Phillip next, but his phone goes straight to mail without ringing. I throw my phone against the dashboard and it bounces back, flying through Jane to land on the seat. The scream that lives in my lungs finally tears free, sliding through my throat like hot oil and spilling into the night.

"Lexi," Jane yells at me. "Cut the shit."

"How are you so damn calm?" I yell back at her.

"Because I have to be," she answers.

I look over at her and see her eyes flash white. She

closes them, curling her hands into fists, and when she opens them they're clear.

"I can't lose it," she says, her voice strained. "Not again, not when we're so close. So would you *please* get a hold of yourself?"

I take a long, shuddering breath. *Don't let it be him. Please don't let it be him.*

"I'm sorry," I say, my throat scratchy from screaming. "I'm sorry, I'm okay. We're going to get through this."

Jane's hands are still fisted tight. "He didn't just kill me," she says. "He stole my life. He took it." She growls the last part and has to close her eyes again. "I want to burn him into nothing. And then I want to burn the world for creating him."

"One thing at a time," I say softly.

She looks over at me and there's the idea of a smile on her lips. "You would burn down the world with me?"

"I'll hand you the matches," I say.

The smile becomes real, if shaky.

"Hey," Trevor says, sticking his head between us. "That sounds good and all, but maybe we deal with the murderer first?"

I can't shake the anger that's fizzing in my blood. I skid into the lot behind Elysium, turning off the engine without a care for how I'm parked. The air is warm and heavy, smoke trapping the last paltry rays of sun. I storm toward the club, zipping up my hoodie like battle armor, Jane and Trevor flanking my sides.

Elysium rises ahead of us, blocking out the lights with its windowless bulk. He was here this whole time, hiding right under my nose, laughing at all of us.

"Stay close," I tell them, kicking hard at the back door.

Georgie flings it open after only a second. "Dammit, Lexi," he swears, "for the last time—"

"Move," I say.

Something in my face makes Georgie shut up and step aside. I'm already moving, punching the elevator number so hard my fingernail bends back. The door opens and I enter, Jane and Trevor following me. Each floor takes an eon to pass.

The elevator barely dings open before I'm barreling down the hallway, the carpet muffling the heavy tread of my boots.

"Ilia," I yell into the empty hall. The door to the office is closed, and I bang on it with my fist. "Ilia, are you in there? Urie?"

I try the handle but the door is locked. I kick at the

wood angrily, wondering if I can break it down with my shoulder. I feel like smashing all those pretty screens on the inside, all those eyes that watched but saw nothing.

"Lexi, come on," Jane says. "No one's in there."

I spin back around, heading for the floor. It's still early and there aren't many people here, mostly the after-work crowd lounging around small tables. Nicole is behind the bar and I go straight to her, waving to get her attention.

"You're not on today," she says, frowning.

"Where is everyone? I need to talk to Urie."

"He's out. But I think Ilia's restocking. Is everything okay?"

"No, it's not," I say. "You need to get out of here. Go get in your car and lock the doors and don't get out until I tell you to. Understand?"

She nods her head jerkily. "Yeah."

"I'll be back."

The ride back down makes me want to scream with impatience. We're so close to facing him, my legs are vibrating with the need to run. When the doors open I spring out, taking long strides toward the stockroom.

The door is propped open with a case of beer, and I can hear male voices coming from within. Who's helping

Ilia? My stomach lurches with the certainty that I'm about to face a killer as I round the door and step inside.

"Lexi?" Phillip looks up at me in surprise and I let out a shaky breath.

"What are you doing here?" Ilia asks, setting down a crate of mixers.

"Where's Jordan?" I ask, my voice echoing strangely in my ears.

"He's back on main floor security," Ilia says. "He's been begging to get to work again."

"*Shit,*" I say, exchanging a look with Jane. He could be looking for a new target already.

"Lex, are you okay?" Phillip asks, looking closely at my face.

"Urie's not here?" I ask.

Ilia shakes his head. "What's going on?"

"You need you to clear the floor," I tell him.

"Why?" Ilia asks, starting up the steps.

"Because Jordan's the murderer, that's why." I turn around and head for the door, but Ilia catches up with me, Phillip right behind him.

"He killed Marcus, and Jane, and all the others," I say.

Ilia shakes his head, looking as ill as I feel. "No."

I believed Jordan. I trusted him.

"Yes," I counter. "Now get out of my way."

"Wait," Phillip says, and I cut him off.

"There's no time to explain," I say. "He's up there with all those people."

"I know," Phillip says. "What do we do?" I feel a flash of warmth for him, that he doesn't hesitate. And I realize that's all that I have left for him, a bittersweet kind of affection.

"We find him. Ilia, can you get his exact location?"

"I'll call Georgie," Ilia says, stepping back to pull out his phone.

"We need to get the police involved, Lexi," Phillip says. "There are too many people missing to take care of this ourselves."

He's right. Jordan dragged those people into this world; their families have a right to know what happened.

"Can you do it?" I ask.

Phillip nods. "I'll call one of our people on the force. They'll take care of it."

Ilia comes back, his face grim. "Georgie doesn't see him on the floor, but he says he hasn't left the building."

"He's here somewhere," I say. "We just have to find him."

I look at Jane, and there's a savage expression in her eyes. Trevor cracks his knuckles.

"Let's go," he says.

It's the longest walk of my life. My hands are trembling with adrenaline, and I can't get enough air into my lungs. I count down the footsteps in my head, my heartbeat pounding so much faster than the numbers.

"Split up," I finally say, my stomach flipping. "Phillip, take the back door. Ilia, front. I'll take the side and check the hallways."

Phillip gives me a tight smile. "Be careful."

"You, too," I say, and he peels off to circle around the back.

"You sure you don't want me with you?" Ilia asks. "He's injured, but he's strong."

I curl my hands into fists and nod. "I'm sure."

He lets out a heavy breath. "Okay. Watch your back."

"I've got it covered," I say, glancing at my ghosts. "Let's go."

I open the door to the dance floor and slip inside the darkened room, blinking until my eyes adjust to the dim. Jane melts through the door after me, Trevor alongside.

"Ilia's right," she says. "He could have some kind of spell that could hurt you."

"I know," I say. I tug back the sleeve of my hoodie and tap on the wheel inked on the inside of my arm. "Protection, remember? Don't worry."

Security is clearing the floor, a line of people waiting to file out the front. It's eerily quiet in here with the music turned off, the multicolored flashing lights cutting through the darkness to a soundless beat.

I move along the floor, my muscles clenched so tight it hurts. The past unspools in soundless pictures in my mind, like I'm watching recorded footage. In another life, a girl danced here with her friends, laughing amid the chaos. In another time, a spell saw something in her and a boy wanted to take it.

I duck behind the bar and slip through the side door, my boots soundless on the ugly carpet. I walk down the hallway, then start to run; I turn the corner and it's still empty.

"Where is he?" Trevor asks.

"He can't have gotten far," I say, pushing myself to go faster. I loop around again, and pull up quickly when I see the backs of two people.

"Stop," I yell, and one of them turns around with awful slowness. I can't make out his face clearly, but I can tell by the way he moves, his body still stiff. I hope he's in pain. I hope it hurts more than anything. I touched him. I tried to *comfort* him. It makes me ill.

"Lexi," Jane whispers.

"I know." There's no mistaking the bright red hair that's next to him.

"Jordan," I say, my voice carrying in the airless hall.

"Hey, Lexi," he says. His voice is easy, his stance relaxed. It's almost enough to make me believe he doesn't know what's going on.

I plant myself in front of him, our eyes level with each other. Fading bruises mark his face, and a cut on his lip has scabbed over. He's thinner than he was the last time I saw him, a yellow undertone to his skin. His jaw is still strong, but his eyes are sunken, dark circles underneath.

"Nicole, are you okay?" She stares back at me blankly and a chill goes up my spine. "Nicole? What did you do to her?"

"She asked me to walk her to her car," Jordan says. "What's going on, why is the floor being cleared?"

"Nicole, get away from him," I say, stepping toward her, but she moves back, closer to Jordan.

"Whoa, Lexi, you need to chill," he says.

"Lex," Trevor says softly. I look over at him, and he

motions to Jane. She's gone quiet, and her entire body is quivering so hard her feet start to lift from the ground.

"That—that voice," Jane stammers, blood spilling down her neck. "I remember that voice. It's like it was inside my head. It told me to leave my friends, to go to the alley alone. It told me not to make a sound."

"Lexi?" Jordan asks, waving a hand in front of my face. "Hello?"

I look back at him. I will never hate anything as much as I hate the man in front of me.

"You told her to stay quiet," I say. "You slit her throat and she couldn't even scream."

Jordan stares at me for a long moment, then I watch his throat move as he swallows.

"How—" He cuts himself off, taking a step back, pulling Nicole with him. "Right. Which one is it?"

"Her name is Jane," I say. "Did you even know their names? Did you care?"

"You wouldn't understand," he says harshly. "I had to. Whoever she is, I'm sorry."

"Sorry? You're *sorry*?" Jane rushes at Jordan, screaming with pent-up fury. She goes straight through him, diving into his chest and falling onto the floor behind him. The lights overhead flicker and buzz, and Jordan blinks up at them as Trevor rushes to help Jane to her feet.

"Nicole," I try again. "Look at me."

"She can't hear you," Jordan says. "Just let us go. I don't want to hurt you."

"You're not leaving this building with her," a voice says from behind me.

"Stay out of this, Ilia," Jordan says, stumbling back.

"Like hell," Ilia says, his face twisted with anger. "I trusted you. Urie trusted you. How could you betray us like this?"

"I betrayed *you*?" Jordan says, lip curling. "No. You've got it backward. You betrayed *me*. All of you, with all your power and your gifts, none of you could save me."

"What are you talking about?" Ilia says.

"I'm dying," Jordan says, voice cracking. "Inoperable tumor. Just like that last girl. I'm sorry for that one; I didn't know until it was too late. The spell only tells me the potential."

Tumor? I suck in a breath. That isn't how he dies; I've seen how he dies.

"You're killing people to extend your own life," another voice says as Phillip appears to our right. Jordan backs up another step, his only exit behind him.

"Why didn't you come to me?" Phillip asks, his face drawn. "Why didn't you go to my mother? We could have helped you, we could have—"

"I *did!*" Jordan yells. "And you know what your mom told me? That her magic couldn't save me. That it was my *time*. So I figured out what my own power could do."

"Magic won't save you from death," I tell him. "Nothing escapes death."

"Maybe not," Jordan says, his knuckles tightening on Nicole. "But it'll help me escape you." He throws his hand out in a wide arc.

"Duck," Ilia yells, but it's too quick.

The spell hits Phillip first and he locks up, his arms clamping to his sides as his eyes roll back. His body falls hard, hitting the floor with an audible crack that's echoed by a louder crash behind me.

The hex hits me like a punch to my chest and I double over, the smell of dirt and wormwood shoved in my face. I can feel it sliding over me, oily and necrotic, trying to find purchase. The magic in my inked wheel flutters to life, the cool tingle of Theo's power a familiar taste. Angry as it is, the curse slips off me and dissipates into the darkness.

I look up and see Jordan's back as he disappears

through the open door, Nicole trotting along docilely.

"Shit," I say, leaning down to shake Ilia. "Wake *up*."

"Leave them!" Jane shouts at me. "We can't let him go."

"I'll stay with them," Trevor says. "You go."

I start to run just as Ilia stirs.

"Jordan's going out the back," I yell over my shoulder at him, not knowing if he's even conscious yet. "Check on Phillip; I'm going after him."

I put my head down and explode into the darkening air, streetlights just switching on.

"Lexi, come *on*," Jane snaps.

I blink, adjusting to the gloom after the brightness of the hallway, and try to follow her voice, stumbling over the asphalt of the parking lot. My eyes begin to adapt, but not soon enough to keep me from slamming into a group of warm bodies.

Deaths wash over me and I jerk away, hugging my arms to my sides to make myself smaller.

"We're losing them," Jane yells again, desperation making her voice high.

"I'm coming." I grit my teeth and plunge through the crowd.

After a moment I can't separate them; the deaths all start to bleed together, images of failed hearts and blackened lungs mixing with mangled steel and empty pill bottles. My stomach heaves and my throat burns, but I don't fight it, instead letting the tide of acid sweep me under and along until I break through to the other side.

Gasping and retching, I sprawl out at the end of the lot and try to catch my breath.

"Lexi?" Jane asks, grabbing my arm and helping me stand.

"Which way?" I ask, my eyes darting around the empty street.

"Alley," Jane says, her voice darkening.

She doesn't need to tell me which one. I meet her cloudy eyes, and I think anger is too weak a word for what's in them.

"He's not getting away," I promise her.

"Just save Nicole. Don't let her end up like me."

We turn the corner, splashing through oil slicks and pools of black water and duck behind Xanadu. It feels like it was always meant to end here, where I found her, where it all began.

The alley looks bleaker in the fading light, the stains darker, the bricks discolored and crumbling.

"Jordan," I yell, and he spins around wildly, his face

pale and clammy. I step forward and he holds up a hand.

"Stay where you are," he says.

"Your spells won't work on me," I say.

"True," he says. "But they'll work on her." He thrusts Nicole in front of him and fear uncurls in my chest, cold and corrosive. I've never touched her; I don't know how she dies. This can't be how she dies. Please don't let this be how she dies.

"She's your *friend*, Jordan," I say. "Leave her alone."

"I can't. I didn't get as much as I should have from *your* friend. And next to nothing at all from the last one. I won't last past tonight," he says, his breathing strained. "The spell picks out the brightest spots closest to me. I didn't know it would be Nicole."

"You mean you don't *care*," I say. "Is it worth it? To kill so many people, just to live an extra few days?"

Sweat shines on his forehead and his shoulders shake as he coughs. He's getting paler by the minute, the life fading from his body.

"Just let me go, Lexi," he says softly. "I'll run. I won't be a problem for you all anymore, and you won't ever hear from me again. I'll go far, as far from here as I can get."

"And you'll keep killing," I say, sliding one foot

forward. "I can't let you do that."

Jordan's face twists and his lips pull back.

"Fine," he says harshly. "I tried to be reasonable." He reaches into his back pocket and pulls out a folding knife. He opens it carefully, the blade long and bright.

Jane hisses at him, throwing out a hand in front of me like she can protect me. I can taste the edge of her rage, like smoke in the air.

But past her, past Jordan, at the other end of the alley, I can just make out the sheen of blond hair, and something else, something that's glinting in the streetlight. And I finally understand what I saw when I touched Jordan that night. Newton's third law of motion: Every action has an equal and opposite reaction. A gun exerts force on a bullet when it fires, and the bullet exerts an equal force in the opposite direction on the gun. Nothing is ever created or destroyed, only transferred.

"When I tell you, kill the light," I whisper to Jane, my fist curling into a fig for luck.

"Lexi," she says, and when I meet her eyes it isn't anger I find, but fear. "He's not worth it. He's not worth you dying over."

"Trust me," I say.

"I didn't want it to be like this," Jordan says, the knife

trembling in his grip. He takes a labored breath and rushes me, lamplight glinting off the knife that's aiming for my heart.

"Now," I say, and Jane opens her mouth and screams. Only I can hear it, but the streetlight explodes into sparks above us.

Jordan flinches and the arc of his knife goes wide. A line of fire scores across my collarbone and shoulder as I drop to the ground and roll. Jordan spins to find me, and that's when he sees Ilia at the other end of the alley.

Jordan grunts when the first shot hits him. The second makes him fall. Then there are the long, awful seconds where he's across from me and our eyes meet over the filthy concrete. He looks surprised; even when his face goes slack he looks surprised. I thought it would be satisfying, to watch him die, but I only feel a kind of numbness.

"Lexi?" Jane kneels beside me and tries to pull at my sweatshirt to see the damage, but her hands just slip through the clothing.

"I'm okay," I say, and my voice sounds muffled to my ringing ears. "It's not deep."

"Good," Ilia says, limping over to me. He holds out a hand to help me up before remembering he shouldn't.

He starts to pull back but I grab it, let the acid wash over me and let him haul me up.

I release it as soon as I'm standing, but he still grins.

"How'd you know I was there?" he asks.

"All that oil in your hair caught the light," I say. "You made me touch him, remember? I saw how he dies, and you're the only idiot I know with a gun."

His grin widens.

"Is Phillip okay?" I ask.

Ilia nods. "He's still a little out of it, but he's going to be fine."

"Excuse me, why am I in an alley? What is—is that Jordan? What the *fuck* is going on?"

I look over at Nicole and breathe a sigh of relief.

"Ask Ilia," I tell her, the numbness refusing to leave me.

Ilia glares at me, but he jerks his head at Nicole.

"Come on, one of our cops should be here soon," Ilia says. "We need to deal with him; I'll explain on the way. You coming?" he asks me.

"Yeah," I say. "Just give me a minute. I'll be right behind you."

Jane is sitting on the ground of the alley, staring at Jordan's body. His blood is pooling out around him, and she moves her feet a fraction to keep them out of the stain, like she doesn't want any part of him to touch her.

I wait until Ilia leaves with Nicole, then sit next to Jane, my leg pressing against hers.

"He's dead," I tell her. "However long you look at him, he'll still be dead."

She swallows, the long line of her throat moving.

"I thought I'd feel different," she says. "I thought I'd feel . . . I don't know, at peace. I thought that's why I stayed, so I could have vengeance. But looking at him . . . he just looks sick. And young. And I don't feel any different."

"Well," I say, "maybe that wasn't why you stayed."

Jane finally looks away from the body. "Then why?"

I shake my head. "I don't know. Maybe you're not finished yet."

She looks back at Jordan. "What if *he* comes back?"

"I don't think he will. But if he does, then he's all yours."

She almost smiles then, and I nudge her with my knee.

"Come on, let's go find Trevor," I say. "You've spent enough time in this alley."

I stand up and hold out my hand. When she takes it I can't help but compare it to Ilia's, how it doesn't hurt me, how warm her fingers are in mine.

"I was wrong about where we met," she says quietly.

"Hmm?" I ask, trying to step around the blood on the ground.

"We didn't meet at the club," she says. "We met here. This you and this me, we met here."

I glance back, remember how she looked when I first met her, like rage barely contained in flesh.

"I guess we did."

"Lexi," she says, her voice solemn. "Thank you. For helping me, for finding him. For making sure he won't hurt anyone else."

"You don't have to thank me," I tell her. "I would rather have saved you."

Her lips tilt up in a sad smile.

"So what now?" she asks.

I don't answer, and the silence stretches between us, something new and painful and tasting of an ending.

21

"ARE YOU READY?" I ASK.

Jane smooths trembling hands down a simple gray dress; I'm still not used to seeing her in different clothes, but when Jordan died whatever he stole from her came rushing back.

"You'll stay next to me?" she asks.

"The whole time."

The morning is overcast, the marine layer heavy and clinging. It'll burn off by the afternoon, but it's fitting for today, the sky sour gray and grieving.

The cemetery is in Mid City, a disordered and crowded stretch of graves. I drive slowly along the curb, pyramid tombs rising next to flat headstones and weeping angels. The grass is dry and brittle and palm trees loom overhead, shadows slicing thin lines across the rows.

"They're so close," Jane says, her face pressed to the window. "The graves. They're so close. This place has no room to breathe."

I nod, my chest tight as the stones fly past. I drive slower, toward a short line of cars parked along the curb. I pull in behind the last one, but Jane makes no move to get out when I cut the engine. Her hands are clenched together in her lap, and when I look at her face her eyes are shut tight.

"Are you sure you want to do this?" I ask.

"Yes," she says. "I just . . . need a minute."

The gray dress ripples, and for a moment I see a bloody shirt. I blink and it's gone, and Jane finally opens her eyes.

"All right," she says. "Let's go."

We walk toward the small group in the distance, a blur of black that slowly comes into focus. Jane's mother is wearing a wrinkled navy blue dress and sunglasses large enough to cover half her face. An older woman walks next to her, strong-jawed and petite, her shoulders stiff in a perfectly fitted dress suit.

"God, my grandma and my mom haven't spoken in years," Jane says. "I guess death is funny like that."

"Yeah," I tell her. "Funerals will heal grudges quicker than apologies."

Jane didn't want to go to the funeral service; she said it didn't feel right, like eavesdropping on someone's private conversation. Funerals are for the living, not the dead. But she still wanted to say good-bye.

The police found her body buried in a remote section of Topanga. They got a tip about someone matching Jordan's description hiking around the area. It was easy enough for the psychics to trace the bodies from the blood Jordan left in the alley. There were six others buried near Jane, young women and men who were missing, all of their wounds matching the knife Jordan had when he died. Marcus had no family to claim him, but he was one of us; we cremated him and Ilia spread his ashes in the ocean.

I see Isaac, dressed like me in dark jeans and a black shirt, and Macy and Delilah standing together. Macy gives me a small wave that I return; we're having coffee next week and I'm taking her to meet Priscilla. Deda is there, his oxygen tank rolling beside him, Ilia and Phillip helping him walk. They said they wanted to pay their respects. Deda looks past me to Jane and gives her a solemn nod.

"A funeral procession brings good luck," he tells us. "As long as you do not cross its path."

"Luck for the dead or for the living?" Jane asks.

"In this case, perhaps both," Deda answers, and Jane

gives him a slight smile.

"That's going to get old real fast," Ilia mutters, and I elbow him in the ribs.

A bright green tarp is tucked around an open grave, a gleaming wood casket held up with metal pulleys. Jane sucks in a breath and I know she's seen what I've seen, her name etched deep in the gravestone. Jane Morris, it reads. Beloved daughter and friend.

"Nice headstone," someone says, and it takes everything in me to keep from jumping. I shoot a glare at Trevor as he comes to stand on Jane's other side, completely overdressed in a tuxedo.

"You came," Jane says, smiling at him.

"Wouldn't miss it, kid," he says, slinging one arm around her shoulders.

A man in a dark suit starts to talk, spouting the usual lines about committing a body to the earth, and my mind tunes out. There's a groaning sound, and then the casket shudders and begins to move. It sinks slowly into the earth, the mechanical buzz loud and ugly in the silence of this place.

Jane's mom begins to cry, the kind of awful, choking crying of someone trying to hide their tears. It sounds like her sobs are tearing her open, ripping her skin until her insides are on display. Her bruised, broken heart, split in half for us all to see. I can't handle this much grief; it's too small, too close, too personal. Pull back, I need to pull back, until I see everything from far away, until humans crawl like ants, until the earth is a blue marble in inky space.

It's impossible to know how many stars there are in the universe. We can only estimate given how many there are in our own galaxy and multiply that by the number of galaxies we think there are. It's a guess times a guess. There are infinity stars.

What is life against that kind of immenseness? What are any of us? We don't matter to the universe; we're nothing. To believe differently is to risk your heart being shredded apart. We're specks of dust, we're atoms; you couldn't find us without a microscope.

And then Jane grabs my hand and holds it so tightly it's just this side of painful. And how can she not matter, if her hand is warm and real, if her fingernails are digging into my skin. There is no way to reconcile the small and the tangible with the vast and the cosmic. Nothing in the wide universe that can compare to the here, to the weight in my hand and the stone in my heart.

I squeeze back and don't let go, not until the screeching of the coffin stops, and not until long after that.

"Mrs. Morris?"

She's getting into her car, half-supported by her mother.

"I wanted to give you something. Jane left it at my place, a long time ago."

I hold the rolled-up paper to her, careful not to let my fingers brush hers. She unrolls it slowly, painstakingly, and I hear the sharp intake of breath when she sees it.

It took the better part of three hours for Jane to finish directing my hand, and my fingers were cramping by the end. It's a sketch of Jane and her mother, both of them laughing, eyes rueful, like they're sharing an inside joke.

"I just thought you should have it," I say, looking away from the emotion on her face.

"Thank you," she says, her voice hoarse.

Jane squeezes my arm, and I turn to leave.

"Wait! Are you— Will you come back to the house?" Jane's mother asks. "Please?"

It's hard to say no to her, and not just because she reminds me of her daughter.

"Um, okay. I'll be there."

"I'm going to ride with her," Jane says, letting go of me. "I'll meet you there, okay?"

I nod and watch as the car pulls away out of the cemetery. At last, only Deda and Ilia remain, still standing at the graveside. I make my way back over to them, trying to step between the graves in the most unobtrusive way possible. They don't care; I know they don't care. To the dead, bodies are nothing more than fingernail clippings; something that was once part of you that has long since used up its usefulness. But I still can't bring myself to step where their faces would be.

"Time to go," I tell Deda. "You want me to take you back?"

"Jane invited me to her house," Deda replies. "It would be impolite not to attend."

I sigh. "Fine. No salty food, okay?"

Deda makes a noncommittal sound and starts back to the car. I glance at Ilia, his eyes studying Jane's headstone.

"Do you want to come?"

"I don't think so," he says. "I can't stay much longer."

"How's Urie?"

"It hit him hard." Ilia shakes his head. "This happened under his watch, with his people. He can't undo any of it. I honestly don't know if he's coming back from this."

"Maybe that's not the worst thing," I say.

"We still need someone to run things," Ilia says. "I can't be the one in charge; I don't even have any gifts."

"So what?" I say. "No one cares if you have magic, Ilia; you're still one of us. You're the one people go to when they have a problem, not Urie. Maybe it's time for a real change."

Ilia lets out a rough laugh. "Well. I guess we'll see. Are you ever coming back?"

"Come on, Ilia, I'm a terrible bartender," I say. "You don't really need me."

"Yes, we do," he says. "People trust you, Lex. Now you're one of the *only* people they trust. If you want me to step up, I'm going to need help. Don't leave me to do this on my own."

I meet his eyes, see the start of crow's feet at the corners.

"Are you going to give me a raise?"

"If you learn how to make drinks," he says, giving me half a smile. "Come on, what else are you going to do? Read tarot cards?"

I screw up my mouth. "I'll think about it."

"Uh-huh. You do that."

We reach the car and I help Deda into mine, shutting the door behind him.

"Take care, Lex," Ilia says.

"Yeah, you too," I tell him. Then I frown. "Did I ever thank you for saving my life?"

That surprises a laugh out of him. "I don't remember."

"Oh. Well, if I didn't, then thank you."

He smiles at me, and he looks like the Ilia I remember. "Anytime."

I leave Jane's house as soon as I can without being impolite. I can't take the handshakes and the tears, the pictures that are proof of a life I'll never be a part of.

"I did not finish my coffee," Deda complains as I shuffle him back into the car.

I drive north, the air humid tonight, the weight of today crushing me farther into my seat.

"There's coffee at the home, Deda."

"It is weak. And you did not say good-bye to your friend."

I left Jane curled up like a cat between her mother and grandmother, her face peaceful in a way I rarely see.

"She's with her family," I say. "She doesn't care if I say good-bye."

"Do you think so little of yourself? Or of her?"

"I thought you didn't want me to have dead friends."

"This one is . . . different," Deda says. "She cares for you. She wants more for you, wants you to have a life. Perhaps I was wrong to be afraid."

I swallow hard, the truth like a stone in my belly. "It doesn't matter," I say. "It's over, now. She doesn't need me anymore."

"That does not sound like the Jane I know."

"You don't know anything about her, Deda," I snap.

"I know she makes you smile. And I know I have not seen that for a long time. I do not think you should give that up."

I clamp my lips together, because he doesn't understand. She isn't mine to give up.

When I pull up outside the home, he turns to me and kisses my forehead.

"I only worry because I love you," he says.

"I know, Deda."

"I left some books in the back for you. Do not forget them."

"I won't. I'll see you tomorrow, okay?"

Deda nods, shutting the door behind him.

"You are a good girl, Alexandra," he tells me. "You deserve to be happy."

I take the long way home, not eager to be alone in my apartment, but I still arrive too soon. I park and sit for long minutes, letting the sun flare through the windshield and bake the entire car. It's just starting to dip low in the sky, turning the clouds electric blue.

My body jerks and I'm awake before I realize I was starting to drift. I shake out my limbs and open the door, cool air hitting my face. I let the breeze chase some of the sleepiness away, get the bag of books from the back, and start the walk upstairs. Maybe I should have said good-bye. But saying good-bye to her only reminds me of the inevitable last good-bye we'll have, and when I think of that the emptiness inside of me yawns, threatening to swallow me whole.

"What the hell, Lexi?"

I jump, and part of me wonders if thinking of her made her appear.

"You just *left*," Jane complains. "I went looking for you and you weren't there."

"I'm sorry," I say, opening my door. "I got really tired."

"Well, you could have at least told me," Jane says,

coming inside with me. "Anyway, Trevor's waiting down by the car; he says we should go to a strip club because people always want sex after a funeral."

"That can't be true."

"Look, I'm just the messenger," Jane says, smiling. "Are you in?"

I sit down on the bed and start to unlace my boots. The apartment looks different with Jane's sketches pinned to one wall, more like a real home.

"Maybe some other time," I say.

Jane tilts her head at me, frowning. "Are you okay?"

"Like I said, I'm tired."

"Oh. Okay." She stares at me for a moment, chewing on her lip. "Well, at least look at your books."

"I'll look at them tomorrow."

"No, look at them now," Jane says, tugging on my arm. "Come on."

I bend down to get the bag.

"What's the big deal, it's just . . ."

"Surprise!" Jane says, bouncing from one foot to another.

I reach in, my mouth dry, and pull the laptop out of the bag, cords dangling down.

"What is this?" I ask.

"It's my computer," Jane says.

"But—how?"

"I told your grandpa to go into my room and get it. He's pretty sly when he wants to be."

"You can't give this to me," I tell her. "Won't your mom notice it's missing?"

"Lexi, my mom would barely notice if her head went missing," Jane says, rolling her eyes. "Trust me, it was only going to waste; she doesn't know my passwords or anything. And now you have a computer." She grins at me, her eyes bright. "You can take classes online if you want, listen to music, and Trevor can shut up about getting a TV."

"I . . ." My throat doesn't want to work. "You didn't have to do this."

"I know," Jane says. "But I wanted to."

I put the laptop gently on the bed and sit down.

"Do you like it?" Jane asks.

I nod. "I love it. Thank you, Jane."

She sits next to me, and I breathe in her smell of frayed wires and the sun hitting asphalt. I taste it in the back of my throat, let it live inside my mouth. She tastes like blood, like life.

"I should be thanking you," she says. "My mother got

to bury my body today. It's finally over."

She closes her eyes, and I sneak a look at her profile, the long line of her neck.

"Jane? Are you okay?" I ask. "Now that it's over?"

"Yes," she says, opening her eyes. "And not just because I wanted him stopped. But because now there are no more reasons to wait."

I knew it was coming; I knew, and it still takes the air from my lungs. The scream rattles the bars of its cage, threatens to burst through my chest.

"I'll help you," I say, forcing the words past my lips. "Say the word, and I'll help you cross over."

"That's not," she says, "what I've been waiting for."

She slides her fingers around the back of my neck, dragging my face toward hers. Her lips part and I tear myself away, scrambling off the bed.

"Jane—"

"It's not because I'm lonely," she says firmly. "It's not because I can touch you. I want to kiss you, Lexi, because it's *you*."

I can't get enough oxygen, the room too small, my heart too vulnerable.

"Jane, this can't work," I say. "You know that."

"Why not?"

"You're a ghost. I'm not. I'll get old."

"Good," she says. "One of us should get to."

"You won't want me then—"

"I'll always want you," she says. "And if I can change my clothes, I can change my face. It's all in my mind, right? Will you still want me if I'm wrinkled and liver spotted?"

"You'll get bored," I say, changing track. "Jane, even if you don't move on, you can go anywhere you want, see any part of the world. You don't want to be stuck in this shitty apartment forever."

She stands in front of me, looking up into my face.

"Lexi, I'd rather be here in this shitty apartment with you for the next eighty years than stuck on a cloud with a harp or whatever. I'd rather watch you eat pancakes every morning than go see the pyramids by myself."

I shake my head. Hope is a dangerous taste on my tongue. "Why?" I ask.

She reaches out and grasps my hands, her warm fingers threading through mine.

"You know why," she says.

"But what if it goes wrong?" I ask, laying everything bare.

I can't have her and then lose her; I'm not strong

enough for that. The scream inside of me is too savage, too desperate, to survive that kind of heartbreak.

"Lexi," she says, and I think I could die happy if I could just hear her say my name that way again. "I can't promise you it will be perfect. But I'm just asking you to *try*. Tell me to go and I'll go. Tell me to stay, and I'll stay."

"Jane," I say, because her name is the only word I can think of. And then I don't talk at all. I lean forward and she meets me halfway. Her mouth is warm and her body is warmer and her kiss smooths something ragged inside me. I plunge my fingers in her hair and press against her and it's better than I imagined it because it's real, because she's pressing back against me and making a sound in the back of her throat, and when she finally breaks the kiss her eyes are glazed the darkest brown I've ever seen.

"Stay," I say.

If two pieces of metal meet in space, they will fuse together. In a vacuum, the atoms can't tell that they're in separate objects. They only recognize that they are the same. This is called cold welding. It doesn't matter that she's dead, it doesn't matter that I'm alive; we dance without music, and with her arms wrapped around my waist, I can't tell where I end and she begins.

ACKNOWLEDGMENTS

I OWE THANKS FIRST AND FOREMOST TO Martha Mihalick, who did some heavy lifting on this book. It's been an absolute privilege to work with you, and if you think I'm going to stop emailing you random nonsense once the book is out, think again.

Thanks to my agent, Heather Flaherty, for constantly talking me off ledges and doing all the real work so I can continue to play in the clouds.

Eternally grateful to the fantastic Greenwillow team: Katie Heit and Tim Smith for editorial prowess, Shannon Cox for marketing, fearless leader Virginia Duncan, Paul Zakris and Sammy Yuen for my gorgeous cover and jacket design. I couldn't have asked for a better group of people to have in my corner.

Thanks to Hope Cook for notes and for saying I made you cry. Thanks to Jen for an insightful critique and for liking my stupid tweets.

To everyone who bought, read, borrowed, or reviewed

Devils Unto Dust: thank you, thank you, thank you. I never thought I would write one book, let alone two, and all the work and revision and stress is worth just a single email from someone saying they connected with the words that I wrote.

To my girls, Adrian, Katherine, Laura, and Leah: y'all know what you did. Eternal love and devotion, etc.

Graham Norris and Lee Arcuri, thank you for dragging me out of the house and forcing me to actually experience LA. I love you both, please send more pictures of the changeling.

To the amazing writer friends I'm made over the past few years, you are so talented and generous, thank you for your advice and commiseration.

To my friends in Texas, California, New Zealand, and all the places in between, I'm so grateful for your enthusiasm and encouragement.

I wrote the majority of this book while listening to Frightened Rabbit, and I can't let the moment pass without acknowledging the impact Scott Hutchison's music and lyrics had on me. I don't know that any other songwriter came as close to capturing what it's like to live inside my head. Scott's music made me feel seen, made me feel less alone, and I only wish someone had been able to do that for him. I wish I could have told him he made tiny changes to my life.

To my family, thank you for your unconditional love and borderline-fanatical (lookin' at you, Hill) support. I'll try to come home more often.

Finally, thank you to Monkee for letting me know when it's time to get off the computer, and to Mike, for always making me coffee. Te quiero.